The Twist of Fate

Anjum Awasthi Mallik

Invincible Publishers

First published in India in 2017 by Invincible Publishers

ISBN: 978-93-87328-16-7

Invincible Publishers

G - 120, Sushant Lok III, Sector 57, Gurgaon-122002

Opposite Kasturba Ashram, Radaur Distt Yamuna Nagar,
Haryana- 135133

Dedicated to my Dada Ji and Dadi Ji

(My Guardian Angels...)

Prologue

Not bothering to wait for the elevator, I started climbing up the stairs of my office. The upheaval going in my mind had affected me to such an extent that I didn't even bother to return the greetings of my colleagues on the way to my cubicle.

"Are you okay?" asked Ankita, peering from the cubicle diagonally opposite to mine as I dropped my handbag on my table.

"Yeah," I lied, because at this moment I was anything but all right.

"Well, all the best for your first presentation," she smiled before resuming to type on her laptop.

My first presentation…

This was the last thing on my mind at the moment. Life is erratic and the most unpredictable thing. It never goes the way we plan. It was still hard to believe that it had taken just a week for my life to shatter to bits.

Why me? Dammit, why me?

I had always embraced whatever life offered me with my arms wide open and I was content with what I had. However, it wasn't like my life was all bed of roses; I had had my own share of miseries and maybe that was the reason I wasn't ready to accept what was now happening in my life. I had always been possessive when it came to my things, perhaps this was the reason why I found myself teetering on the brink of an abyss. It was something I just couldn't let go, period.

I felt my legs wobbling and hands trembling as I pulled my phone out of my handbag. I knew that nothing could recuperate my condition until I got to know what was going on in his life, for which it was important to talk to Dev—his roommate. He was the only person I could rely on at this moment. I called Dev with a gaggle of queries hovering in my mind. He rejected my call. I called him again and just as the last attempt, he cut my call off in first ring. Now why the hell was he avoiding me? Why was everyone around me on a mission to test my patience? I was stopped short from calling again when his message popped in: **I'm in a meeting. Will call you shortly.**

My presentation with my manager was due over the next hour. I prayed for Dev to call me before that, dreading the restlessness which otherwise threatened to mess with my concentration over my first presentation. I kept my phone aside and waited for his call. Why does it happen that a few seconds seem like an eternity when you are frenziedly waiting for something to happen? I kept checking my phone every few seconds, but nothing appeared on my notification bar. It was getting hard to curb the urge to call him again, but I restrained myself...*somehow*, as I didn't want to come across as some frantic girlfriend stalking her boyfriend.

It had been fifty-one minutes since his message had popped in, but still I didn't get any call from him. Clenching my phone in hand, I made my way to the washroom. I felt a certain heaviness in my chest and dryness in my sleep-deprived eyes. As I entered the freshly cleaned washroom, the smell of disinfectant made me nauseous. Covering my nose and mouth, I stood in front of the washbasin. The pale, fragile and sullen reflection that I saw in the huge mirror mounted on the wall in front of me, looked anything but me.

If just two weeks ago, when I first came to Noida, someone had told me that my image in the mirror would look like this, I would never have believed them.

"Why are you doing this to me?" my aching heart asked, hoping for it to reach him.

"Why are you letting him do this to you?" my subconscious snarled, pointing back at me. And I stood there… *numb*, as a silent tear peeped over the brim of my eye.

Chapter 1
The Departure

"Raahi..." I heard my father call my name.

"Yes, Paa?"

"Are you done with the packing?"

"Yes Paa, almost," I said loudly, standing out on the porch, carefully studying the blooming buds on the potted plant that I had planted only a few months ago. I had eagerly been waiting to see the flowers and now when they were finally blossoming, I had to leave the city. It was getting really hard for me to keep my focus on one thing. All kinds of thoughts had been hovering in my mind since the day I got the call letter for my first job in Noida. I really had no idea how I would acclimate to a new city, among new people and in a new environment.

I was confused...*utterly confused*. I didn't know whether I was excited, anxious, scared or frazzled, as this was the first time I was going to stay away from my home. Till now, every time I felt agitated, my Paa was always there beside me, but all that was going to change. Contrary to expressing my nervousness this time, I was actually hiding it from him, not because I was afraid of him, but because I knew that he was way more petrified than I was. I tried to calm him down by being confident myself.

Let me tell you a bit more about my Paa, Professor Hitendra Sharma. He is obsessed with only two things in his life. First is me, and the second is his work. He was working as a professor of mathematics at the government Degree College then and was famous in town for his passion for teaching. In his whole career, he hadn't missed a single class, not even the day when my mother met with an accident and was fighting for her life at the hospital. She didn't survive. I was only four years old then. I hated him sometimes for this, but it didn't mean that he didn't love my mother. He loved her with all his heart and he still does. He could have married again after my mother's demise as he was pretty young at that time, but he committed himself to look after me and provide me with all that he and my mother would have given me.

I have always been a bright student and after 12th standard, I had much better options at hand than to study at a private engineering college in Solan, but all those demanded me to move to other cities and my Paa wasn't in favor of it. Consequentially, I had to abdicate all other opportunities. He wanted me to stay here in Solan with him and he gave me the weirdest possible reason for his disapproval, saying that I was too young to stay alone. I wanted to argue, but kept my mouth shut. I was 18 years old then, an adult according to the constitution of India, but these parents, I tell you. If it were up to them, they would still feed us with bottles, well into our adulthood.

But things had changed now; one, I was twenty-two year old and two, I had completed my graduation and was placed in a Noida-based IT company. Initially, my Paa was quite reluctant to the idea of me shifting to Noida, but had to kneel in front of my obstinacy.

The idea of living independently in a metro city had always fascinated me. When my best friend Shreya took admission in an engineering college in Chandigarh, I tried my level best to coax my Paa to let me take admission there too, but he was dead set on his decision to make me stay and I had to capitulate. Shreya used to share stories from her girls' hostel and their frequent hangouts with friends in Chandigarh and I listened to all of them attentively. I too wanted to experience that life and that kind of fun at least once if not often, but to my dismay, Paa never allowed me to go anywhere except to a few relatives'. To hangout with friends was a big NO-NO for me.

When I broke the news of my placement in Noida to Paa, he even came up with an idea and offered to leave his job at the college and move to Noida with me, but I refused; One, because then I would never get to experience the hostel life, and two, I knew how passionate he was towards his work and I didn't want to snatch that contentment away from him. I was eagerly waiting for this day hitherto, but as the time of departure approached, I started getting cold feet.

"Raahi, go and check your room once again if you missed something," Paa reminded me again.

"I have already checked, Paa. Get ready, we have a train to catch in three hours," I told him entering the living room.

"Hmm," he said without looking at me and ambling towards his room. I was well aware that he was worried and was trying hard to hide his emotions. It was justified too; after all, his only daughter, or rather his only family, was moving to NOIDA, the city that had always been in the limelight for less-than-good reasons. His only concern was my safety, and thanks to the news channels across the board, not a single day passed by when there wasn't some flashing news regarding cases of molestation, rape and murder in the NCR.

"Paa, did you talk to Raj *mamu*?" I asked to divert his mind.

"Yes," he said and added after a brief hiatus, "He has already had a word with Mr. Kashyap; we shall go to his place straight away."

"Oh! And what about the PG?" I inquired.

"He will suggest once we reach there," he responded, fidgeting with his already packed bag.

Mr. Suresh Kashyap was a childhood friend of my maternal uncle Raj. He was a renowned doctor and ran his own clinic in Noida. He was also associated with all the major hospitals across NCR. He had been settled in Delhi for the last twenty years and had recently moved into his new flat in Noida. Raj *mamu* insisted for Paa to go directly to Mr. Kashyap's house and assured that he would gladly take care of my accommodation, as Paa and I both were unacquainted with that city.

"Paa, I'm ready," I shouted, dragging my bags to the living room. He called for a cab to railway station, while signalling at me to sit quietly and wait. Our train to Delhi was to depart from Kalka, which was around fifty kilometers from Solan. Soon the cab arrived and we started loading our luggage in.

"Paa, let me check the house one last time before leaving," I said and sprinted inside the house. I wasn't there to look for my belongings, I just wanted to see my home for one last time before I left. Until yesterday, these walls had seemed like an immurement, but today I felt like my heart was ensconced within those walls. I had spent a great deal of my life here. *Did I really want to leave this house?* A part of me asked. I hastily dismissed that thought because I knew it would make me frail. I checked everywhere for the last time and locked the house. As I turned to leave, a beaming rose in my potted plant caught my attention, newly bloomed as if only to bid me goodbye. I sat down near it and titillated its velvety petals; after all, it was my baby and I whispered, "Keep blossoming, you are a symbol of my love, see you soon."

"Raahi, come soon *gudiya*, we are getting late," Paa called me from inside the cab.

***

I woke up with a jolt as my head hit the window pane in the train. I heard Paa talking to Kashyap uncle over the phone. We were about to reach the New Delhi railway station, I conjectured, as the train compartment was abuzz with other passengers unloading their luggage from the racks overhead.

I looked outside the window, each and every person seemed to be in a hurry. Isn't it strange? We all are running to reach an ephemeral destination; I call it ephemeral because as soon we reach there, another thing enters the pipeline and we begin again, rushing towards this new goal, without realizing that the ultimate destination is beyond the scope of one's wits. While the journey is eternal, why don't we cherish it without thinking too much about the end?

"Hurry up, Raahi...our station is here," Paa called out, pulling me out of my reverie. I stretched and straightened my back in response. The train hadn't stopped yet, but the corridor towards the gate was blocked with people ready to get off already. They pushed and shoved about to be out the train as soon as possible. Didn't I tell you? *Everyone was in a hurry.* But I was not. Though Paa was incessantly intimidating me with his stare to get up, I still lazed about on my seat, ignoring Paa's stare and munching on some leftover chocolate. Oh! Did I tell you? I love chocolates and I can eat them anytime anywhere. I never got fat, however. I have superb metabolism.

As the train crawled to a stop at the New Delhi railway station, we started collecting our belongings and sauntered towards the exit door to alight from the train. As soon as we clambered down, I saw a middle aged man approaching us. He was tall and sturdy with prominent cheekbones, a fair complexion and a partly bald head.

"Hello Sharma Ji, welcome to Delhi," he said.

This was indeed Kashyap uncle, I could tell from his looks. Even without the vocational garb, there was something about his demeanor that exuded the aura of a doctor. He had come to receive us at the station. After exchanging some generous pleasantries, we headed towards Kashyap uncle's home in Noida. Peeking through the window of his car, I tried to scrutinize and gauge for myself the capital of India—Delhi.

'Delhi is like that beautiful girl in town who has enticed everyone; few are her true lovers who love her just as she is, few love her covertly because they don't have the courage to approach her, and few are the cynic who can't afford to get her and try to annihilate her image by slander.' I grinned as I recalled one of my friend's epiphanies regarding the city.

'Miss Raahi Sharma, finally you are in the city of your dreams. Be ready to embrace your new life,' I told myself and updated my Facebook status.

Soon we reached our destination—Oasis Apartments—the sumptuous and aesthetic interior of the building complex welcomed us to Kashyap uncle's flat on the eleventh floor. A lady in her early fifties opened the door. Kashyap uncle introduced her as his wife, Reena. I folded my hands to greet her. She looked at me lovingly and caressed my head. I held her gaze and was struck by the charisma of her personality.

She had a remarkable aura of positivity around her which always makes the surroundings jovial, a kind of energy that makes someone find reasons to love and smile. She didn't seem like a stranger at all. I instantly took a liking to her.

When we entered the living room, everything looked palatial; from textured walls to the wooden flooring, the colossal sofa with delicate satin cushions, hand carved antiques, stupendous paintings, from velvety sheer curtains to the gorgeous hand woven Kashmiri carpet. I must say, she had good taste.

"Whoa! What an exceptionally beautiful house!" I couldn't stop myself from appreciating aloud.

"Really? You like it? We shifted to this flat only a few months ago and got the entire interior done by professionals," she said excitedly.

"Yeah aunty, it's the best interior I have ever seen," I replied, really meaning what I said.

Just then, a girl in her twenties came in with glasses of water on a tray and offered it to each one of us. Reena aunty introduced her as Kanchi, who helped around with the domestic chores.

"Come, I'll show you the other rooms," Reena aunty said and turned to the other side, beckoning me to follow her. First, she took me to the master bedroom which had a king sized bed and the walls were beautifully decorated with a collage of their family pictures. Then she showed me the next room that had pink textured walls with a huge framed picture of two kids, hanging right behind the bed. The girl in the picture was chubby and cute with an exquisite smile, while the boy had an impish glint in his eyes paired with a mischievous smile. Reena aunty told me that the girl was their elder daughter Aisha and the boy was their younger son Aadit. The picture was almost twenty years old, she said.

She also told me that Aisha was now working as a Senior Editor at a Delhi based publishing house. She was engaged to be married in the next six months, whereas Aadit had been working as a Business Analyst in a New York based Investment Bank for the last three years. Of the rooms that she showed me next, one was Aadit's room and the other, a guest room.

***

Soon, the lunch was served on the dining table and we had the afternoon meal together. Kashyap uncle told us various funny childhood stories of his friendship with Raj *mamu*. I also learnt that Kashyap uncle knew my mother well and that he used to treat her like his own younger sister. However, once he moved out because of his studies, he lost all his contacts, except for Raj *mamu*. I love it when someone talked about my mother; it helped me create an image of her in my mind.

After the lunch, Paa asked Kashyap uncle to suggest some good PGs, as I was to join office from the coming Monday and he wanted to finalize my accommodation as soon as possible. He also shared his concern for my safety, as Noida wasn't considered very safe for girls in popular opinion.

Oh God! Not again. I rolled my eyes.

"Stop worrying Paa, I'll be alright. I can take care of myself," I tried to soothe him, despite knowing that it wouldn't make any difference.

"You won't understand a father's concern, Raahi," said Kashyap uncle, supporting Paa. "We have been living here for the last twenty years, yet Aisha isn't allowed to stay out after ten in the evening. This is the least we can do as parents to ensure her safety."

"I wish I could stay with her," mumbled Paa to himself, looking down at his clasped hands.

"I have a suggestion Sharma Ji. If you agree to it and Raahi feels comfortable, she can stay here with us. At least till the time she gets well settled in the city," he suggested.

Please say no, Paa. I closed my eyes and crossed my fingers.

"No, No, Kashyap Ji, you are already doing so much for us. We can't hope to bother you anymore," said Paa. I heaved a sigh of relief.

"*Nahi nahi, Bhai Sahib*, we haven't done anything and Raahi is such a lovely girl, I already feel connected to her. I'd love to have her stay here. Moreover, Aisha will be married soon and Aadit visits us barely once a year. We could use some young company in the house," said Reena aunty.

"Whatever you are saying is true, but—"

"No buts Sharma Ji, it's decided now," Reena aunty cut him off and said authoritatively with both her hands raised, "No more discussions, she is staying with us."

And with that, my dream of staying independently in a big city got shattered, but I did hear them say 'till the time I get settled', so I still had hope.

***

It was around six in the evening when the doorbell rang. Kanchi opened the door. It was Aisha.

"Aisha? How come you are early today?" asked Reena aunty, surprised at the sudden arrival of her daughter.

"Maa, I was famished and the thought of delicious food at home was driving me crazy. So, I came back," said Aisha.

Aisha was beautiful. She had golden streaked dark brown hair that cascaded down the sides of her head and over her shoulders in loose wavy curls. She was of a bubbly personality and cheerful character. The black trousers which she had paired with a sleek grey shirt complementing her shapely figure well. Reena aunty introduced her to Paa and me.

I found Aisha an independent and understanding girl, as we chatted for some time. She was quite loquacious too and I hardly got a chance to speak in her presence. Her thoughts rolled off of her tongue like a freight train, making her talk incessantly. In a short span of time, we got acquainted well.

***

Chapter 2

A New Beginning

It was my first day to work. My excitement however was streaked with nervousness. I took a shower early in the morning and got carefully dressed in a crisp blue cotton suit contrasted with yellow *churidar*. I tied my hair in a tidy braid. Then I arranged and rechecked the documents that I needed to submit that day. After arranging my bag, I looked at the watch; it was still only 6:35 AM. I had gotten up quite early that day as I couldn't sleep properly the night before. Whether it was the anxiety or the new place, I don't know. I was eagerly waiting for the clock to hit seven, so that I might rush to Paa who was sleeping in the neighboring room. Kashyap uncle was going to drop us, me at my office first and then Paa at the railway station. Yes, he was going back the same day and it was bothering me, since I was still unsure of how I would manage without him.

I still remember clearly the day a few months ago, when it was my farewell event at college. The dress code for the farewell was saree for all girls. Paa insisted on buying a new one for me, but I was adamant to wear one of my mother's old sarees. He had preserved all my mother's belongings perfectly and he was quite emotionally attached to them. With anguish on his face, he took out a black silk saree with a golden *zari* border and handed it over to me.

Later when he saw me dressed in that saree, he couldn't control his emotions. I noticed tears twinkling in his eyes, which he wiped away quickly and feigned that something was troubling his eyes. I had instantly run to Paa and hugged him tight. I knew that he still missed my mother a lot. They had been so much in love that they fought with their families to be with each other, but destiny had planned something else for them. He told me that he saw my mother's reflection in me. For me, it was the biggest compliment I could ever get. I had seen my mother's pictures. She was extremely beautiful and I was nowhere even close, but I was delighted to hear him say it nevertheless. I can never forget that look on Paa's face when he said it. It had an essence of satisfaction, as if his entire arduous, tiring and lonely journey was worth living for that one moment alone.

Growing up, there were so many occasions when I needed my mother more than my father. Transforming into a woman from a little girl, I had so many queries to ask her, but I couldn't. There were many things that I would have loved to share and experience with her, but couldn't. It was challenging for me as well as for Paa. I still remember that day when I had my annual day at school, every other girl in my class came carefully dolled up in a satin gown. Their mothers had adorned them with all the matching accessories, whereas I was dressed in a simple cotton frock, with my hair oiled and tied in a ponytail. My class teacher made me stand at the rear during our dance performance because I wasn't dressed properly. I was so shattered that day, and so was my Paa, completely heartbroken when he saw me burst into tears asking, 'Why don't I have a mother? Everyone has a mother except me. Why is God so unfair to me?' He tried his level best to calm me down, but all was in vain. He then took me to an orphanage to make me realize that I at least had a father, there were so many kids who neither had a mother, nor father.

A sudden knock at the door jolted me out of my trance and I wiped my moist eyes hastily. I opened the door, expecting to see my Paa on the other side but it wasn't him. It was Reena aunty.

"*Arey wah*, you are already dressed up," she said, carefully examining me from top to toe. "You look so pretty in blue". Then she quickly reached for the side of her eye, smudging some kohl from her eye and onto her ring finger, she proceeded to place a black dot behind my ear. "*Nazar naa lage kisi ki,*" she said dotingly.

"Thanks Aunty," I blushed. It was the first time someone had done this for me to oust the evil eye. The gesture made me feel loved.

"Now come quickly and have your breakfast," she said as she walked hurriedly to the kitchen. I followed her.

After breakfast, when Paa and I were about to leave, Reena aunty came to me, holding in her hands a bowl of sweet curd.

"It's auspicious. This is your first day, may God bless you with lots of prosperity and success," she said, feeding me a spoonful of curd. I was deeply touched by this gesture of hers.

"Thanks Aunty," I whispered, "I have no memories of my mother, but I feel that she would have done the same."

She kept the bowl on the table and cupped my face with her hands. Reading the unshed tears in my eyes, she kissed my forehead and said, "I'm also like your Maa, ain't I?"

"Then, can I call you Maa?" I asked, as a tear started to roll down my cheek.

"Of course," she said and hugged me affectionately. No

one can compensate for a mother's love and I had really been longing for that. Soon, we left with Kashyap uncle in his car.

As we reached my office, I climbed down the car and looked at the building, not because I was particularly amused by it, but because I didn't want to look at Paa, who's unbroken gaze was on me standing near the door of the car. I knew that I wouldn't be able to hold my tears if I looked at him. He drew closer and patted gently on my back. As I turned my gaze towards him, I couldn't control my tears any longer and they started streaming down my cheeks. I pulled him into a hug and said with a muffled voice, "I love you, Paa." I could sense his body relax upon hearing those words, as if all his perturbations were gone. I knew that all this time, the only one thing that kept him going was to see me growing, chirping and smiling. He kissed my head and wrapped his arms around me.

"I'll miss you, Paa," I sobbed.

"So will I. But this is what you have always dreamt of, isn't it? Take care of yourself and always remember one thing, I'm always with you and I'm proud of you," he said, gently caressing my back.

He released me and went to sit inside the car, his eyes still locked with mine. I felt a sting deep down my heart, as the car started moving away. My eyes followed the car till it disappeared from my sight. *Nothing comes for free.* For my dreams, I had to sacrifice his presence in my life. I sighed.

As I entered the premises, I prudently observed each and every little detail around me. It was like a dream come true for me, as now I would have my own identity, my own office and my own earnings. I had been waiting for this moment since forever and it was finally happening.

My first day went by just completing the formalities, filling various forms and meeting the other personnel from my department. I liked my cubical, my desktop and my neighbors. As the clock struck five-thirty in the evening, I picked up my bag and walked out of the office. I called up Kashyap uncle to inform him that I had pooled a cab with some people from my office, who were on the same route and had offered to drop me home.

***

When I came back, I found Reena aunty talking to someone over the phone and I could bet it was Aadit, because she always had a unique glint in her eyes while talking to or about Aadit.

"Achha, listen…I'll talk to you later, Raahi is back," she said over the phone and disconnected the call.

"How was your day?" she asked, turning to me.

"Tiring…but I liked the people over there, especially at my department," I replied cheerfully.

"That's nice. What will you have, tea or coffee?" she asked.

"Let Aisha di come back too, then we will have some together."

"I have to go to see a friend of mine today. She is admitted in the hospital," she said.

"Oh! What happened to her, Aunty?" I asked.

"Aunty? I guess you were going to start calling me Maa," she said, raising an eyebrow.

"Ah! Sorry, what happened to her, *Maa*?" I repeated. A tingling sensation rushed up my body as I said 'Maa'. It's a sacred word and only they know its worth, who are still yearning to experience the emotions allied with it.

"Appendicitis," she informed and smiled lovingly at me.

A little later, Aisha got back from her office and joined us too. Maa left soon after instructing Kanchi what to cook for the evening.

I was sitting there in the living room, flicking through

TV channels to find something interesting to watch. Just then, Kanchi brought two cups of coffee with a bowl of dry fruits and called for Aisha to come to the living room.

"Aha! It is the best feeling when you have someone to serve you hot coffee after a hectic day, isn't it?" she asked without expecting any answer from me. As I had mentioned earlier, she didn't give another person a chance to speak.

"So, how was your first day, Raahi?" she asked, turning her attention to me. But before I could answer, she replied to her own question, "First days are generally very hectic. You have to complete all kinds of formalities, filling all kinds of forms and run around from one person to another needlessly, isn't it?"

"Yeah...that's true di," I replied with a smile.

"Humph! Don't call me *di*...call me Aisha. 'Di' makes me feel so much older," she grimaced.

"Oh! Sorry... Aisha," I apologized and corrected myself.

"Aww...you are such darling. For me, it's the commute that drains all the vigor out of me. Gosh! I don't know how much time I spend just on the road, waiting for traffic signals to go green, listening to the nonstop honking of vehicles and breaking my back on bumpy roads,"— she paused to sip her coffee— "Things will run better once I shift to Girish's place. It will take just a few minutes from his house," she said, looking at her coffee.

"Girish?" I asked as it was the first time I was hearing that name and had no idea who he was.

"My fiance. His name is Girish. I don't know when they are going to fix a date for the wedding. I don't understand why people behave so weird sometimes. I mean, who waits for someone's physical presence just to fix a date, that too in this era of technology. They are waiting for Girish's paternal aunt, who is in Dubai, to arrive. She will visit around Diwali and then they will decide on the date."

"Aren't you nervous?" I asked.

"Nervous? For what?" she said with a clueless expression.

"For spending the rest of your life with a stranger."

"He isn't a stranger. I have known him for almost 18 years now."

"18 years!?"

"Yeah...actually, we studied in the same school, and then the same college too. After college, he joined his family business, while I landed up in a publishing house. Girish's father and my papa are friends. One day, Girish's father came with a matrimonial proposal asking my hand for Girish. Papa asked me and I said 'yes' instantly as we had already been dating—" she stopped suddenly and caught the tip of her tongue between her teeth, as she had blurted out something she wasn't supposed to say.

"Dating? But uncle said it's an arranged marriage," I took the opportunity to interrogate.

"Yeah, you see, nobody here knows that we were already seeing each other, so please don't tell this to anyone," she requested.

"Sure, why would I?" I smiled to assure her.

"You know, papa is cool otherwise, but in these kind of matters, he is no better than century old people. And he has become all the more strict after what happened with Aadit." she said, letting out a deep breath.

"What happened with him?" I asked inquisitively.

"Four years ago, he was dating a girl from his college. After graduation, she went abroad for higher education, whereas Aadit took a job here. One day, she told him that she was not interested in their relationship anymore.

Perhaps she found someone else there. She was just using Aadit. I never liked her, to tell you the truth. But Aadit was mad after her. You won't believe, he turned into a complete maniac after their breakup. He was so depressed that he looked marginally suicidal. He used to stay locked up in his room all day and stopped going anywhere. He started avoiding everyone, even his own family. It was a really hard time for all of us." She paused for a while, as if to reminisce about that time better and continued, "He had to see a psychiatrist. But thank God, with each session, he recuperated wonderfully and after about six months of treatment, our hunky dory Aadit was back to being himself and everything came back on track."

She kept the empty cup on the table and shrieked all of a sudden, "Oh my God! It's 7:35 already, I have to leave for my workout." She got up and rushed to her room to change into her workout clothes. I remained sitting there, trying to make sense of what she had just narrated to me. It must have been a really difficult time for all of them. I couldn't comprehend how Aadit could be so dumb to trust someone so blindly.

Soon Aisha was back, wearing her Adidas workout pants with a neon bright tank top. "I need to reduce at least 5 kgs before my wedding," she said and rushed out of the house. She looked quite perfect to me already, I didn't see why she needed to lose the extra 5 kgs.

Chapter 3

Trapped In The Past

AADIT

It was an unusual evening; I found myself rambling the streets of Madison Square Park. The entire street was empty. I tried to look around for other people, but there was no one. I decided to take a cab and go back to my place. As I started walking, I noticed a girl in a long white dress. Her face was partially hidden behind locks of her long black hair. I started walking towards her, but despite walking briskly, it seemed ineffectual to cover the distance. All of a sudden, a familiar tune drifted in the air as she started moving towards me. The distance between us started diminishing with each step that she took. It appeared as if she was trying to say something, asking for my help perhaps, but I was unable to hear her because the music that was reverberating in my ears.

Suddenly, my eyes flashed open and I sat up on my bed. *Damn, it was just a dream.* I heard the same tune again and noticed that my phone was ringing. It was Maa. I looked at the watch and reckoned the India time in my head. 'It would be around six in the evening there,' I thought. I received the call.

"Hello Maa, how are you?" I asked groggily.

"Are you still sleeping, Aadit?" she asked, astounded as if sleeping at five in the morning was a crime.

"Maa, it's still very early in the morning here."

"Oh... Yes. So, what are your plans for Diwali?" she asked again, despite knowing well enough that I wouldn't be able to visit India during that time this year.

"Maa, I told you I have some important assignments here that I need to complete before Aisha's wedding, so that I may get leave at that time," I tried to explain the umpteenth time, in a modulated voice.

"Okay...I understand that, but....you know...that means, this Diwali will go by without you..." she trailed off. I knew what was coming next. She would start crying to make me feel guilty.

"Come on, Maa. Now don't try this emotional blackmailing again. You know what things are like here," I said in a calm tone.

"Hmm, a mother's love is always labeled as emotional blackmail. You will realize its worth when I am no longer around," she bounced her potent weapon.

"Ah! Please drop this topic now and tell me, how is your new business going?"

"What new business?"

"I came to know that you are turning our home into a PG"—the sarcasm in my voice was palpable—"I mean, who does that, when you already have so many facilities of PGs and hotels in the city? She isn't a kid who needs a guardian to look after," I said.

"Can't you ever say something nice to me? I hate this sarcastic tone of yours. Anyway, she is Raj uncle's niece and she isn't going to stay here forever, it's only till she gets settled in the city. This is the first time she is staying away from her father," she said infuriated.

"Ok Maa, cool down! I was kidding," I tried to pacify her.

"She is really a very nice girl, you know. she has an impeccable face and a beautiful smile. Her candidness and innocence can touch anyone's heart. Whoever will marry her will be the luckiest guy in the world," she declared convincingly. *Now why is she praising her so, all of a sudden*? I scratched my head.

"If it were up to me, I'll never let her go. You know, she has already started calling me Maa," she continued.

"Already?" I quizzed. *Now what did that mean*? It sounded as if she was looking forward to the girl calling her Maa in some time, which she started to do already.

"I mean…she calls me Maa. Her mother died in an accident when she was very young. Maybe she is trying to find her mother in me," she paused for a moment and then added, "Shall I send you a picture of her?" Then it dawned on me, why she was praising her so and what was going on in her mind.

"NO," I said instantly, raising my voice a notch. "I think I should disconnect now because I know which direction this conversation is going to take." I wanted to put a stop to whatever was running through her mind.

"And what's the problem in thinking that way? She is a nice girl," she said.

"All girls are nice MAA…but right now, I'm not interested in anyone. I have already told you very clearly, that I don't want to even think about marriage and you promised me we wouldn't talk about it for at least two more years. I need some time." I couldn't quell the impulse of my exasperation.

"I'm not asking you to get married today. You take your time, but there is no harm in just seeing a girl. I know"—she snorted—"I know, it's all because of that girl Ruhani, isn't it? I don't know when she will let us live peacefully."

"NO. For God's sake Maa, it's not about her. It's about me. I don't want to get married at this moment. Is it that hard to understand? I have moved on, I don't even think about her anymore. It's you who always brings her up in our conversation..."

"It's not me who always brings her up...but the fact remains that she still affects you. That is the reason you turn down all the proposals that I bring to you," she said impetuously. I squeezed my eyes shut and tried to calm my nerves down.

"I'm sorry, Maa...but I'm really not ready for this. End of story," I said, but soon noticed that she wasn't listening to me anymore, as something else had caught her attention.

"*Achha*, listen...I'll talk to you later, Raahi is back," she said and disconnected the call hurriedly.

I don't know what's wrong with Maa, her daughter's wedding is on the cards and she is still worried about my marriage. Every other day, she would start talking about some random girl she met recently and send me her pictures. I don't understand why parents get so anxious for their kids to get married. I mean, marriage isn't the ultimate goal of life; there are so many better things to do and isn't it too early to get married when you are just twenty-six? I argued in my head, because arguing with Maa on this topic was clearly irrational and pointless.

Every time I would say no to a girl she had selected, she would start blaming Ruhani. How did she fit into our conversation in any way? It has been four years since I last saw her, then how could she affect any of my decisions. I know I behaved weird after she broke up with me. Everyone assumed that I was mad after her, but I wasn't. Rather, it was she who was madly in love with me. She used to treat me like her most prized possession. It was she who used to entwine and depict the dreams of our future together. Perhaps I too had started to envision our future through her eyes and when that crumpled, I was shattered. I felt like something had died inside me and that I would have no future without her. I had lost all my confidence and hope.

But the day I saw the reflection of my pain in my Maa, papa and Aisha's eyes, the pain of losing me, the pain of seeing me dying bit by bit, I decided to pull myself out of all the mess and they helped me. They held my hand during the toughest time of my life. For the first time in life, I realized the importance of having a family.

I clambered out of my bed and switched on the coffee maker in the kitchen. I opened the Facebook app on my phone. I wasn't an active user of social networking sites, but I did log-in occasionally. I learnt that my mom and sister had both added a new friend to their list. It was Raahi Sharma from Solan, Himachal Pradesh. I opened her profile. With rosy lips, a fair complexion and beautiful dark brown long hair, she looked cute…a typical *pahaadi beauty*. Her cover picture was a group photo with six girls, all in sarees. I recognized her in a black saree with golden border. From the comments I inferred that it was from her farewell event. Her latest status read: *Finally in my dreamland!!* which she had posted a day before yesterday.

I closed the app as I received a text from my friend, bringing me up to speed with the day's visit to the orphanage. We loved going there and spending some quality time with those little intelligent minds. It was always a rewarding experience and gave me immense satisfaction.

***

Chapter 4

Surprise Or Shock

A week had passed since I came to Noida. Throughout the week, I went through a grueling training schedule that seemed to drag on forever and sapped all the energy out of me, but on the upside, I managed to make some new friends at my work place. One day I was alone at home, since everyone else had gone to attend a live concert by Sonu Nigam at Siri Fort auditorium with Aisha's in-laws. Aisha and Maa had insisted on me to join them, but I refused because of two reasons: One, I was too tired and two, I wanted to spend some time alone at home.

All relaxed, I plonked on the sofa, devouring some melted Cadbury's Silk with one hand and browsing through WhatsApp messages with the other. Due to my tight schedule throughout the week, I barely got the time to check or reply to messages. The first contact I opened to reply to was my bestie, Shreya.

I had received more than a hundred messages from her in the span of a week. I didn't dare to read all of them, as I anticipated some obvious abuses and chiding for not having attended to her calls and replied to her messages. I grinned as I scrolled through our chat and replied to her texts. Throughout my school life, I had just one best friend—

Shreya. It was only after 12th standard that we parted ways, as Shreya joined an engineering college in Chandigarh and I stayed back to study in Solan. But we were always in touch through phone calls and messages and met whenever she was in town.

Shreya was the most desirable girl at school. It wasn't her beauty that made her 'the chick' of the school, but her attitude. She was absolutely dauntless and the boys thought twice before approaching her. She was damn protective over me and I followed her blindly. She had two *funda*'s of life she followed by: One, test everyone who wants to be your friend and two, teach a lesson to whoever messes with you. Somehow, a few of her qualities ended up rubbing off on me, but I could never match her way of doing things as she was way too gutsy, while I was of a shy demeanor.

Going through the messages, I came across a video shared in one of my new WhatsApp groups. It was a CCTV footage of a house at some foreign location. The camera was installed at the top of the main door, which showed a courier boy approaching the house. Then a lady came to the main door and took the parcel through small window carved into the door. But the courier boy coaxed lady to open the door, pretending that he needed to have her signatures on some documents. As soon as the lady opened the door, the courier boy attacked the lady and went inside the house to loot. The video really frightened me. I typed a quick comment:

These days you can't trust anyone.

I also made a mental note to not open the door for any stranger at any cost. Going through the other messages, I didn't realize when I fell into a deep slumber.

The continuous ding at the doorbell interrupted my sleep. In a half sleep, I got up and pulled opened the wooden door to see who was outside. Through the grill of the safety door,

I saw a boy, who seemed to be in his mid twenties, standing outside. He wore a collared white T-shirt and blue denims. One of his hands was resting on the wall near the doorbell, while the other was on the handle of his huge suitcase.

'*Courier boy?*' I wondered, looking at his gigantic bag.

"Yes?" I asked in a groggy voice, rubbing my eyes.

"Um…you are Raahi, right?" he asked, cocking his head to one side.

"Hmm," I gave a confused and suspicious nod. *Strange! How does he know my name*?

"What do you want?" I asked in a stern voice.

"Well... I want you to open the door for me," he said smiling.

Why? Are you the president of somewhere? I was shocked at his audacity.

"And why would I do that? Do I look like a fool?" I said sarcastically, raising my voice a bit.

"NO. Well…I would say you look quite edible, especially with the delicious chocolate all over your mouth, and trust me"—he placed his right hand over his stomach—"I'm damn hungry right now too," he said smirking facetiously at me.

And then it occurred to me that the way I had been licking the chocolate, assuming that no one is watching me, might have spoiled my face. I hastily wiped it off with the sleeve of my T-shirt, ignoring his astute grin.

"Are you here to deliver a courier?" I said, perplexed at the way he was talking to me.

"No…even better… let me in and you will get to know soon," he replied charmingly.

I smelled something fishy in his way of talking. His gigantic bag looked like the one that Shahrukh Khan's character had used in the movie Baazigar to hide the dead body and this guy was trying to be prodigiously charming too, as if he had some hidden motive behind it. My mind was beeping high alert.

"Look mister...who ever you are...I don't know you—" I started rudely, but he cut me off.

"But I know you very well Miss Raahi Sharma from Solan, working at Northern Software Tech."

Oh no! He must be a stalker. I was appalled at all the information he had on me.

"Doesn't matter...no one is at home right now, so please fuck off," I retorted. I was damn terrified, but didn't let it reflect on my face.

"Language, Miss Raahi Sharma," he furrowed his brows. "Don't you think you are being too rude to a charming guy like me," he teased with his wicked grin. I was confounded, as he had now started to get on my nerves.

"CHARMING!! MY FOOT...get lost from here otherwise I'm going to call security," I declared loudly, trying to scare him away.

"Okay, okay...I think it's going too far. Let me introduce myself," he said with both his palms up in a conciliatory gesture. "I'm Aadit...Aadit Kashyap... I hope you have heard my name," he said persuasively.

"Wow!" I faked a laugh and shook my head. "I must say you have done your homework quite well. But for your kind information, Aadit is in USA and you can't bluff me by his name," I said sardonically, folding my arms over my chest. *I'm not a fool mister stranger.*

"DAMN!! I can't believe I'll have to go through a security check to enter my own house now," he murmured under his breath. "Do you want to see my passport?" he said annoyed, as if it was I who was tormenting him.

"NO, I don't want to...I know it's not very difficult in this country to duplicate a passport or any other document, for that matter," I said bluntly with my brows rutted in anger.

"Argh! Look, I'm damn tired and I'm in no mood for an argument, so please let me in," he appealed.

"Never," I scowled and shook my head in a clear refusal.

"Okay...then let me at least use your phone. My phone battery has drained down," he pleaded.

"I know all these tactics MISTER, but I'm not falling into your trap."

"TRAP? And why would I do that!?" he asked quizzically.

"May be"—I paused to gather the appropriate words in my head and then continued —"to rob, rape, or perhaps you are a psycho serial killer. Who knows?" I vituperated and before he could say anything else, I slammed the door shut in his face.

As I walked in, I heard the continuous ding of the doorbell again. It didn't sound like he was going to leave anytime soon and that got me damn terrified. I picked up my phone and dialed Maa's number, but it was unreachable. Then I tried Aisha and uncle's numbers too, but without success. Perhaps there was a signal problem at the auditorium, I inferred. With no other option left, I informed the society's security office before it could get any worse. Soon, I heard a low-pitched argument right outside and after a few minutes, there was complete silence. *They must have taken him away*, I thought and breathed easy.

Half an hour later, I called the main gate security to track the whereabouts of that stranger boy. Though he wasn't bothering me anymore, I felt a little restless regardless. The security guard at the other end told me that the guy was still there and said that he was waiting there for his parents to come back. He had also tried to call his parents repeatedly using their phone, but couldn't reach anyone. I disconnected the call.

I got even more restless after knowing this. If he was truly an intruder, he could have just run away as soon as I called the security, but the guy was still here, waiting.

What if he really is Aadit?

I bolted upright and hurriedly tried to search for his picture in all the three bedrooms. All the pictures hanging on the walls or on shelves and tables however were his childhood photos. I tried every possible way to know whether that stranger boy was Aadit or not, but couldn't get any clue.

Then I opened Facebook on my phone and searched for Aadit Kashyap. The search result listed numerous Aadit Kashyap but only one contact showed two mutual friends underneath the name. I quickly tapped on it and his profile started to load on my screen. The two mutual friends were Aisha Kashyap and Reena Kashyap. When I opened his profile picture, I was stunned to see the same stranger boy. With my heart in mouth and hands trembling, I called the security office number again and told them to let the boy in, as it was indeed Aadit Kashyap. This was the first time that he had come to his new house, so none of the security guards recognized him.

"Are you sure, madam?" the security guard asked to ensure.

"Yeah...pretty sure." I said, nibbling on my lower lip.

My heart started to throb ten times faster as the doorbell rang. I closed my eyes, took a deep breath and opened the door. He stood about half a foot taller than me, with an appealing lean yet masculine frame. His deep brown eyes were gazing at me unfathomably.

"Hi," I managed to say somehow, with a smile plastered on my face. He didn't reply and sauntered in, dragging his gigantic bag behind him. Without uttering a single word, or looking at me again, he walked briskly to his room and shut the door behind him.

Gosh! I messed up. Sometimes, being too cautious is also dangerous. I wished I hadn't seen that video right before dozing off, then I might have given him a chance to explain. But now, I had to placate him before everyone arrived, as I didn't want to get embarrassed in front of them all.

Suddenly, an idea flashed in my mind. I tiptoed towards the kitchen, placed a glass of water in a tray and waddled towards his room. I knocked on his door. There was no response. I knocked again. No response again. 'May be he is in the washroom,' I tried to assuage my disappointment and counted till thirty in my head with my eyes closed. This time, I decided to knock louder with a heavy hand, just to ensure that the sound reaches his ears even if he is in the washroom. As I lifted my hand and was about to hit on the door, he unlocked the door and swung it open; I lost my balance and splashed half of the water on his clothes. *Crap! Another mistake.*

He was taken by surprise and immediately started to shake the water out of his clothes. He looked noticeably miffed now. With a disgruntled expression, he looked straight into my eyes. I shuddered. This meeting had definitely started on the wrong foot.

"You need some water?" I tried to sound confident, though my voice jittered.

"NO, I don't. Anything else?" he asked, narrowing his eyes.

"Um…err…actually I…I'm sorry, I'm so sorry for everything. For all the drama I created and now this," I stuttered, gesturing towards his drenched shirt.

He took the glass of water and gulped down the little water that was left in it. His cold stare was still stuck on me and I was looking anywhere but at him.

"It's okay," I heard him say as he kept the glass back on the tray.

"What will you have? Tea? Coffee?" I asked timorously.

"Nothing, and thank you so much MISS RAAHI SHARMA, but you have already done a lot for me. I don't know when I'll get a chance to reciprocate the favor you did by allowing me in my own house," he mocked.

"It wasn't my fault," I said looking down.

"Yeah…I agree...it was actually my fault. I wanted to surprise everyone and got the shock of my life."

"Are you sure you don't want anything?" I asked for a final time, uninterested in the discussion of whose-mistake-it-was.

He shook his head, still looking into my eyes. With a dead-tired expression he said, "I'm exhausted, can I sleep in peace for some time?"

"Yeah…sure," I said and took my leave.

After a few hours, when everyone was back home, the environment was beatific as never before; everyone was thrilled to bits by the sudden arrival of Aadit. No one was expecting him. Maa was in seventh heaven and her face came aglow with glee. She made all the possible dishes she could think of. I thanked my stars that he didn't recount the incident from before to anyone, or I would have died of embarrassment.

***

Chapter 5
Shared Secrets

It was ten-thirty in the evening already and I was desperately waiting for a call. I kept my phone on the table and started changing out of the dress that I had worn to office that day. I put on some pink knee length shorts and was about to grab my top when my phone rang. I quickly put on a white T-shirt with a Minnie Mouse printed on it and scurried to the balcony of my room. This was my patent place to talk. I was about to take the call, when I noticed a silhouette of a man smoking at the far end of the balcony. I rejected the call as I recognized who this person was.

"Aadit?"

He swiftly turned on his heels, startled by my sudden appearance. He put out the cigarette in a haste and threw it in the corner. The way he was standing, as if he had been caught red-handed, made me guess that no one else at home knew that he smoked.

"What are you doing here in my balcony?" I asked him.

"Our balcony. I think we share this balcony." he corrected me, gesturing at the doors of our rooms that were connected through a common balcony.

"You were smoking here. Didn't—"

"Huh? No. I was out for some fresh air," he answered without letting me complete my sentence.

"Answering too quickly or taking too much time to answer, both are the traits of a fibster. I saw you. You were smoking here, so don't lie."

He didn't say anything and looked away.

"Don't you know it's injurious to health? How can you be so careless?" I chided.

"Oh please...I'm not a regular smoker. I just do it occasionally," he said exasperated.

"Does Maa know about it?" I asked. Smoking and drinking had always been things that turned me off.

"No, she doesn't. Don't tell me you are going to complain to her about this."

I raised my brow at him roguishly.

"Hey! Wait a minute. *Haan?* Are you expecting me to bend my knee and beg you for mercy?" he chuckled. "I'm not going to do any of that Miss Raahi Sharma."

He looked deep into my eyes and said, "If you are thinking of telling this to Maa, then let me tell you that I may also disclose your secret."

"Oh really?" I faked a laugh, "And what will you tell her?"

"I'll tell her about your boyfriend," he said with his tongue in cheek, halting me in my tracks. The sudden change in my demeanor told him that his arrow had hit right on the target.

"Answering too quickly or taking too much time to answer, both are the traits of a fibster. I heard someone say this just a moment ago," he mocked.

"It is nothing like that. I was just—" I stopped and as my phone started vibrating in my hand. It was his call.

"And he is calling you right now," he added, mischievously pointing at my phone.

Glowering at him, I took the call and whispered, "I'll get back to you in five minutes."

"It's okay, dear...I'm going out with a friend. Let's talk in the morning," I heard him say over the phone.

Aadit looked at me expectantly for a reply, but I preferred to keep my mouth shut, as I had no idea whether he really knew about him or if it was just his speculation.

"He is just a friend," I said, nodding my head in an attempt to convince him.

"Who? Abhimanyu?" he snapped.

He knew his name!

"How do you know?"

"I heard you talking to him over the phone yesterday," he said and waved his hand gesticulating the balcony, "Here."

"Were you eavesdropping?"

"Not exactly. When you were talking to him yesterday, I was about to come here, you know, for some fresh air,"—he air-quoted the 'fresh air' by flexing his fingers—"but unlike you, I didn't barge into your personal space."

I narrowed my eyes at him in response.

"By the way, why are you hiding him? Aren't you sure about him?" he asked.

"I can never be surer than this, but I want my father to know it first. So don't tell this to anyone," I blurted out the truth.

"And why haven't you told your father yet?" he tried to probe further.

"I tried many times...like seriously," I pinched my throat to swear, "But couldn't."

"Why so?" he asked.

"I don't know. Maybe I'm scared of his response. He has always been quite strict. Though I won't be able to hold it in for long. Abhimanyu is coming to meet me the day after tomorrow and he told me that he wants to talk about our future," I said and blushed, looking down at my clasped hands.

"Ahem...ahem...so that means I'm the first one to know about your love life," he teased.

"Um, second one. First is my friend Shreya; after all, she was the one who had planned and designed the whole test approach," I said and then crinkled my nose, realizing that I was giving him too much detail, but I couldn't control myself as I had finally found someone to whom I could talk about my boyfriend after so long.

"Test approach?" he asked, puzzled.

"Yeah...actually, when he proposed to me two years ago, Shreya and I made him go through various tests before I said 'Yes.'"

He sniggered at the way I said it. "So, Shreya is your relationship guide, eh? Care to explain, what kind of tests were these?" he needled further.

"Like background test, intelligence test, sincerity test, compatibility test, loyalty test and blah. Shreya and I made a complete checklist that time. Shreya is in Chandigarh and he is from Patiala, so she did a background check on him through her friends who stay at Patiala."

"Hmm…and how did you test sincerity and compatibility?" he asked, stifling his laughter.

"Well, it was Shreya's idea. In fact, everything was planned by her and I just followed her commands. For sincerity, she instructed me to meet him in my absolute worst look, so I went on a date wearing literally my pajamas and a T-shirt, with my hair tied up in a messy bun. For compatibility, she told me to throw various tantrums and see how he reacted."

"What about the loyalty test?" he tittered.

"For that, she called him over the phone and made him believe that she was deeply in love with him. She tried everything to lure him, but nothing worked. He clearly told her that he liked me." I beamed excitedly at the memory.

"Don't tell me, you actually tried all of this on him? Poor guy." He shook his head in disbelief and I nodded sheepishly in response, while we laughed.

"Interesting, Miss Raahi Sharma...you aren't that naïve as I was told. But why all these tests?" he asked.

"Because I didn't want to take a chance. Once I say 'yes' to someone, I don't want there to be any looking back, and I'm lucky I have him. He is my first and will be my last," I said. Aadit opened his mouth to say something and then decided against it.

"So, what about you?" I asked, curious to know his part of the story.

"What about me?" he asked.

"This isn't fair. I told you everything about me. It's your turn now," I said in mock anger.

"There is nothing to know about me. I'm single," he faked a sad expression.

"No way... you look like the kind of boy who must have many girlfriends, you know, the flirting kind," I mocked.

"Is it? Then I must say that looks can be deceptive, Miss Raahi Sharma. I'm also a one-woman kind of man. As for flirtation, only a few special people earn it," he smiled.

"Then, should I feel privileged?"

"Did I flirt with you?"

"Kind of. Remember the day you arrived here, if you had talked to me normally I would have gone easy on you."

He pursed his lips. "Did I ruin my first impression?"

"Not really, and you should thank your stars for that," I said. "So, you are still waiting for your miss perfect, right?"

"Not really...mine is a found and lost case, from a long time ago."

"Oh! I'm sorry." I knew his story to some extent as Aisha had told me that day, but I assumed he had moved on. I didn't want to scrape at his wounds, but unintentionally I had done just that.

"Don't be. It's all in the past. I believe that everything happens for a reason. May be, there was something good in that too," he said looking at road under our balcony and got lost in his own thoughts. None of us spoke for a few minutes. Then Aadit broke the silence and said, "It's getting late now, I think we should sleep."

"Indeed...so now that we know each other's secrets, I feel it would be wise to accept each other as friends," I tried to make light of the moment and extended my right hand for a handshake. He responded with a smile and shook my hand. Then both of us returned to our respective rooms.

As I slipped inside my blanket and closed my eyes, the first thing that appeared behind my closed eyelids was his face, Abhimanyu Singh, the love of my life. Thinking about him before sleeping had become a ritual now. He was my batch mate: the same college, the same batch and the same stream. We had become friends on the very first day of our college. I still remember that day, both of us arrived late for our first lecture and the professor didn't allow us to enter, so we had to spend the entire one hour of that lecture at the college canteen and that was how we got acquainted to each other. We connected instantly and so well that the one hour felt more than enough for us to know each other. With every passing day, our relationship grew from just friends to best friends and then we routinely started to spend each and every minute of college time together.

I would never have realized my feeling for him if he hadn't proposed to me just the day after our second year session exams at college got over. It was the time when Shreya was in town too and together we planned a complete strategy to test him. Though it seems stupid now, but back then, it was a matter of life and death. He passed each and every test totally unaware of the fact that he was being tested, and that was just the thing which made me fall in love with him even more. But as they say, no story is complete without its twists and turns.

In my love story, the first twist came when he got his call letter two months before I got mine, and left for Hyderabad. We both had filled Delhi as our first preference for posting, but he got Hyderabad, whereas I came to Noida, and our all-time-together-relationship changed to a long distance one.

It got worse with each passing day, as we became so entrapped in our new jobs, that we hardly got any time to talk to each other the way we used to before. It wasn't like I didn't understand his situation, but somewhere deep inside, it was smiting my heart.

Ever since he had told me that he had to tell me something very important regarding our future, my excitement was at its pinnacle. His words were still reverberating like music in my ears, sweeping me off my feet. *Was he going to propose to me for marriage? Or was he thinking to move out of the country?* I remembered him saying that he wanted to get settled in Australia. I knew that whatever it would be, it was going to change my life and I would happily say yes to anything he asks me for. I could never let my love become a bondage for him because we weren't committed to each other's lives, we were committed to each other's dreams. I smiled and envisioned myself with him. *Just a day and a few hours more, and he would be here, right in front of me.*

***

Chapter 6
A Date To Remember

AADIT

"Who is it, Kanchi?" I heard Maa's loud voice as Kanchi rushed to attend to the door. Lying on my bed in my room, I had been in deep slumber when the doorbell rang and interrupted my sleep.

"Raahi Didi *hain*!" Kanchi replied.

"Raahi, how come you are early today? What happened?" I heard Maa asking her.

"Maa, remember I told you I have to go to meet my college friends today?" she reminded. I knew she was lying. She had revealed only half the truth saying that a few of her friends from college had planned a get-together in Delhi and she was going to meet them.

"Oh, yes. You did tell me. It slipped out of my mind. You get ready. I'll tell Kanchi to bring tea to your room." I heard Maa's voice fading as I covered my head by clenching a pillow tight around my ears. Since the day I arrived, I had been fighting hard to cope with the jet lag. The buzz on my phone just then failed my endeavor to get any more sleep.

"Hey, handsome, how have you been?" she said as soon as I picked up the phone.

"Hey Sakshi, I'm good. How are you? It's been a long time. Where are you?" I said, sitting up in bed.

"Yeah, true. Well, I'm here in Delhi today. Let's catch up?"

"Tell me time and venue, I'll be there."

"I'll message you as soon as my shoot is over."

"Yeah, Sure."

"Okay, I gotta go. See you soon."

"Bye."

Sakshi had been my friend, right since we started learning A-B-C. We went to the same school, were in the same class, shared the same birthdates and even the school's Mr. and Miss Farewell titles; and as if it weren't enough, the major setbacks in our lives had also happened at the same time. When I was struggling to get out of depression, she was also struggling with her family's disapproval with her career choice. She wanted to be a model and she did it anyway without any support from her family. She was now one of the top models in India. Tossing my phone to the side, I tried to elicit a little more sleep from my heavy head and tired eyes, and I finally succeeded.

When I opened my eyes, it was already quarter to seven. Rolling over to my side, I checked my phone for Sakshi's message and there it was, with the venue and time for our meet-up. Had I done a little math, I would have known that I was already running late. Getting up from the bed, I grabbed my towel and ambled to the bathroom for a quick shower.

As soon as I was ready, I grabbed my car keys from the dining table and was about to leave when the creaking sound of the door made me turn my head towards it and the sight I was greeted with, changed something inside me...*forever*. I saw her, dressed in a white chiffon Anarkali suit that hugged her carved body perfectly, a delicate red chiffon Duppatta was draped over her left shoulder, her long dark brown hair were untied and cascaded down her back in perfect loose curls, and the shimmer of her silver *jhumkies* and the tinkle of her silver metallic bangles was in perfect cadence with her steps. My gaze was stuck on her like a partridge staring at the moon awed by her beauty, as if everything besides her had ceased to exist. Sidling up to me, she tucked a lock of her hair behind her ear and arched up her brows at me, while I savored her fragrance in response. She was humbly dressed, yet looked so damn gorgeous! She was covered top to toe in that delicate white fabric, yet looked enticing enough that one could declare it unlawful to dress that way. Standing just an inch away, she supported herself up on her tippy toes to reach my level and leaned slightly closer to me.

Fuck! She is going to kiss me, I thought as my breath hitched in anticipation.

She tilted her head a little and whispered in my ear, "Stop gawking senselessly at me, Mister Kashyap. Don't behave as if you are seeing a girl for the first time." A smile crept onto my face. *God! What was I thinking!*

"Nah! You are mistaken, Miss. I was just wondering what kind of makeup you've put on? Smudged black eyes and painted red cheeks, what happened to your face, by the way?" I asked slyly.

"WHAT?" she grimaced and rummaged through her handbag for the phone. Pulling it out, she opened the front camera, as I tried to stifle my laughter at her sudden reaction. As soon as she noticed me snickering, she understood my mischievous escapade.

"You…stupid!" she said and lifted her hand as if to punch me, but stopped midway.

"Well...I don't want to say this, but someone is going to feel like the luckiest guy in the world tonight. You look stunning." As soon as my words reached her ears, she bloomed feverishly and her cheeks turned a richer shade of pink.

"Aha! Someone is looking beautiful today!" Maa exclaimed as she saw her.

"Thanks Maa," Raahi said, all flattered. "I'm leaving now."

"Maa, don't you think it's too late for her to go out alone? I think you should go along with her," I snapped, knowing full well where she was going, but I couldn't help but make her escape a little unpalatable. Raahi instantly glared at me, but I was in no mood to stop.

"Your unsolicited advices aren't required here," she muttered under her breath, with a taut jaw.

"What will I do there with her friends? But what Aadit says isn't wrong either. Why don't you go with her, Aadit?" Asked Maa, looking at me.

"What will he do there, Maa? He doesn't even know my friends. I'm not taking him," Raahi shrieked.

"Why not, Maa? Don't worry. I'll accompany her. After all, she is our responsibility, isn't she?" I said, placing my hand softly at her back. She squirmed out of it instantly in irritation.

"You know, you are a demon. I regret the day I shared my secret with you," she grumbled as we entered the elevator.

"Do you even know why I want to come with you?" I asked.

"To ruin my date," she snarled.

"No, because I am really eager to meet this great personality, you know, your tested, tried, verified and certified boyfriend," I said.

"Abhimanyu is a black belt in Karate, you know," she said, crossing her arms over her chest. The way she expressed her contempt and anger made her look all the more cuter.

"Are you trying to scare me?" I said, mirroring her gesture.

"No. I'm warning you, just in case. He won't tolerate any shit around me," she snorted.

"Language, Miss Raahi Sharma," I warned. It wasn't like I didn't use swear words myself, but when it came out of her innocent mouth, it felt odd. As we approached the car in the parking, I opened the passenger door of my car for her, but she pulled the back door open and climbed in.

"I don't like to sit with over-smart people," she mumbled as an explanation.

The whole way I kept exasperating her, keeping my eyes on her in the rear view mirror. On reaching her destination, she quickly got off the car and started walking, ignoring me completely. I went after her and quickly grabbed her arm to stop her. The look on her face at that moment told me that she would land a punch straight on my face any second.

"Hey, don't worry, I'm not coming with you. Go ahead and enjoy your date," I said.

"Then, what was all that drama for?"

"Because, I love teasing you. I like you more when you are pissed at me," I winked at her as if it was a matter of pride.

She shook her head in disbelief and then smiled, giving me a glimpse of her carved and beautifully glossed lips.

"Actually, I have to meet a friend too. So, I thought I'd drop you on my way. What time shall I come to pick you up, Madam?"

"No need. Abhimanyu will drop me back," she replied.

"Aye, so the princess will come back with her prince charming, huh?"

"Shut up Aadit," she blushed again at my remark.

"Okay, don't forget to call me before you leave this place. As you know, I won't get entry at home without you."

"Yeah sure," she said and ambled towards the entrance of the restaurant.

***

It took me fifteen more minutes to reach the place where Sakshi was waiting for me. I forgot to mention this before, another similarity between us is that she is the same height as me as well, six feet and an inch high.

"Hey Aadit, it's so nice to see you!" Sakshi exclaimed, getting up from her seat and raising her left arm in invitation for a hug as I approached her.

"Same here. It's been a really long time. Celebrity now, eh?" I teased her.

"Ha! It's only glittery on the outside, inside it's all dark."

"I don't agree. I mean, just look at you. You have achieved what you always wanted to. I feel very proud seeing you on the cover page of the top magazines."

"Yeah, it's all good for now. But the one thing I have learnt about this industry is that once you are at the top, you should start preparing yourself mentally for the downfall."

"Why so?"

She shrugged. "Let's not talk about that right now. Tell me, what has been up with you. By the way, I have already ordered for starters and drinks, I hope you don't mind."

"That's perfectly fine. And as for me, everything is going perfectly smoothly."

"That's good. Hey, when is Aisha's wedding?"

"Most probably in February. And you have to come!"

"Stop me if you can," she chuckled.

We spent the rest of the evening talking about everything and nothing over dinner. As I sipped my drink, I noticed a couple at the next table feeding each other across the table and wondered what would Raahi be doing. It was quarter to ten already and she still hadn't called.

"Where is your mind?" Sakshi asked, dragging my attention back to her.

"Ah! I'm supposed to pick a friend up. She must be waiting for me."

"It's okay, we are almost done here."

Soon after, we bade adieu and I was back in my car, still waiting for Raahi's call. 'I'll wait for another fifteen minutes and then I'll call her,' I told myself. I beamed as I recalled my conversation with Raahi on the balcony the other night. The childlike enthusiasm in her while she talked about her love life was pleasantly amusing. Although she had been trying to prove herself clever and agile through her words, I could clearly see the glint of innocence in her eyes that surpassed everything else. That innocence was still alive in her because she was yet to experience life. I wished for the trust she had on her love to never be broken and that she might never be made to see the ugly side of love. My own life was testimony to the fact that the wounds that love causes can never be healed completely, they always leave an everlasting mark. It drains all the innocence out of you and makes you see the world through a different lens, not allowing you anymore to trust someone so blindly again.

When I didn't receive a call even after half an hour, I called her up myself. No one picked up the phone. Then after five minutes, I called again and a stranger's voice answered this time.

"Hello, *kaun bol rha hai? Ye jis madam ka phone hai wo auto mein hi bhool gyi hain* (Who is speaking? The Madam who owns the phone has left it in my auto)," I heard him say.

"Hello *Bhaiya, kahan hain aap aur madam kahan hai* (Where are you and where is madam)?" I asked.

"Madam *ko to hum chhod diye the unki building mein kareeb aadha ghanta pehle. Aap madam se kahiye phone le le apna, hum unki building ke samne aata hu* (I dropped her at her building around half an hour ago. You please tell Madam to come and collect her phone, I'm coming to the front of her building)," he said.

"Okay Bhaiya," I hung up and dialed my mother's number so that I might convey the message to Raahi. She was already home and hadn't even cared to call me.

"Where are you and Raahi, Aadit? It's already so late. Come home soon," my mother said as soon as she picked up her phone. I had presumed that Raahi was already at home, but apparently she wasn't. I called Raahi's number again. The auto driver picked up the phone. I inquired him again regarding what building he had dropped her at. It was indeed the Oasis Apartments. Then I told him to wait for me at the main gate. I had started to get really baffled now. The auto driver repeated that he dropped her at building half an hour ago, then why hadn't she reached home yet? I tried to make sense of things, but to no avail.

"Where the hell are you, Raahi?" I banged my fist on the dashboard of my car.

I reached the place in the next twenty minutes. I took her phone from auto driver who I found waiting for me right at the entrance of my apartment.

"*Madam ander gyi thi naa, pakka* (Are you sure, Madam went inside)?" I confirmed again.

"*Ji sir, koi dikkat hai kya? Madam bhi bohot ro rhi thi* (Yes sir, is there any problem? Madam was weeping all the way here)," the auto driver said.

"*Nahi Bhaiya,* thank you," I said and handed over a hundred-rupee note to him for the inconvenience he had to go through.

I unlocked her phone and her WhatsApp conversation with Abhimanyu flashed on the screen. A chill ran down my spine as I read her last message to him, which was delivered almost an hour back. I rushed inside and asked the guard on duty about her whereabouts. The guard confirmed that she had gone inside and had taken an elevator. Every guard was familiar with both of us, since that stranger boy fiasco.

"Is the terrace door open?" I asked the guard.

"Yes, it's open," he replied. "It's the festival season and some lighting work is going on at the terrace. That's why we have kept it open."

I didn't pay attention to what he was saying anymore. My instinct was telling me that something was wrong, *damn wrong*. I took the elevator till the 18th floor and climbed up the stairs, leaping over two at a time, to reach the terrace. As I made it there, gasping for breath, I saw her. She was standing near the edge of the terrace, resting her hands on the cement parapet. As I approached her, I saw her staring blankly into the distance; her eyes wide and blood shot, and her eyelids swollen. It was evident from her face, which had the black streaks of dried tears running down her cheeks, that she had been crying for a long time. She seemed to be in utter despair. I had to shake her repeatedly by the shoulders to bring her back to her senses. She looked at me with her gloomy eyes; I took a deep breath and asked her in a calm voice, "What happened, Raahi?"

She kept on staring at me numbly. Distraught, I could not understand how a girl who was so cheerful a few moments ago, could have crumbled to such a crestfallen stupor. I asked her again, "What happened, Raahi?"

Before any words could escape her lips, fresh tears started streaming down her cheeks. Soon, the silent sobs transformed into painful groans. I felt shattered to see her in this condition.

"Raahi…Raahi…please look at me," I held her face in my palms. "Now tell me, what happened? See...I'm here with you," I said, standing in front of her. I held her tightly as she staggered on her weakened knees.

"Aadit…he… he…" she choked on her tears.

"Yes, Raahi. Tell me, I'm listening." I comforted her by caressing her back.

"He broke up with me, Aadit," she howled, "Everything is finished. My life is finished."

She clutched me tightly, holding the front of my shirt in her clasped fists and buried her face in my chest to muffle her sobs. I enveloped her in my arms and started caressing her back incessantly. She kept on crying and I let her weep her heart out. Who else could have understood her better than myself? This reminded me of my own state from a few years ago, the only difference being that I didn't cry, but buried and suppressed all the pain deep down my heart.

A buzz on my phone snapped me out of the daze. I made her sit on a cemented platform on the terrace as I took the call. It was Maa. I excused myself and went at the other end of the terrace.

"Where are you, Aadit? It's eleven already, what are you guys up to?" she exploded as soon as I picked up her call.

"Oh Maa, I forgot to tell you. Actually, Raahi and her friends wanted to see a movie. So we are here at PVR. You don't worry, I'm with her," I made an excuse, as taking Raahi home in her condition wasn't a good idea.

"Okay then, we are going to sleep and I'm keeping the keys under the potted plant outside," she said and disconnected the call.

I came back to where Raahi was and sat beside her. She rested her head on my shoulder. Neither of us spoke for a while. I knew that nothing could comfort her at that moment. Nothing could mend a broken heart. Only time has the power to heal such wounds and yet, the scar remains. She wasn't crying anymore, but I could still hear the muffled sobbing sounds.

After a few moments, she broke the silence, "You know Aadit, when I was a baby, I used to think that one day, someone will come into my life, who will love me with all his heart, just the way my Paa loved my Mom. He never remarried. He says he can still feel my mother's presence. He was so much in love with her that there was no room for anyone else. I used to think that the love in my life would be eternal, it would know no boundaries, and even death won't be able to separate us. I had never thought it would end this way," she sobbed.

I placed my hand on the back of her head and caressed her. She continued, "He had been behaving strangely for the past few weeks, but you know, love is blind, how could I have seen what was coming my way. I thought maybe he was having a rough time adjusting to the new city. I was so blind, I was so…so…blind," she blubbered.

"It's okay, Raahi…" I tried to console her.

"NO. IT'S NOT OKAY!" she bawled, lifting her head up and looking directly into my eyes.

"I can't let him go, Aadit, I can't...I have to stop him. I have to stop him now. He can't leave me," she started looking for her phone in her bag.

"It's here, you left it in the auto," I took out her phone from my pocket.

"Oh, did he call me? Let me check..." she asked and extended her hand towards me.

"He didn't," I said. He was such a douche that he hadn't even cared to reply to her last message.

"It's okay. Maybe he is busy. He had to catch a train to Patiala. He was already running late. He told me. Let me call him," she rambled, trying to take her phone from my hand but I withdrew it out of her reach.

"It's late, Raahi...let's call him in the morning," I tried to coax her out of her desperate attempt to call him.

"What if it's too late by then? I need to call him now," she insisted.

"NO!" I raised my voice.

"Please Aadit, please please, let me do it once. Just once," she pleaded.

I handed over the phone to her and told her to keep the call on speaker. No one picked up at the first attempt, neither at the second. The third time, Abhimanyu picked up.

"Abhi, I'm sorry Abhi...please talk to me. I promise, I'll listen to everything you say. We need to resolve this matter. It can't end this way," her voice cracked.

"What's your problem, Raahi? Please, please stop this non-sense. Why don't you understand? There is nothing to resolve. Our relationship has already fizzled out, there is nothing left anymore," he paused for a moment and then added, "See, if you want we can still be friends, but don't expect anything more than that. It's over now and you have to understand that. Stop behaving like a kid." There wasn't a single tinge of emotion in his voice. I started to get skeptical about her claim that he ever loved her.

"Don't say that, please. I'll die. You promised—" she sobbed.

"You know, I hate this…all the drama that you always create. You know, you suffocate me sometimes. Loving you was the biggest mistake of my life. I can't understand why the hell you are making such a big deal out of it? You aren't the first one to ever go through a breakup. Stop acting as if you are a victim and I'm the culprit here. I have never done anything wrong to you," he snorted. "Now stop calling or messaging me please, otherwise I'll have to block your contact."

As I heard their conversation, blood rushed to my eyes. I clenched my fist in anger, took the phone from her hand and said in calm but firm voice, "Hey look, let me tell you one thing, you are an asshole. I know that if not tomorrow, then surely sometime in future, you are going to realize the worth of what you have lost. But do keep one thing in your mind, if I ever, EVER see you around her again, even in a one kilometer's radius of her, I promise I'll kill you in the deadliest way you can think of," I said and he disconnected the call.

"Why did you say that? What if he takes it seriously and never calls me again?" Raahi asked distraught.

"I won't let anyone treat you like that, Raahi. It would be better for you if he doesn't call you anymore. You definitely deserve better."

I took her hand in mine, looked into her eyes and said, "Raahi, promise me that you won't talk to him again." She shook her head and sobbed, "No, I can't, I can't promise that, Aadit."

"Okay...then promise me that you won't be the one to make the move first," I said. She nodded reluctantly.

***

Chapter 7

Going Through The Pain

"Raahi…are you still sleeping, *beta*? Aren't you going to office today?" asked Maa, as she entered my room and saw me still lying in bed. She shook me slightly by the shoulder to wake me up. I tried to open my eyes and get up, but failed miserably. My eyelids felt heavy, even my chest felt heavy, as I woke up to another depressing day.

"What happened, Raahi? Are you fine?" Maa asked, touching my forehead. It was warm. "Oh! It looks like you have a fever, Raahi…let me check," she said in a worried tone and got up to fetch a thermometer. I was running a hundred and one degree fever but this wasn't the thing that was troubling me, it was the cold attitude of Abhimanyu that I had been subjected to the day before. Did it really happen or was it all just a bad dream? Just a few hours ago, I had a perfect life and now I was all devastated.

Maa brought in a glass of warm milk along with a toast and instructed me to eat, since I couldn't take medicines on an empty stomach. I followed all her commands without uttering a single word. Maa caressed my head and kissed my forehead. "I think you are tired, take rest. I'm just a call away if you need anything. Everything will be alright," she said and took her leave.

'Nothing will be alright anymore,' I thought. I looked at my phone expectantly, but there was neither a message nor any call from Abhimanyu. My heart sank once again. *How could he? How could?* It took him just a day to forget two years of our togetherness and move on. Did it mean that everything he said to me and everything he did for me, all the promises that he made to me was nothing but pretense. I curled up on my bed and didn't realize when I fell asleep again.

***

"Just leave me alone, Abhi," I said furiously, climbing down the stairs.

"No, I won't. Until you say you love me," said Abhi, trying to catch me ardently from behind.

"NEVER EVER. I'm breaking up with you," I said, irately.

"Aaah…don't say that. I'll die." He pretended to be massively hurt.

"Stop following me, for God's sake, we are in the college campus," I exploded.

"So what? Let everyone know how much I love you," he said playfully.

"Go and tell this to all the girls you were flirting with a moment ago. This isn't going to work on me."

"Ah! You know I love that,"— he suddenly came to the front of me and blocked my way— "seeing you get jealous like that."

"Stop presuming, Abhi. I'm not jealous. Now will you please stop following me? I don't want to be the next hot potato of college," I chided, pushing him away.

"Say 'I love you' and I'll do as you say."

"And what if I don't?"

"Then, you know how stubborn I can be!"

"That means you will follow me everywhere. Right?.... What if I go there?" I pointed towards the ladies' washroom.

"Obviously, I'll wait outside. Come-on. I'm not that dumb."

I laughed at the way he said it.

"Um, what if I go to the principal's room?"

"I'll follow you in and complain to him that you are refusing to say what I want to hear."

"Haha, and then he will throw you out of the college. Dumb. What if I die?"

He wrapped his arms around my waist and whispered, "I'll follow you there too. Nothing can separate you and me, not even death. My love has that power to cross any boundaries for you."

A silent tear escaped from the corner of my eye, reminiscing one of my special moments with Abhimanyu in college. I was still lying on my bed. It's the hardest thing to get out of love, while falling in love doesn't take any effort at all. It's impossible to expunge the memories that you create while in love. They will always haunt you, despite all your endeavors to go away from them.

I lifted my head and looked at the clock, it showed five past two in the afternoon. *What was wrong with me?* I wondered. I had never dozed off for so long and that too when sleep should be evading me. I held my head up straight and opened my eyes wide. My head hurt as if I was under the influence of some drugs. The persistent heaviness was making it difficult for me to keep my eyes open. *Is it something that always happens to people when their heart breaks*? I wondered. I grabbed my phone from the side table and opened Abhimanyu's WhatsApp contact. He hadn't replied to my last message from the previous night. It was a verse:

With a broken heart, you left me alone
It's still reverberating in my ear, your frigid tone
Reminiscing your love that felt so great
I'm lost in the darkness, with endless wait
I was elated to be in your love-girth
And now, I'm here, doubting my own worth
My soul is dead, though my body is alive
And from here, I see the end of my life
Please come back, we aren't destined to part
And hold me again, I'm falling apart

Every time, he got mad at me, all I had to do was write a poem for him and he would melt like wax in a jiffy. I tried this yesterday too, but it didn't work this time. Did that mean it was the end of our relationship? 'No!' my heart screamed. 'I won't give up on this relationship. Mr. Abhimanyu Singh, no matter what you said and how you behaved yesterday, my love won't let you abandon this relationship so easily. I know you will come back following me and I'll wait for that day,' I consoled myself. A rap at the door pulled me out of my reverie. It was Aadit with a bowl of fruits that he had brought for me.

"Hey… how are you doing? I heard someone is getting quite hot today," he said wryly.

"Yeah, yeah…hot and now single too," I responded with a smile that didn't reach my eyes. "I need to go to the washroom," I excused myself and clambered off the bed.

As I entered the washroom, I looked at myself in the mirror. My eyelids were puffy and there was a slight swelling all over my face. I washed my face.

"So, slept well?" he asked as soon as I stepped out.

"Well! I slept like never before…I don't know what's wrong with me," I replied, wiping my face with a towel.

"Hmm, it happens sometimes. You will be fine soon," he replied.

"I don't know. I'm still feeling sleepy," I said.

"Mind if I confess something?" he asked, making a puppy face. He looked cute.

"Go on."

"Actually, I know what's wrong with you… I had dissolved a sleeping pill in the water that you drank last night, just to make sure you sleep well. Otherwise, you would have spent the whole night sobbing," he confessed.

"Silly me! I thought it was one of the side effects of a breakup."

"Breakup isn't a disease," he chuckled.

"Yeah, it's worst. You can't even take medicine for it," I sneered.

"But I must say Raahi, you are very strong," he said in a genuine tone.

I looked down; a tear escaped, wetting my eyelashes and falling onto the floor. "I'm not," I mumbled.

"It's okay to cry, Raahi. Tears aren't a sign of weakness, they signify your strength."

I smiled at how the tables had turned in my life. Call it fate or coincidence; it leads us to meet new people that influence our lives in unexpected ways. Just three days ago, Aadit and I were complete strangers, but today, he knew everything about me and was even making an effort to soothe my pain.

***

It was quarter past ten in the evening, when I received a message from Aadit:

Hey, I'm here in the balcony. Care to join me?

Yeah…wait a minute, I replied, but hardly took twenty seconds to make my way out.

He had arranged two chairs in the balcony, with a small table in the middle, which had a decorative candle nicely placed at the centre, along with two wine glasses and a white porcelain plate. On the plate, there was kept a delectable chocolate pastry with creamy vanilla frosting and a cherry on the top.

I cupped my face in amazement and asked, "What's all this?"

"I think we should celebrate."

"What's there to celebrate?"

"Um, one of my friend's status recently changed to single, so now I can finally hit on her. Isn't it an amazing reason to celebrate?" he said frivolously.

"You are incorrigible, Aadit," I shook my head.

"Miss Sharma, will you please do the honor of cutting the cake now?"

"Yes, Mr. Kashyap," I said, cutting the pastry in two and feeding a little piece from it to Aadit. He did the same for me.

"I was thinking of getting wine, but I wasn't so sure about you," he said as he poured a soft drink into the wine glasses.

"I think I should start drinking wine now. Isn't that what people do after they breakup?"

"Miss Raahi Sharma, I can see your sense of humor has surely improved in the last few hours," he chuckled.

"Maybe it's another side effect of the breakup," I said, tongue in cheek.

Both of us laughed and then sipped our drinks in silence. I could hear the chatter of people strolling on the road below. The kids were noisy as always and their parents were adding to it all the more by instructing the do's and don'ts to them loudly. Both of us were lost in our own world for some time before I broke the ice.

"Isn't it strange, Aadit? How life changes in a jiffy? We plan something and something entirely unexpected happens." I exhaled a deep breath and continued after a pause, "You know Aadit, what was the most hurtful thing for me...when I tried to find love for myself in his eyes, and didn't see even a hint of it. He gave me endless reasons to justify his cold behavior, but they were all vague and warped. I know he was just looking for an excuse to run out of this relationship. I was so confused, I still am, but I waited patiently, hoping that he will soon realize the ridiculousness of what he was saying and everything will fall back into place. But I was wrong. I was so wrong..."

Tears threatened to stream down my eyes again, but I hastily wiped them away and continued, "I tried to make him understand my perspective but all my words fell on deaf ears. He wasn't ready to hear anything, as if he wasn't there to discuss, but only to pass the judgment. He had already made up his mind. He felt like a stranger to me. I loved him dearly and this is what I got in return," I sobbed.

"You know Raahi, everything that happens in life has some significance. Sometimes, the things that happen appear to be meaningless, but they have their own significance, that we come to know of later. It's our own inability that we fail to understand the deeper connotations behind the events that occur in our life. Nothing happens out of context. When something in our life ends, it helps us to grow mentally, as well as emotionally, and enriches us with experience. Emotional growth is not possible without going through pain. So it's always better to accept things, let go and move on. One more thing, no one comes into our life by chance, it's all planned. Everyone around us is here to teach us something and it improves us as a person," he said.

"Whoa! I wish I had that kind of positive attitude. Things would have been far easier then," I said, wiping the corner of my eye.

"I have experienced such a situation very closely myself. It really takes a lot of effort to move out of the love that you hold for someone, but it's not impossible. There is no use crying over someone who doesn't appreciate your worth. I wasn't always like this. But…yeah, life teaches you everything. It either breaks you or makes you. It's up to you, which side you choose to be on. Negativity and an unbalanced mind is the crux of all the troubles we create for ourselves, as well as for the people around us. Hence, maintaining sanity in an adverse situation is always favorable."

"Ingenious, Mr. Kashyap. I'm impressed," I patted his back lightly.

"So, do I have a chance with you now?" he winked.

"Stop it, Aadit. I don't feel comfortable when you talk like this," I spoke my mind.

"And I like making you uncomfortable," he said, studying my face with a wicked grin on his.

"You are extremely hopeless," I said and punched his shoulder mockingly.

***

Chapter 8
A Ray Of Hope

"No...Raahi...you have to come with us," Aisha exclaimed.

"But what will I do there, Aisha? I don't even know anyone," I reasoned.

"You know me and you know Aadit, that's enough. Don't you want to meet Girish?"

"Of course I want to, but—" I started, but she cut me off.

"Please Raahi, am I asking for too much?" she pleaded.

I hated it when someone made an emotional appeal like that, I was left with no option and I was terrible at arguments anyway. But how could I go to a random place and be amongst random people? Even Paa wouldn't have allowed it if I had asked for his permission to go to a party that late at night.

One of Girish's friends had arranged a pre-Diwali party for his friends at his house. He had invited Aisha along with Girish, and she was insisting Aadit and me to join in with her.

"You know Raahi, papa will never allow me to stay out this late at night without you guys with me and I really want to attend this party," she implored.

"But why will he not allow you to be with Girish? He is your fiancé," I argued.

"That's true, I'll get the permission to go out but will have to stick to the time limits, which he won't extend beyond 11, and these kind of parties actually start after 11." She took a pause and repeated, "Please, Raahi."

"Okay," I said as I was left with no choice, but to comply with her.

"Thank you, thank you, thank you so much." She stretched the 'so' and kissed me lightly on the cheek.

"Now get ready, we have to leave by nine," she said and rushed out of my room.

It wasn't like I didn't want to go, but something inside me was stopping me. Perhaps it was the diffidence, as I wasn't used to going to these kinds of parties, or perhaps it was guilt, as I knew that Paa would never have approved of it.

'It's okay Raahi, you are a grown up now and don't need explicit permission for each step you take. Besides, you don't have much to do here anyway and this party could serve as a well-deserved break from your monotonous routine,' my inner voice made an attempt to coax my mind into going, as if I had a choice to disavow anymore. Aisha would definitely have killed me, had I tried to refuse after all that. So finally, I made the decision to go with Aisha.

The next substantial issue was what I should wear. At first I chose to wear jeans, but soon realized that it wouldn't be entirely appropriate for a party like that. So I rummaged through my closet and after rifling through almost everything I owned, I picked out an evening gown that Shreya had gifted me on my last birthday. I dolled myself up in that royal blue flowing gown, with a slightly deep V-neckline. I tied my hair in a side bun and left a few loose tendrils to fall softly over my shoulder. I completed the look with blue studs and silver stilettos that added another four inches to my already 5'6" height. After spending an hour on adorning myself with such trinkets, I finally felt pleased when I looked at myself in the mirror. All of a sudden, I had an urge to take a picture of myself and send it to Abhimanyu. The thought that if he would see me all dressed up, he would want to come back to me, flashed through my mind.

"Raahi, are you ready?" Aisha rapped the door with her knuckles.

"Yeah, just a minute," I shook my head at the foolish thought and stepped out of my room. As I entered the living room, Aisha exclaimed, "Oo-la-la...someone is looking damn sexy!"

The way she said it, made me feel extremely embarrassed. I wasn't habitual of such compliments.

"Let's go now, Girish is waiting outside," Aisha said, picking up her bag.

I turned my gaze to Aadit, who was standing in one corner, leaning against the wall. He was dressed casually in a blue tee and denims, yet he looked damn handsome. He gaped at me admiringly and I smiled in response.

When we came out of the building, I saw Girish waiting for us, leaning against his white Audi, his gaze buried in his iPhone. Aisha introduced me to him. He was tall, but a little fat. Not a little fat; if you ask me, he was quite fat. Aisha was way prettier and smarter compare to him. But yes, he was a rich businessman and looks don't matter if you have palatial house, big branded cars and a wallet full of money. 'Aisha should start working on gaining weight rather than losing it, otherwise they'd look so odd together on stage on their wedding day,' I thought.

"Hey Aadit, you know the way to the club, right?" Girish asked.

"I'm not sure. You guys go ahead. Raahi and I'll follow you," Aadit said.

'Did I hear club? Wasn't Aisha saying that we were going to Girish's friend's house?' A doubt popped up in my mind.

"Are we going to some club?" I asked Aadit as I made myself comfortable on the front seat of his car.

"Yes, we are going to a club. Aisha lied. Otherwise, we wouldn't have gotten the permission to be out. Is there a problem?" he asked, putting the car into first gear. I shook my head.

"You look wonderful today. Though, I like you more with your hair untied," he grinned.

"Thank you," I said. Now what did that mean?Wasn't I looking good in the hairstyle I spend an hour on?

We started following Girish's car. Some random Bollywood songs were playing on the FM. I quietly peered outside the window, a little upset as I hadn't informed Paa about going out and the club added more to the guilt that had already been haunting me. I had never been to such a place before. Although I had always been eager to experience it, but now that I actually got a chance, I started feeling penitent.

"What's going inside that head of yours?" Aadit pulled me out of my thoughts.

"Nothing," I shrugged.

"You look a little lost today."

"No, I'm not," I lied.

"You are! It's written all over your face. What's the matter?"

"Actually, this is the first time I'm heading out this late, that too for this kind of a place," I stuttered. I didn't want to sound fogeyish, as hanging out at clubs was not an unusual activity in the city for girls of my age.

"So? What's the problem? You are with us," he snapped back.

"That's true, but I haven't told Paa, I mean my father, about it and I know he would have never have approved of it," I replied.

"Hmm, it's okay. Although, there was no harm in telling him that we are all going together, not to the club of course, but just going out, same as Aisha told Papa," he said, looking straight at the road ahead, occasionally glancing towards me.

"He worries, he worries a lot and I know if I had told him he wouldn't have slept until I was back, that's why I avoided," I avowed.

He nodded, still looking at the road.

"Don't worry; tell him once you are done with it. He will understand," he advised.

***

We entered the club, and I noticed that there were many people already present there, most of them in couples. The place was dimly lit from the inside with purple and green lights hanging from the ceiling, partially illuminating the hall. The blaring music hit me as soon as we entered the place. The ambience inside was euphoric. Though the music was on, the dance floor was still empty. It was a private party, so most people were busy with drinks and chitchats. Girish and Aisha introduced me to their friends. Many of them were acquaintances of Aadit. I instantly forgot who was who as I was least interested in the introductions.

Soon Aisha, Girish and Aadit got busy with their friends. I started to feel a little out of place amongst all the strangers, so I grabbed a seat on a black leather couch in one corner of the room and started scrolling through my Facebook newsfeed on the phone. Smart phones are truly the saviors when one is caught in such a predicament, where one is neither entirely comfortable, nor has the option to leave. Some bustling beside me distracted me from my activity just then, as I saw a guy grab the seat next to me.

"Hey, you are new here. Aren't you?" he asked as soon as he plopped down.

Yeah, I'm new here, but I'm not new to such lines that guys use just to start a conversation, I thought, but didn't say it out loud. Instead, I just nodded in an uninterested manner, quickly turning my gaze back to my phone's screen.

"I'm Kabir, and you?" he asked. Now why the hell was he making advances at me? Couldn't he see that I wasn't interested? He extended his hand towards me. I couldn't decide whether to take it or decline, but just shifted my gaze from his hand to his face.

"Hey Raahi, what are you doing there?" I suddenly heard Aadit's voice. I looked over my shoulder and saw him standing just a few feet behind me. I quickly got up and trotted towards him. I didn't even bother to look back at Mr. Kabir's face.

"Who was he? Do you know him?" he asked as soon as I reached near him.

"No. I don't."

After that, Aadit never left my side. Perhaps he sensed that I wasn't very comfortable talking to those aliens around me. I knew that most of the people around us might have mistaken us for a couple, but I didn't care. We took another booth and relaxed there for some time. We didn't have much to talk about so we just ensconced ourselves there and enjoyed the crowd silently.

"So, you are here and I have been looking for you all round," a guy said as he approached us and patted Aadit on the back. Aadit stood up buoyantly and hugged him. Aadit introduced him to me as Utkarsh, Girish's younger brother. He looked a lot like Girish, but a little less fat. Aadit also told me that he was working in Hyderabad. The mention of Hyderabad brought back the memories of Abhimanyu once again and I couldn't concentrate on their conversation any further. Aadit excused himself for a bit and went somewhere with Utkarsh.

I unlocked my phone once again and opened my last conversation with Abhimanyu. I scrolled up to read the messages that we had shared before the breakup. It made me nostalgic. I noticed that he had changed his profile picture. I tapped my finger on it, but it took some time to load as the network was weak indoors. As his display picture became clearer, a burning sensation rushed through my body and I felt a certain tightness in my throat. The picture had a girl standing behind him while he was sitting on a chair. Her arms were wrapped around his neck, her chin resting on the top of his head; they looked rapt and content. *Has he started dating some other girl?* The thought poked my mind and a stinging soreness brimmed over in my heart. A gentle tap on my shoulder startled me and I almost jumped in reflex, looking over my shoulder. It was Aadit. I turned my phone screen down and clenched it in my hand. "Let's go out for some time?" he asked. I nodded and followed him.

We moved out of the club and walked away from the congregation of unknown faces and booming music. The image of Abhimanyu with that girl continuously flashed in my thoughts and haunted my mind. My eyes were about to betray my effort to repress my emotions. All I wanted in that moment was to run away and hide somewhere.

Aadit's voice pulled me out of my thoughts.

"Can I use your phone?" he gestured towards my hand.

"Sure," I handed my phone over to him.

He unlocked it by swiping right. Abhimanyu's profile picture flashed on the screen. Without paying much attention to it, he quickly tapped on the home screen button and then opened the camera.

Camera? But why?

Before I could ask him, I felt his hand on my waist as he suddenly pulled me towards him. I placed my hand on his shoulder to maintain my balance. I was a little addled because of his sudden proximity.

"What are you doing, Aadit?" I mumbled.

"Smile."

"Huh?"

I noticed that he had stretched his other hand out, with the camera pointing at us for a selfie. I smiled squeamishly and he clicked our picture. He then proceeded to change my WhatsApp profile picture with the one we had just taken and returned my phone to me. All this happened so quickly that I couldn't immediately comprehend his motive behind this.

"Why did you do that, Aadit?" I asked, puzzled.

"He should feel that he has lost you, the same way you are feeling, looking at his picture," he replied, gesturing towards my phone. "Don't let him treat you like just another option in his life. Remove yourself from his life, only then will he realize your worth…and it's not called ego or arrogance, it's self-respect. You can't expect others to respect you, until you recognize your own worth." He stopped when he heard his phone vibrating; he picked it up and started talking to someone.

I didn't have anything to say in response. I wasn't sure if Abhimanyu would ever even check my profile picture or get jealous to see me with someone else. He used to be so possessive about me before, but I doubted if he would even care where I was, let alone whom with anymore.

"Let's go in, Aisha is calling," Aadit said as he disconnected the call.

We found ourselves inside the club; the blaring music started to pierce my eardrums again. When your mind is upset, even the most melodious music sounds like abhorrent clamor. As we entered, the panorama inside seemed quite different than before. People had started to hit the dance floor. Our booth, where we had been sitting earlier, was already occupied by another group. I started looking for another table, while Aadit went to look for Aisha. My hunt for the seat was still on when a boy about my age approached me and asked me for a dance. I was about to decline when I heard Aadit's stern voice from behind, "She is with me."

My savior…

I tried to stifle my laughter as the boy apologized and left frisking for another availability. Once he was well out of earshot, I started laughing out loud.

"Am I responsible for this smile on your face?" Aadit asked, cocking his head to one side.

"You may say that," I said, without realizing that I was tapping my foot to the song being played.

"I'm glad to hear that," he said locking his gaze with mine. "So?" Aadit raised his brows.

"So?" I asked, mirroring his expression.

"Do you like to dance?" he asked, looking at the dance floor.

"Yeah, why do you ask?" I tried to act oblivious to his intentions.

"Let's dance," he said, gesturing towards the dance floor.

I took a while to respond. It wasn't that I didn't like to dance; in fact, dance had always been a way for me to release my bridled emotions and vigor. It held such power over me that it used to engulf all my worries and take me to another world altogether. However, I didn't feel so sure this time. Before I could reply, Aadit had already started to guide me towards the dance floor. As we reached there, the music started showing its magic. Our feet started tapping automatically to the beats and our bodies started swaying to the accent of music. After a few minutes of dancing, the music changed from a peppy dance number to a slow romantic song. He turned to me elegantly with a glint in his eyes and offered his hand saying, "Dance with me."

I decided to revel in the moment and blow out all the worries and thoughts clouding my mind. I placed my hand in his, as he raised his other hand and rested it gently at my waist and I placed mine on his shoulder. We started dancing to the music with our gazes locked at each other and our feet moving perfectly in sync with the music. With each passing beat, I felt more relaxed and a smile crept over my face, which reflected on Aadit's face instantly. He twirled me around and my flowing dress swirled out across the floor, creating a perfect magical moment. Other people on the dance floor stopped for a moment to look at us. We continued to dance, lost in our own world. The thundering applause from our newfound audience brought us back to the real world and we separated.

"Wow! That was awesome," Aisha shrieked as she hugged me from behind. At that moment, I knew that people who were even a little dubious about our relationship before, were absolutely certain thereafter. I didn't care one bit however, because I felt gratified and blissful living in that moment, which had successfully dragged me out of my blues. I was genuinely ecstatic. I stepped off the floor and grabbed a seat. Aadit got busy talking to his friends.

I checked my phone; the notification bar said '5 messages from 2 contacts'. As I tapped on it, I found that two of the messages were from Abhimanyu and others were from, well...I didn't care to check.

At 11:14 P.M.

Abhimanyu: ***Who is this guy with you?***

At 11:26 P.M.

Abhimanyu: ***Is he the same guy who was with you that day at that hour?***

I typed a reply and was about to hit send when I recalled my promise to Aadit. But I wasn't making the first move; I was just replying to his texts. So, I hit send without a second thought.

Me: ***Did I ask about the girl in the picture with you?***

Abhimanyu: ***She is just a friend***.

He replied immediately.

Me: ***So is he. JUST A FRIEND***. I replied back, purposely typing 'just a friend' in bold. I checked my profile picture again, as I hadn't paid much attention to it earlier. It didn't seem a 'Just-my-friend' kind of a picture from any angle. The way Aadit held me, the look on my face, the expression on Aadit's face and the overall effect of lighting around us perfectly captured a very 'Deeply-in-Love' kind of a frame.

Abhimanyu: ***I asked because I care. Delhi isn't a place where you can trust someone blindly***. He replied almost after ten minutes. As I read it, a sudden smile appeared on my face. This was the smile of hope and pleasure that he still cared for me, that it still bothered him to see me with someone else. *Isn't that the irony of love? Even a hazy ray raises hope for the sunny days of love again.* That ray of hope was evident on my face— my lips stretched in a wide smile and my eyes brimming with tears of longing. I then saw

Aadit at a distance, waving at me to catch my attention. He must have noticed the glimpse of happiness in my eyes or I must have been looking like a lunatic, staring at my phone and smiling at the screen with moist eyes. He raised his eyebrows, gesticulating his curiosity. I gestured at him to check his phone and then proceeded to message him.

Me: *Abhi messaged me and asked about you?*

Aadit: *Told you* ☺

Now don't reply immediately to him.

Me: *But why?*

Aadit: *He will think that you have purposely done this to attract his attention.*

Me: *Oh! But I have replied already. What to do now?*

He shook his head and grinned.

On our way back home, Aisha blabbered, "You know, everyone was asking me about you two. They all presumed that you guys are dating."

She was sitting on the front seat with Aadit and I had occupied the back seat. "You guys should seriously think about it. You look so cute together," she continued despite our discomfort, shifting her gaze back and forth between me and Aadit.

"And you guys look so odd together. Why don't you tell Girish to lose some weight?" Aadit snapped, snubbing what Aisha was saying.

"Now that's something next to impossible. He is already too occupied with his business to spend time at the gym," Aisha tried to reason with him.

"Give these lame excuses to someone else. He has time to party, but not to work out?" He paused and then added, "Tell him to lose 20 kgs in the next three months or else you'll call off the wedding."

"You have completely gone mad, Aadit. It's better not to talk now," grunted Aisha and turned her face to the other direction, disregarding Aadit completely.

The brother-sister fight went on for some more time, but my mind was somewhere else entirely. It was already past twelve and I had to catch a train to Solan early the next morning. It was Diwali time and my Paa was eagerly waiting for me, because all his celebrations were incomplete without me.

***

Chapter 9
Home Calling

"Hey, happy Rose day."

"What's this, Abhi?" I asked as I saw him approaching me, holding a sapling with its roots concealed in a handful of soil wrapped in black polythene.

"A rose plant," he replied, smiling.

"Dumb-o, you are supposed to present roses on Rose day, not a rose plant." I made a face, trying to pull his leg.

"I don't think so. Only those who think that one day their love will fade away just like the fragrance of a rose, present a rose. They know that their love is temporary and will die some day, just like a flower gets withered with time. But I know that my love for you will only grow with each and every day, just like this plant. It won't fade away with time, it will never," he said with the glister of love in his eyes and a promise of forever in his voice.

"Really? Then I'll look after it just like my baby," I said and carefully took the plant in my hand.

A teardrop travelled down my cheek, rested on a petal of the rose and shone like a dewdrop. I had just reached my home in Solan and was kneeling next to the rose bush that I had planted just a few months ago. It had a fully blossomed rose and two blooming buds. It reminded me of the day when Abhimanyu had gifted it to me. Time had changed, his words had changed, even our relationship had changed, but it was still growing, unaware of the fact that the love it symbolized had already fizzled out. Words are such traitors...they change their meaning with time and according to situations. Soak them with a tinge of emotions and they will conquer any heart. They will make you fall for the person who owns them, despite knowing that they are nothing but just sugar coated venomous words that are going to shatter everything one day. But what can one do? Few things are only meant for brain, beyond the understanding of heart, just like mine. My heart was still beating for him. I still had faith in my love. I still had faith in his words, and that was the only hope left in my life. I still believed that he had just strayed away from the right path, from my path, and the day he would realize this, he would come back to me.

Paa had messaged to say that he had a class and that he wouldn't be home before five in the evening. He had left the house-keys with our neighbors, so I took the keys from them, unlocked the door and entered my home. There was a bouquet waiting for me on the dining table with a note that had 'Welcome back, my Doll' scribbled on it in red ink. Along with that, there was a pack of Ferrero Rochers too. I hunted the refrigerator for food. I found inside a bowl of Rajma-Chawal, my favorite, cooked by Devraj chacha. Devraj chacha had been our cook cum caretaker for as long as I could remember. I took out the bowl from the refrigerator, reheated it in microwave oven and satiated my hunger. It was only a quarter past two in the afternoon, so I headed to take a nap in my room, as I was tired from the previous night's party and hadn't sleep properly even after coming back because of all the excitement of coming home.

I woke up to the clank of utensils in the kitchen. I checked the time; it was around seven in the evening, which meant that Paa was back home. I rushed to the kitchen.

"Good evening Paa," I sang, as I hugged him from behind. "Thanks for the flowers and chocolates."

"I hope you haven't eaten them all," he raised his eyebrows.

"No. I have saved one for you," I said mischievously, lifting myself up to sit on the kitchen platform.

"Hmm...one out of ten, not bad, huh?" he said with a hint of sarcasm in his voice. I giggled.

He poured some milk into a mug, stirred bournvita into it and offered it to me.

"Paa, I need to tell you something," I started hesitantly as I took a glass from him.

"I'm all ears," he said as he placed another vessel on the burner for tea.

"Um...actually...last night I went to a party with Aisha and Aadit to one of their friends' place. It was all of a sudden, so I couldn't inform you," I mumbled, expecting him to explode with annoyance any moment. I clenched the mug tightly in my hand, as I noticed the lines that appeared between his eyes.

"Oh! I thought you were going to tell me about someone special," he said without looking at me.

"Someone special?" I confirmed with my mouth hanging open, unable to digest the fact that he was actually asking me about my boyfriend.

"Yes...your Prince Charming, if there is one? Or will I have to find one for you?" He looked at me this time.

"Paa, are you all right? Let me remind you, I'm your daughter," I said, with my mouth still open.

"So? My daughter is all grown up now. She is independent. I don't see any harm in discussing these things now," he said the words that I had never expected to come from him.

It was the golden opportunity that I wouldn't have missed for the world. I had been waiting for a long time for a chance to tell Paa about Abhimanyu. Should I tell him now? But what would I tell him, that I loved a boy who ditched me and that I was still waiting for him to realize his mistake and come back? Would he even understand this? *Never.*

"I'm still waiting for your reply," he reminded me.

I shook my head in a 'no' and started sipping my milk quietly, keeping my gaze locked deep into the glass to avoid any further discussion. I was surprised to see my Paa suddenly acting like a cool Dad, so unlike how he used to be before.

"Raahi, I forgot to tell you, Shreya called when you were sleeping. She said that she would come tomorrow morning to see you," he said.

"Oh! Really? I'll call her," I said and headed to my room to call Shreya. As I picked up my phone, I saw three-missed calls; two from Shreya and one from Maa. I called back at Maa's number first.

"Hello, Miss Raahi Sharma," a male voice responded and the way he had addressed me, I recognized it instantly.

"Hello Mr. Kashyap," I replied in the same tone. I heard him chuckle.

"How have you been? You didn't even bother to tell me that you would be leaving today," he chided.

"Oh! Didn't I? But Maa and Aisha already knew."

"Yeah, I came to know later," he said, nonchalantly.

"Why do you sound like you have been missing me?" I teased.

"What if I say, I actually am."

"Aww, no problem...I'll be back the day after tomorrow."

"Ha! I'm leaving that morning."

"Don't tell me." I felt bad about not having met him before leaving.

"Yup, but it's okay. You enjoy your Diwali."

"Hmm, you too."

"Well, I have bought something for you. Actually, I was buying gifts for Maa and Aisha and I bought one for you too."

"Really? That's so sweet of you, Aadit. It's my lucky day today. First, I got chocolates from Paa and now a gift from you too. Thank you so much."

"Ah! Thank God...I thought you would act like a typical girl. You know, the I-Don't-Accept-Gifts kind of a girl."

"Naah...let me tell you one thing, your 'typical girls' never actually say no to gifts, they just pretend," I said, making him chuckle again.

"Okay, so I'll keep your gift in your drawer. Is that fine?"

"Yes," I said and then there was a silence.

"Are you okay now?" he asked after a hiatus with a hint of concern in his voice.

"Yeah," I opened my mouth to say more, but then decided against it, as I wasn't sure whether he would understand me or not.

"Raahi, you can tell me anything. You should know this by now," he said, reading the dilemma in my silence.

"Um, I was thinking of going to Hyderabad." I spoke my mind.

"Why?"

"During the journey here, I thought a lot about it...and I...I know him; he would never have talked to me that way if there weren't a reason. Maybe he is going through some kind of problems, a tough phase and pushed me away just to keep me safe. I don't know, but I need to know why he did it." My voice cracked towards the end as I tried to convince him, but more than him, I was trying to convince myself.

"Raahi, whatever you are saying, it only happens in movies and stories. In real life, people share their problems with the ones they love, instead of pushing them away. Stop being blinded by your love for him."

"Hmm, where is Maa?" I tried to change the topic, as I realized my mistake of telling him what had been occupying my mind.

"She is inside. We are here at Girish's house to finalize the wedding date."

"Really? Do inform me as soon as it gets finalized," I laced my voice with intended excitement.

"Sure-" he was about to say something else, but I interrupted him because I knew what he was going to tell me next.

"And don't forget to send me the pictures of Diwali celebration at your place… I'll send mine too."

"Definitely…and don't do anything stupid. He is a closed chapter now, the sooner you accept that, the better. Okay?"

"Hmm…bye, I have to go. Take care."

"You too," he said and I disconnected the phone.

***

The next morning, I woke up to the feeling of something crawling at the back of my ear. I hastily shrugged it off and pulled my blanket over my face, exposing my feet below. My eyes were still closed as I was lying on my bed. Soon I felt something crawling on my right calf. The thought of crawling lizard provoked me to act aggressively and I started yanking my legs out of fear. I then heard her laughing vigorously.

"I'll kill you Shreya, you took my breath away," I seethed, gasping for breath.

"Oh! *Meri jaan*...don't you know how much I love teasing you," she said and her words immediately made my mind drift to Aadit.

"Why are you smiling like that?" she asked, noticing the grin that had crept onto my face.

"Nothing, I'm just happy to see you," I replied.

"Aww..." she said and closed the distance between us, pulling me into a hug.

"You know, I have so many things to tell you," she said with a glimmer of excitement in her eyes.

"Even I have so much to tell you," I said in a dim tone.

"About Abhimanyu, right?" she said, glancing at me.

"Yeah! How do you know?" I frowned as no one knew what had happened between Abhimanyu and me, except for Aadit.

"Ha! Because this is what you always do, talk about Abhimanyu. But"—She paused for a second as if she was about to declare the result of some reality show finale—"today we...I mean I'll talk about someone and you'll have to listen."

"Okay, go on," I said, straightening my back and sitting crossed legged on my bed.

"I have a boyfriend now," she said with an amused face.

"Really? Who? Where? When? Why didn't you tell me before?" I smacked her back.

"Wait, wait...his name is Kartik. It happened last month in Chandigarh. He is my batch mate at the coaching centre and works for Infosys. I wanted to tell this to you in person, so I didn't tell you before," she answered my questions in one go.

"I'm really happy for you," I kissed her cheek. "So, did he pass all your tests?" I asked curiously.

"No, I didn't test him," she shrugged.

"Impossible! Shreya Mehta, who doesn't even make a friend without testing, now has a boyfriend! Do you want me to believe this?" I argued.

"Yes darling, trust me," she said squeezing my face between her palms. "Actually, I have realized Raahi, you don't need a test to recognize that one person whom you love with all your heart and who loves you back unconditionally. The testimony of my heart was enough to recognize him."

"Do you really trust him enough? I mean, it's only been a month since you met him. What if—"

"It's not time Raahi, it's the love and trust that matters most in any relationship. If there is love and trust between you two, you'll move mountains to save your relationship," she said, emphatically cutting me off and her words hit my heart hard. Did I love Abhimanyu enough to move mountains to save my relationship?

"Back to earth, Raahi." Shreya pulled me out of my thoughts.

"Tell me everything," I said. She told me everything, from their first meeting to his proposal, from their first date to the first parting, from their first kiss to the first fight...each and every thing. Though I was listening to her, with every first she mentioned, my mind drifted to my own firsts with Abhimanyu. Isn't it funny? You can relate your love story easily to anyone else's love story. The story itself may be different, but the emotions linked are always the same. I wanted to tell her all about what happened between Abhimanyu and me, but it wasn't the right moment then. She was so ecstatic and I didn't want to ruin her mood. My phone buzzed. It was a message from Aadit: **So, the wedding date is 22 Feb.** ☺

***

Festivals are the soul of us Indians and the atmosphere is specially zealous if it's Diwali. I spent the whole day decorating my home with flowers, *Rangoli*, lights and earthen diyas. I had gone to Shreya's house early that morning, where we decided that we would both go to Chandigarh together the following Monday, as she wanted me to meet Kartik. From there, I would take a bus to Delhi. Much to my surprise, Paa permitted me to go and even booked a Volvo's ticket from Chandigarh to Delhi himself. My Paa was playing extra cool those days. *Has he started dating someone?* The thought arose in my mind and I dismissed it instantly, as I couldn't envisage him romantically involved with anyone else.

I clicked pictures of my decorated house and sent them to Aadit, asking him to send some photographs from Noida in return. Paa was busy arranging the sweets and other accessories for the Diwali Puja, so I got the chance to open and close Abhimanyu's WhatsApp contact on my phone many times throughout the day. I wanted to wish him Diwali, but I was expecting him to wish me first. I really had to fight the urge to text when I saw him online, but somehow, I bridled my desire. It was evening already, but my heart was still hoping for his message to arrive. A wave of happiness washed across my heart as I heard my phone vibrating. However, it soon vanished when I saw that the message was from Aadit, not Abhimanyu.

Aadit: ***How about showing your face rather than the walls, floor and furniture?***

Me: ***How rude! I spent the whole day decorating these walls, floor and furniture.***

Aadit: ***I'm sorry...well...beautifully decorated.*** ☺

I clicked a selfie and sent it to him immediately. I had put on a peach and pista green lehenga, with all the traditional jewelry on. I got his reply immediately, as soon as the double tick turned blue.

Aadit: ***Nice... where is the groom?***

Me: ***Which groom?***

Aadit: ***Aren't you getting married today?***

Me: ***Shut up. I wore this for Diwali.***

Aadit: ***Oh! And here I am thinking that you forgot to invite us.***

Me: ***It's not funny...it's my Mom's jewelry. Paa wanted me to wear it. You know, everyone who teases me these days, reminds me of you.***

Aadit: ***Does that mean you are missing me?***

Me: ***I didn't say that.***

Aadit: ***But you meant it.***

Me: ***Okay bye...Paa is calling me for Puja.***

Aadit: ***Yeah, take care.***

***

Shreya and I were roaming the streets of Sector-17 in Chandigarh the following Monday. We had reached Chandigarh just that morning. Though Kartik had already informed us that he was caught up in some work and wouldn't be able to meet us, we kept our program intact. We did a lot of shopping and gossiping together. At one point I noticed that Shreya was a bit restless during the shopping.

First, I thought maybe she was upset with Kartik's sudden change of plans, but later I realized that it wasn't Kartik that was bothering her.

"What's it, Shreya?" I asked her finally.

"Raahi...have you noticed something?" she whispered in my ear.

"What?" I said, looking all around.

"Keep walking and don't move your head here and there," she chided. "That guy in the blue tee is following us."

"Really? Which guy?"

"He is standing to your left. Don't look there right now and just keep walking," she instructed.

"Let's ignore him," I said.

"No. Let's teach him a lesson," she said, exactly as I had anticipated. It was her favorite pastime and boys always had to pay a heavy price once they fell into Shreya's teach-a-lesson trap.

"Shreya, following someone isn't a crime. We aren't even sure if he is following us. It may be a coincidence," I tried to make her understand, but deep inside, I knew that Shreya could never be wrong in judging people. She had that gift of insight.

"It's not a coincidence. I noticed him clicking our pictures too. I have been watching him for the last hour. What world are you in, Raahi? Stalking is a crime!" she retorted.

"Now what?" I asked.

"I have a plan," she said and I saw the all too familiar wicked grin on her face, as she opened her bag, took out her phone and switched it off.

"Keep your phone either switched off or on silent mode. And remember, you don't have a phone," she ordered. I did as she said.

"Now look at him and smile," she instructed.

"Are you mad? It's like inviting trouble. I won't do it," I grumbled.

"Raaaheee! DO. AS. I. SAY."

"NO."

"Dumbo, once he's taught a lesson, he will never dare to stare at another girl. You have the kind of face that people fall for easily. Now do it fast," she said.

The plan was completely preposterous, but once Shreya had her mind set on something, it was next to impossible to wheedle her out of it. I started giving him furtive glances. He smiled. I smiled. My smile disappeared when I saw him approaching us. I clenched Shreya's hand.

"Don't worry," she assured me.

"Hi, actually I think I have seen you somewhere." he threw a typical line at me. Before I could say anything, Shreya piped in, "Even she was saying the same." She turned her gaze from him to me. "Isn't that what we were just discussing right now?"

"Really? I'm Sidharth." He offered his hand towards us to shake.

"She is Priya and I'm Meera," said Shreya, faking our names and shaking hands with him.

"Do you want me to drop you girls somewhere? I have my Honda CR-V parked close-by," he bragged, trying to impress us with the mention of his luxury car.

"No. Actually, we are planning to have lunch," Shreya said.

"Can I join you? The lunch is on me. What say?" he said.

"Yeah, why not? Let's go," Shreya said.

A few minutes later, we found ourselves at a posh restaurant. We carefully picked the most expensive dishes from the menu and ordered till the bill reached to a heavy amount.

"...and a chocolate brownie with ice cream and hot chocolate sauce for dessert. That's all," Shreya said to the waiter, who looked flabbergasted by the amount of food we had ordered. Sidharth was looking at us dumfounded, with his mouth hanging open.

"Don't worry, we will split the bill. We are starving actually," I said, looking at his expression.

"No, no, there's nothing like that. It's perfectly fine," he stuttered.

For the next half hour, we chatted as if we were long lost friends. When the food was about to be served, Shreya nudged me with her elbow. She then got up holding her phone in her hand and feigned an upset expression, looking at her phone.

"Shit. My phone's battery is dead and I need to make an urgent call. You don't have your phone, do you?" she asked me with a tinge of worry in her tone. I shook my head. Both of us looked at Sidharth.

"Yeah, take my phone," he said, unlocking his Samsung S7 and sliding it towards Shreya.

"Actually, a friend of mine is waiting outside. I need to hand over these bags to him," she said and picked up the shopping bags. The moment Shreya was out, the waiter started serving the food. I pretend to wait for her, looking occasionally at my watch.

"I think I should go to look for Meera," I said, excusing myself.

"Wait, I'll also come," he said as I turned to leave.

"Actually, I don't think that's a good idea. It's her boyfriend outside and he is very belligerent. We haven't told him about you. I hope you understand," I spun an excuse on the spot.

"Sure, I'll wait here," he said and sat back down on his seat.

I rushed outside. Shreya was waiting for me there.

"I told you he clicked our pictures. I have deleted them all and also destroyed his memory card. Let's go now," she said and handed over his phone to the doorman standing outside the restaurant. We took an auto and came to Shreya's PG straight away. As soon as we entered her room, we couldn't help but roll on the floor with fits of laughter, envisioning the expression on Sidharth face, with loads of food on the table and the devilish girls gone missing. We laughed till our stomachs and jaws started to hurt.

"Oh God! I hope he at least gets his phone back," I said, catching my breath.

"Now, don't mention this to Abhimanyu. Remember, how mad he got when you told him about the last teach-a-lesson stunt we pulled. He was so furious," she tittered.

Suddenly, my laughter evaporated and tears of grief replaced the tears of glee. I literally started crying, having wraped my arms around my folded knees.

"Hey...hey...Raahi, what happened?" Shreya rushed to me on her knees.

"There is no Abhimanyu anymore, Shreya. He left me," I blubbered.

"What do you mean, he left you?" she interrogated, holding me by my shoulders.

"He broke up with me," I sobbed.

"What? When? And you are telling me now?" she castigated.

"I wanted to tell you before, but you were so content with your life, I didn't want to spoil your mood," I groaned.

"Are you mad? Now tell me what happened?"

I narrated the whole incident to her. She hugged me tight as I cried my heart out. Shreya couldn't control her tears either and soon it was I who was consoling her. That's the reason people say that friendship is the most unadulterated relation and lucky are the people who find a true friend. Friendship doesn't need words to understand the state of the other. Once your hearts are linked, a single look in the eyes can tell what's going on in another's mind. Shreya was hurt and was blaming herself because she hadn't been able to read my eyes and was so engrossed with herself that she didn't bother to listen to me. I made her understand that it wasn't her fault and that I was actually feeling better after having shared everything with her.

After an hour, we made our way to the bus stand and waited for my bus to Delhi. It was scheduled to depart at 2:40 P.M. and we still had ten minutes before it started. We were both sitting quietly on a bench at the bus stop when Shreya broke the silence.

"Raahi."

"Hmm?"

"I think we should teach him a lesson."

"No. It's silly. I don't want to do anything now that I regret later."

"What does that mean? Are you still expecting him to come back?"

"He will, Shreya. I'm sure he will come back."

"You are mad, Raahi. I can't let him live in peace, not after knowing all this at least. Give me your phone."

"No way Shreya, you aren't going to call him from my phone. I have promised Aadit that I won't call him."

"Who is this Aadit? And how does he know about Abhimanyu?"

"He is Kashyap uncle's son. He was with me the day it happened and he knows everything."

"Hmm...I won't use your phone then, mine neither. I just want his number."

She jotted his number down on the palm of her hand and walked up to a middle-aged Sardar uncle sitting on the next bench. She requested him to let her use his phone, feigning that she had forgotten her phone at home. She took his phone and went to a corner, out of the earshot of people around us. I followed her there. She called Abhimanyu and he picked up at the third ring. As soon as she heard him say 'hello', she hurled a load of swear words at him in all the languages she knew. She started in English, then moved to Hindi, then Punjabi and finally in Haryanvi too. I looked at her slack-jawed. She didn't give him even a fraction of a second to speak. Soon he disconnected the call, but she continued for another few seconds.

"Where did you learn all this?" I asked, astonished.

"Why? You need a coaching?" she snapped back.

I shook my head. She returned the phone to the Sardar uncle and then turned to me.

"Now go, your bus will be leaving soon," she said and pulled me in for a final hug.

***

Chapter 10
The Bride

The extremely euphoric aura of a festival turns the next few days into a complete humdrum affair and that day was exactly one of those kind of days. I was sitting in my cubicle at office. For most people at my work place, the Diwali hangover wasn't over yet. A very few people had turned up. I took a round of my floor and counted the number of desktops that were awake; the result was only about five out of eighteen. Even at home, the environment was no different. Aadit had already left for USA and Kashyap uncle left that day for a conference in Kolkata. I started browsing through different websites on my desktop. It appeared as if an effect of apathy had engulfed everything around me; even the social networking sites weren't helping me get rid of that insipidity. They all showed the same monotonous Diwali pictures, the decorations, the rangolis, the lights and diyas. Now I realized exactly how Aadit must have felt when I sent him the pictures of my house.

I decided to leave early because it was better to sleep than to wander around in an almost unoccupied office. But I had to pass the time at least till 1 P.M., so that I could mark my half-day attendance. Just then I heard a clank in a cubicle diagonally opposite to mine. It was Ankita.

"Hey Ankita, how come you are late today?" I asked, leaning backwards and stretching the backrest of my office chair.

"Actually, I was on leave. We were supposed to go to my maternal home today, but the plan was annulled at last moment. So I came here," she said jaggedly.

"Oh!" I responded. I could guess that something was wrong with Ankita; the happiness, the radiance, the exhilaration that should be a newly wed girl's companions, had never made an appearance on her face. Perhaps I was being presumptuous because all I knew about her was through her conversations over the phone that I had unintentionally earwigged, being in the cubical diagonally opposite to hers.

She was beautiful, a little shorter than me but had a chiseled figure, which was twine thin. She still had the red and white bangles on her wrists, that signify a newly wed bride.

The rough way that she was dealing with the things on her table, betrayed her agitation. So many times I had heard her arguing with her husband on the phone about typical domestic stuff. Today as well, it seemed like she had had a fight at home, as she looked baffled. I decided not to probe her about the matter; getting into someone's personal life just to while away the time wasn't a good idea at all.

I got up and spent the rest of my time at the library, reading newspaper.

***

I was in my room when I heard Maa calling out to me from her room. Only Maa and I were at home then; Aisha was still at office and Kanchi was on leave. As I entered her room, I saw around 6-7 jewelry boxes lying open on her bed. Each and every piece of jewelry looked magnificent and traditional, finely studded with diamonds, Kundan and pearls.

"Aha! Are these for Aisha?" I asked, carefully examining the jewelry.

"No. It's not for Aisha," Maa said, softly touching the necklace as if reminiscing old memories related to it. "You know, I wore this on my wedding day."

"You must have looked like the most beautiful bride ever. Hadn't you?" I asked and I noticed her blushing in response.

"It's an ancestral piece of jewelry. My mother in law gave this to me on my wedding day and I'll bestow it upon my daughter-in-law," she said looking at me.

"You mean Aadit's wife?" I inferred.

"Yes," she nodded smilingly.

"My Paa also says that he will give me all my mother's jewelry on my wedding," I smiled back.

"Come, sit here," she motioned towards the chair in front of the dressing table. I followed. She took out the same necklace that she had worn for her wedding and placed it around my neck. It exquisitely covered the base of my neck, going all the way across my collar bones on either side. The pearls hanging at the outer circumference of the necklace, strikingly complimented my neckline.

"Why are you making me wear it, Maa?" I asked, looking over my shoulder as she was standing right behind me.

"I was just curious to see how it looks on you," she replied, still looking at my reflection in the mirror.

"It would look good on anyone. It's so beautiful," I said, brushing my hand lightly over the necklace.

"Hmm, wait," she said and turned to pick another piece of jewelry. It was the earrings that went with the same necklace. She carefully removed the studs that I had been wearing and put the earrings in my ears. Then she parted my hair from the center and placed a *maang teeka* in it.

"Oh God! I look like a bride," I blushed as I saw my reflection in the mirror.

She beamed and rested her hands gently on my shoulders. I couldn't take my eyes off myself. I was actually looking beautiful, without any makeup or dress either. The shine of gold was enough to add a special glimmer to my face.

When I was young, I used to envy my friends when their mothers dressed them up. Today, I too finally experienced the same feeling.

"Thank you, Maa," I said and turned slightly to wrap my arms around her waist and hug her. "Thank you for making me experience this beautiful feeling. I wish I were your real daughter."

"Do you really mean what you just said?" she asked, holding my chin with her fingers. I nodded.

"Then be my daughter-in-law," she said simply. I had not anticipated this and her words felt like a dagger piercing my chest. I couldn't believe what I had just heard. I turned my face, wriggling out of her arms.

"Raahi, look here and tell me," she said and turned my face towards her again, holding my chin. "Do you like Aadit?"

"What are you saying, Maa? It....it's just impossible," I spluttered and hastily started removing the jewelry she had just adorned me with.

"Why? It's possible every which way. I'll talk to your father. But first, you tell me; do you like Aadit? I have seen both of you together and I know there is great tuning between you two," she said convincingly. There was a glint of hope in her eyes that I didn't want to ruin, so I decided to drop the ball across to Aadit's court.

"Maa, why don't you ask Aadit first?" I proposed. I was sure he would never agree to this.

"I have already asked him and he said 'yes,'" she said assertively.

I felt like someone had pulled away the ground from beneath my feet. I couldn't believe my ears, he had said 'yes' despite knowing that I love Abhimanyu? I removed the remaining jewelry from my head and placed it neatly on the dressing table.

"Why did you remove all this, Raahi?" she asked.

"Because this isn't for me"—I paused for a second and closed my eyes to regain my composure—"I don't want to give you any false hopes. I can't do it." I swallowed a lump in my throat.

"But Raahi—" she started, but I cut her off.

"Please Maa, let's not discuss it if you really want me to stay in this house," I said in a firm voice and rushed back to my room. I latched the door shut.

I couldn't grasp what had just happened. Aadit could never say 'yes'. I was damn sure that it was just a misunderstanding. I dialed Aadit's number without caring about the time. It would have been past midnight there. He picked up.

"Hello," I heard his husky voice. It was evident from his tone that he had woken up mid-sleep.

"Hello, Aadit, I am sorry to disturb you at this time, but I need to talk to you urgently. Can we talk now?" I asked him.

"Yeah, is everything all right?" he asked, a little worried.

"What did you say to Maa?"

"Umm…like what?"

"Did you tell her that you like me?"

"Yeah, so?"

"She mistook your 'like' as a 'yes' to a marriage proposal. She is planning to get us married. Please clarify this confusion as soon as possible," I blurted out in one breath. I waited for his response, but only heard his breath as he let out a sigh.

"Are you there, Aadit?" I asked.

"Hmm…"

"Why are you so quiet, Aadit? Please say something."

"What if I say that I actually said yes, knowing full well what she was asking me about?" he conceded.

"WHAT?" I was stunned.

"See Raahi, I wasn't expecting Maa to bring this matter up so early. Actually, I wanted to talk—"

"How dare you, Aadit?" I didn't let him complete his sentence.

"Raahi, listen."

"I really don't understand, why all the people whom I start trusting, have sworn to make my life hell. How could you even think about it, when you are well aware of the fact that I love someone else?" I paused to clear my choking throat. "What were you trying to do, *haan*? Taking advantage of my situation?"

"Listen Raahi…I…"

"NO. You listen to me, Aadit. I trusted you. You knew everything about me and Abhimanyu, and yet you did this." I started sobbing.

"Raahi, Abhimanyu is not in your life anymore."

"Who are you to decide that? You have no right, Aadit. Let me make one thing very clear, I don't need a rebound. I do believe in destiny, and if my love for Abhimanyu is true and if we are meant to be together, love will lead us back, no matter what." I could hear him breathing heavily.

"Raahi, you are taking me wrong…"

"I don't need your kind of people in my life, who pretend to be my friend on my face and stab me in the back when I'm not looking. I'll never forgive you for this, you have broken my trust..." I snivelled.

"Raahi..."

"I don't want to hear anything. It's enough, now. I'm so done with this so-called friendship. From now on, don't ever try to call or contact me, neither will I," I said and disconnected the call.

Somewhere in my heart, I knew that the anger that I had just lashed out on Aadit, wasn't wholly for him. I had taken out on him the entire wrath that had been building up since the day Abhimanyu broke up with me. But Aadit had played with my reliance on him. He could have talked to me first; he could have asked about my opinion first, instead of talking directly to Maa. And how could he expect me to fall for him in just five days?. He knew what I was going through, and still expected me to move on from one relationship to another in such a short span of time. I heard my phone buzzing in my hand, but I didn't care to check. I knew it would be Aadit calling. I hurled my phone on the bed in fury and sat on the floor, resting my back against the side of the bed. I counted the number of times he called. Thrice.

"Raahi... open the door," I heard Maa knocking at my door. I quickly pulled it open. She gave me her phone and motioned at me to attend the call. *Oh...so now he was calling on Maa's phone.*

"What's your problem? Can't you understand a simple thing?" I chided, once I was out of Maa's earshot.

"Raahi, Aisha here," I heard a female voice.

"Oh! Sorry Aisha...I was expecting someone else's call," I apologized.

"Expecting someone else's call on Maa's phone?" she probed.

"Is it Maa's phone? Oh! I didn't realize," I made an instant excuse, unmindful of whether she believed it or not.

"Where is your phone? I called you so many times. *Achha* listen, is Maa around?"

"No. She is in her room."

"Okay, so one of Girish's friends has organized a party and I want to attend it. Will you accompany me?"

"No…I'm not feeling well today," I lied. After having such a dreadful day, going to a party was the last thing I wanted to do.

"Umm, then will you help me sneak off with Girish to go to the party?"

"But that's wrong, Aisha."

"Don't lecture me, just say yes or no. Don't worry, I have a plan."

"Umm...okay."

"Fine…I'll tell you the rest once I am home," she said and disconnected the call.

I checked my call log. All the calls were from Aisha. There wasn't a single call from Aadit, neither a message. *Wasn't that an indication that he was wrong? And he knew that.*

***

"Why are you behaving so weirdly today?" Maa asked, as she saw Aisha fidgeting with her office bag.

"Maa, because I have a lot of office work to finish today. I'm going to Aadit's room. Please don't disturb me till morning," she said, collecting a bundle of sheets from her office bag.

"Why Aadit's room? What's the problem with yours?" Maa asked.

"The AC isn't working in my room," she said and went straight to Aadit's room. "And please don't disturb me. I won't open the door no matter what happens." She went in and latched the door from inside.

Maa and I were still sitting at the dining table, having our dinner in silence. Aisha had gobbled down the dinner in haste before heading to Aadit's room. I still had no idea what she was going to do and what her plan was.

"Maa, I'm sorry for being rude today," I said, as I saw her getting up from her chair. She smiled meekly and went to the kitchen without saying anything. I knew that she was hurt, but what else could I have done? I picked up my plate too and went to the kitchen. I saw Maa arranging the dinner utensils in the dishwasher. I started helping her.

"Maa, are you still angry?" I asked.

"No. Why would I be? You go and take a rest. You must be tired. Kanchi will do the rest of things tomorrow." She sounded normal. I heaved a sigh of relief.

It was around ten at night when I heard a knock at my balcony door. I opened the door and saw Aisha in a bottle green knee length dress.

"Raahi, please go to Maa's room and check whether she has slept or not," she said, adjusting her stilettos. I checked Maa's room and gave her a go-ahead nod.

"I'll be back around twelve and you have to open the door for me. I'll call you," she said and tiptoed to the main door.

"Take care and come early," I said.

"Hey, keep this with you. It's not going well with this dress." She removed her wristwatch and handed it over me. Once she was out, I closed the door as cautiously and quietly as possible.

I came back to my room and opened my drawer to keep Aisha's watch in. I saw a deep purple Tanishq jewelry box along with a sealed envelop inside. I recalled that Aadit had bought a gift for me and had kept it in my drawer. I had completely forgotten about it. I opened the envelope first; it had a two-page handwritten letter.

Hey Raahi,

I wish I could have seen you before leaving, but perhaps it wasn't in my fate. I wanted to say all this in person, but couldn't. So I decided to write a letter. And guess what? I realized that writing a letter is a way better idea of conveying your feelings than telling them in person.

Remember the day when you were dressed in that white suit, that was the first time when I thought about you the other way. I was awe-struck by your beauty. I tried hard not to gawk at you, but I couldn't help it. Shallow, isn't it? Liking a girl just because you find her attractive. But that's not the only reason. I feel the same comfort with you as I feel with Maa. I feel like home with you and trust me, this is a superlative emotion that any guy can ever experience.

You won't believe this but I actually felt jealous of the boy you were going to meet. And the same day when I saw you shattered, I felt as if something was dying inside me too. I wanted to wash away all your pain because I know how much it hurts. I felt like killing that boy the moment he talked to you uncouthly. I know that you love him genuinely, but I strongly feel that he doesn't deserve you and there is no rationale in wasting your life for someone who doesn't care for your feelings.

Remember our dance…trust me, it was the best thing that ever happened to me. Don't you think that it was a real moment for us? It seemed like the whole aura was carefully planned by the almighty himself just for that one moment to happen. And the next day, when I didn't see you around, I felt…lost. I pined for you, Raahi. Literally. What have you done to me in just a few days?

I like you, Raahi. I know it's too early to call it love, but sometimes it's just an instant connection that you feel with someone, which even time fails to build up, and the one thing I'm damn sure of is that I would love to spend the rest of my life with you.

I don't want you to take a decision in haste, take your time and think about it sagaciously, I know, what your mind's state is now. But Raahi, what has happened has happened, there is nothing you can do that would change the nature of this situation, and it's always wise to move on in life because it doesn't stop for anyone.

I hope you get this letter before Maa asks you. I don't want you to be dumbstruck when she talks to you about me. And one more thing, whatever your decision be, we will always be friends.

-Aadit

I opened the gift box. It was a beautiful pair of earrings studded with diamonds. I shut the box immediately. There was no chance I was going to accept this gift. I would never have gotten so close to him, had I known his intentions. I was still firm on my decision to break all ties with Aadit. Keeping any kind of relations with him would have meant encouraging his feelings. Everything had started to make sense now, why he made me promise him not to keep any contact with Abhimanyu. He even threatened Abhimanyu that he'd kill him if he ever tried to approach me. He purposely put that photograph as my profile picture to plant a doubt in Abhimanyu's mind. Oh God! While I told him everything, considering him my close friend and confidante, he was secretly wishing the exact opposite of what I wanted. I was so stupid to trust him. He never wanted Abhimanyu and me to reconcile and just because of him, I never tried to clear things up between Abhimanyu and myself either. I held my head in my hands as all kinds of thoughts started tormenting me.

'*It's enough now, I need to take control of my life before it's too late. I can't simply sit here and wait for Abhimanyu to come back. It's time to take some action. It's time to move mountains to end the differences that fate has put between us,*' I told myself and grabbed my phone to call Abhimanyu. I dialed his number. The first attempt was futile, as he didn't answer. I knew that he wouldn't pick my phone, so I decided to message him. He had removed his profile picture and even his 'last seen' wasn't visible to me. I typed a message: **Abhi please pick up the phone, it's urgent**. It didn't get delivered. I dialed his number again and kept my gaze on the screen that flashed: *Abhi dialing*. My hand trembled as the call timer started counting. I frowned upon hearing a female voice at the other end.

"Hello," I heard her voice.

"Um, hello… err… Is it Abhimanyu's number?" I stammered.

"Yeah, may I know who this is?" she asked in a chirpy voice.

"Umm, can I please talk to him?" I said.

"He is in the washroom right now, so you can tell me if it is something urgent," she said.

"May I know whom am I talking to?" I asked, mustering some confidence in my voice.

"Umm, just wait a sec," she said. I heard a bustling in the background and then overheard their conversation as she asked Abhimanyu, "Maan, there is a call for you."

"Who is it?" I heard his muffled voice and an instant nostalgia gushed through my heart.

"Don't know…the number isn't saved," she said.

Had he deleted my contact number? And who the hell was this girl? What was she doing with Abhimanyu at this hour? Why did she call him 'Maan'? My mind was clogged with numerous questions that only Abhimanyu could answer.

"See, he is busy right now. He will call you back once he gets free and if you are calling for an advertisement or some insurance policy, let me clear one thing right away that we aren't interested," she said and disconnected the call.

'*We aren't interested*'? Why did she use 'we', instead of 'he'? I could sense myself going crazy. '*I should trust him; he is already staying so far away from his home. He needs company too. Maybe she is just a friend, as he told me.*' I tried to calm myself down.

My message was still undelivered. *Has he blocked my contact?* Another question disturbed me. I searched for his profile on Facebook and that was the final nail in the coffin. He had unfriended me and on his profile, nothing was visible to me. I clutched my phone tight and cried my heart out. I hadn't bothered him at all. Since the day he broke up with me, I hadn't called him even once. Then why did he unfriend me? Was I too bad to even deserve an insignificant place in his Facebook friend list? My head throbbed as all these questions started tormenting me. I made up my mind to call Dev instead of Abhimanyu. Dev was our senior from college. He was also working in Hyderabad and was one of the three roommates Abhimanyu had. I knew that Abhimanyu wouldn't like me to have called Dev, so I decided to call him during office hours the next day, when Abhimanyu wouldn't be around him.

***

Chapter 11

When Hope Dies...

I couldn't sleep that whole night. Aisha came back around 1 A.M. Everything had gone smoothly on her part, as Maa didn't come to know about her going out with Girish, but for me, the entire day had been ominous. So much had happened; my relationship with Aadit had completely been altered, I had truly considered him as my friend. On the other hand, the hope of getting Abhimanyu back in my life was weakening with every passing moment. All these things were stinging at my heart. I called Dev as soon as I reached office. He said he couldn't talk to me then as he was busy in some meeting. I had a presentation too that day and I wanted to talk to Dev before that. He told me that he would call me as soon as he would get free, but he didn't call even after an hour and the time was running at the pace of light.

"Hey Raahi, let's go," said Ankita, getting up from her seat. She was the team leader of our group. I switched my phone to silent mode and kept it in my drawer. I knew that if I took it with me, I would keep checking it every few seconds and ruin my first presentation.

The presentation went smoothly, though I stammered a bit because of anxiety, but everyone took it as my hesitation of being a newcomer. The presentation was followed by lunch and that was the time I cursed myself for not having brought my phone, as I had ample of time after the presentation to receive a call. After lunch I came back to my cubicle, unlocked my drawer and checked my phone. There was a message from Dev: **Hey, mind if I call you in the evening around five? I'm a bit occupied right now.**

No problem ☺ I replied. *So now I had to wait till five,* I sighed.

It was 4:35 P.M. when my phone flashed, 'Dev Calling'.

"Hey pretty girl, I'm so sorry to have kept you waiting for so long," he said in his typical flirtatious tone as soon as I picked up the phone. This was the reason why Abhimanyu never liked me calling at his number.

"That's perfectly okay...even I was caught up in a presentation," I tried to sound normal as if I hadn't been waiting for his call all day.

"So, how is life going?" he asked.

"It's good. How about you? How do you like Hyderabad?" I asked.

"I'm good and Hyderabad is a cool city if you ignore the food and the distance from the hometown."

"Yeah, that's true. I'm lucky that way," I said.

"You bet. How come you called me today? Anything urgent?" he asked.

"Not really...just like that." I scolded myself for not coming to the point. But I couldn't bring myself to start the conversation without the fear of being judged.

"Hmm, *yaar* I really felt bad on hearing about you and Abhimanyu. I mean, you guys looked so perfect together, just like a dream couple. At least, that's what we used to think," he said.

"It's okay." I was surprised that he knew all the details. *Did that mean that Abhimanyu had announced our breakup to everyone?* My heart sank.

"You know, I tried my level best to coax him, but he was dead set on his decision. He said he is too young to be in a committed relationship."

"Hmm..." I responded just to let him know that I was listening. Saying anything else would have completely shattered me. Had Abhimanyu been feeling smothered by me? *You suffocate me sometimes.* I recalled his words.

"But I think that's what we call destiny, all your efforts fail if you aren't destined for something," he continued. *Really? If we were destined to separate, then why did God unite us in the first place?*

"How is he?" I asked.

"I don't know. He doesn't live with us anymore."

"Then where is he?" I frowned.

"He has moved in to Neeti's flat, almost two weeks back."

"Who is Neeti?" I rubbed the pain in my chest that had started to claw at my heart. *Was it the same girl I talked to yesterday?*

"Oh! Didn't he tell you? I think it's something you should ask him, not me," he replied with a tinge of ruth in his voice.

"Please Dev, I need to know this. He isn't returning my phone calls," I pleaded.

"Well...these guys have been dating for the last two months and now they're in a live-in relationship."

I felt like I was falling into a dark and never-ending inferno. This was something I hadn't imagined even in my worst dreams. *He had been cheating on me.* The light of faith started becoming hazier with each word he said and my world started collapsing around me.

"They work at the same office. Abhimanyu had been talking about her since the first day they met. Then slowly, Abhimanyu started staying aloof. His long late-night calls started growing, I was under the impression that he was talking to you, but one day I realized that it wasn't you. I talked to him; I even threatened him to tell you everything," he paused for a moment before adding, "I was stunned by his response that he had made up his mind to leave you and go ahead with Neeti. I know it's very hard for you to hear all this, but I think you should know it. He isn't worth it, Raahi…you definitely deserve someone better."

Oh! So that was the reason behind his strange behavior. And he accused me of being too possessive and arduous. Now I understood, why he used to be so disinterested while talking to me at night, because he was fervent to talk to someone else. My heart scorched at the thought of Abhimanyu and Neeti living together. Despite his rude behavior, I had still assumed that we would be fine one day, but that day, the last thread of hope was also broken. Despair started coursing through my blood and apathy clouded my eyes. A sob escaped my mouth and he heard it.

"Are you okay, Raahi?" he asked.

"Yeah…I need to go…" I said and disconnected the line.

I couldn't breathe in that moment. I froze where I was standing. My mind was slipping into an abyss of grief. His words had crumpled my heart to such an extent that it was mangled beyond recognition. *Was this real? It couldn't be.* I closed my eyes and said a little prayer, all I wanted was for it to be a nightmare that I would soon wake up from. Standing there at that moment, I saw no future, no answer to any of my sufferings. I felt worthless and numb to life. They say that sleep is the only escape from any kind of emotional pain, but I didn't want a temporary escape; I needed a permanent one. I lost all my sense of thought and analysis. I didn't even realize when I took out a paper cutter from my drawer and reached the office washroom, which was on the same floor. I stood in front of a large mirror and looked at my reflection. All I could see was a soul trapped in a corpse, struggling to get out, screaming to get rid of the pain that this body was causing it. *What's this body without hope anyway? Nothing, it's just nothing...except an effigy of flesh and blood.* I slowly pulled out the blade and kept it against my wrist and closed my eyes; my hand trembled and knees wobbled but I kept my spirit strong. I didn't let a single tear escape my eyes. *Isn't it something that happens when hope dies?* I was about to slit my wrist when I felt someone's hand on my shoulder.

"Raahi, is everything okay?"

I turned in reflex and saw Ankita behind me. The paper cutter slipped down from my hand, leaving a scratch on my wrist. I kneeled down to the floor, exclaiming my misery and cried; not just cried, but howled. Ankita quickly latched the washroom door from the inside so that no one else could come in and see me in that state. She held me firmly around from my shoulders and sat beside me on the floor. I collected myself somehow, as it wasn't good to break down in front of one's office colleagues.

"I'm okay now," I muttered.

"Are you sure? Is everything all right? I saw you talking to someone on the phone and somehow, I sensed from your expressions that something was wrong. That's why I came to see you," she said.

"Yeah...actually, I lost someone very close to me," I said and my eyes welled up with fresh warm tears.

"Oh! I'm so sorry to hear that," she consoled as she took my words in a literal sense. I didn't care to clear the matter either. "Come with me, I'll drop you home," she added. I nodded. At that instant, I wasn't feeling all that stable mentally. It felt as if someone else had taken over my body, whom I couldn't trust. So I decided to go with her.

On the whole way back, I tried hard to hold myself strong. I shook my body back and forth continuously to keep myself together, at least until I reach home. When we reached my place, Ankita patted me on my back and said, "Be strong, Raahi."

I clambered down the car and smiled at her wanly.

As I entered the house, Maa sensed my miserable and devastated state immediately. She asked me about my condition and I told her that I wasn't feeling well. I came to my room, didn't even bother to switch on the light or fan, but just coiled on my bed, clutched the pillow tight between my arms and cried.

I learnt a very important lesson that day. So many times we ignore the people around us, thinking that it's none of our business to interfere in their personal matters. We keep ourselves so occupied in our own world, that we don't even care what the people around us are going through. Perhaps, I had also done the same throughout my life. So many times I had seen Ankita baffled, anxious and even crying, but I never went to her to talk. All I thought was that it was her personal matter. What if she too had thought the same way today, would I even be alive? I knew that taking your own life is the biggest offence one could ever commit. It's a misconception that your life belongs only to you. Rather, it belongs to those who have brought you into this world. I couldn't even imagine what my Paa would have gone through, had I done anything wrong to myself. But that was just a bad moment when my intellect gave up and my heart took control of my body; all I could see in that moment was complete darkness, such darkness that nothing was visible to me. It seemed as if the only relief to my pain at that moment was to release the soul entombed in the painful body. The moment Ankita tapped my shoulder, I felt like someone had pulled me out of the darkness and jolted my senses into me. Meddling in other's lives could sometimes actually save them, as the one suffering from emotional pain may not ask for help outright, but that doesn't mean that one might not need it.

Maa called me out for dinner, but I refused. She still fed me forcefully. She also gave me a few medicines to get rid of the headache, which is what I had told her.. I didn't go to office the next day and spent the entire time lying in bed; without a shower, without eating properly and without even talking to anyone.

"Raahi, what happened, *beta*?" Maa asked when she came in to feed me. I shook my head, but my eyes brimmed over with tears. She held my face in between her palms and asked, "Is it because of me? Did I do anything wrong, talking about you and Aadit?" I saw remorse in her eyes.

"No…no…Maa…" I shook my head vigorously. *Oh God! Where was all this going?* "I'm feeling homesick. I just want to go back home for a while. I can't live without my Paa," I said and sobbed. She hugged me tight and I responded back with the same intensity.

I kept myself confined in my room for the next day too, and in the same state. I had made up my mind to go back to Solan. These big cities weren't for me. I was folding my clothes to pack them when Aisha entered my room.

"Hey, is there something wrong with you?" she asked.

"No… all's well," I said wanly.

"Please Raahi, you are scaring us," she said.

"There is nothing like that…"

"Look Raahi, I told you not to call me 'di', but you can consider me your elder sister. I'm here to listen; you need not to suffer in silence. Is there something wrong at your office? Tell me what's troubling you?" she insisted.

"I had a bad breakup," I pursed my lips and looked up with eyes wide open to avoid fresh tears come out. I didn't know why, but I told her the truth.

"It's okay Raahi…he must be a loser. Why are you suffering because of that asshole?"

"I'll be fine. I just need some time. But please don't tell this to Maa," I said. She nodded and took her leave.

***

It was around midnight, when my phone displayed 'Shreya calling'. I had been deprived of sleep those days and it was evident on my face, in the form of dark circles around my eyes. It had been five days in a row, since I last saw the sun. I had completely stopped taking any calls on my phone, except for my Paa's. Ankita at office and Aisha at home were being a great support to me. Ankita had applied for medical leaves on my behalf and Aisha told Maa that I was going through some severe PMS. Maa took my illness seriously and started treating my PMS with her home remedies. She made me drink ginger, basil and cinnamon tea thrice a day and also gave me a hot water bottle to relieve the muscle cramps. I felt really bad lying to her.

My phone buzzed one complete cycle and then went silent. She had been calling me since morning, but I was in no mood to talk to anyone. I curled up on my bed again and tried hard to fall asleep. I even searched for sleeping pills in Aadit's room that he had given me the other day, but couldn't find them anywhere. Engrossed in my anguish, I didn't realize when the first ray of dawn entered my room through the window. I heard a loud clatter on my door.

"Raahi, there is a call for you," said Maa as she entered my room. I checked my own phone, but there weren't any calls from Paa. *Who could be calling me on Maa's phone?* I wondered.

Aadit?

"Who is it, Maa?" I asked, puzzled.

"Why don't you check yourself?" she said and handed the phone over to me. I took the phone from her. She went out of my room, closing the door behind her.

"Hello?" I said.

"Hello, Raahi…what's wrong with you? Why are you not answering my calls?" she yelled.

"Shreya, actually…"

"Did Abhimanyu do something?" she asked, cutting me off.

It was really hard to hide anything from her. I told her each and every detail of what had happened that day and cried. She scolded me for not letting her know earlier.

"What could I have told you, Shreya? Nothing will make a difference now. He is gone. No one can do anything," I sobbed. "I can't explain how I'm feeling right now. I can't explain this pain that I'm going through. It is so deep, so intense that even if I cut my limbs off, that physical pain would still be nothing compared to this," I blubbered.

"Shall I come to meet you there?" she asked.

"No, I'm kind of stable now. And I won't try to do again what I was about to do, the biggest mistake anyone can ever commit," I spluttered.

"What do you mean?" she asked.

"I was about to kill myself. Can you believe it, Shreya? I don't know what happened to me in that moment. But don't worry, I won't do anything stupid like that again. I have realized that my life is far more precious than that infidel relationship." I replied.

"I really think I should be there with you."

"No...in fact, I'm coming back to Solan. I have decided. I'm done with all this."

"You take care Raahi...I'll call you again," she said and cut the line abruptly.

Just an hour later she called me again. This time I answered her phone.

"Hey Raahi...I need your help," she said. Just an hour ago she was talking about helping me and now she needed my help. *Oh God! Would I ever be able to understand this girl?* I sighed.

"I'm sending you an address, you have to go there today by six in the evening. There will be this lady there, Mitali. Please hand over a cheque for five thousand rupees to her. It's really urgent," she said and waited for my answer.

"Why handover a cheque? Why can't you just transfer it online?" I argued.

"No, I can't. She doesn't have a bank account."

"Shreya, I don't want to go anywhere. I'll do it some other day."

"You are so mean, Raahi. Do you want me to miss my classes and travel 250 kms, just because you aren't in the mood to move a few meters?" she chided, "It's really urgent Raahi, I wouldn't have asked you otherwise. You know that." Her voice was a bit calmer now.

"Okay...baba... I'll go," I capitulated.

"Now that's like my girl. Muaaaah," she effused. She really behaved weird sometimes.

***

Chapter 12

The Sixteen Sheets

The feeling of being in a perfidious relationship is something that excruciates your mind and wrecks your inner peace. But, who is to blame? It was entirely my fault, I granted this relationship the power to devour my worth and make me feel like a loser. The most essential thing gone was my sense of self. Still lying on my bed, I continued to question myself: *Why did this happen to me? What had I done to deserve this? I loved him with all my heart, my God knew, I had never ever thought about anyone else, then how could he choose someone else over me?* The feeling of rejection is something that can make you feel worthless and humiliated; it's the worst thing that can happen to anyone.

I looked at the time, I still had an hour before going to the address that Shreya had messaged me. I got up from my bed to take a shower. I quickly put on an oversized tee with denims. Then I took a leaf out of my cheque-book, filled in all the details and out of habit, I was about to cross it when I recalled Shreya's words that she didn't have a bank account. I also grabbed some cash in case she refused to accept a cheque. I tied my sticky hair in a braid and put on my sneakers.

As I came out of my room, I saw Maa cooking in the kitchen while Kanchi was sitting at the dining table, mincing onions. Maa had asthma, for which reason, she usually avoided cooking.

"Why are you cooking today?" I asked Maa, standing outside the kitchen.

"Suresh is coming back today, so I thought of making all his favorite dishes," she turned pink as she said that. She looked so enthusiastic. Who says love fades away with age? I smiled and gesticulated a thumbs up.

"Ah! Thank God, you are looking a bit normal today," she said, looking at me in between stirring vegetables in the frying pan with a spatula.

"Actually, I'm going to meet a friend's friend. I need to hand over a cheque to her. I'll be back in half an hour," I said, fidgeting with the strap of my handbag.

"Okay, take Kanchi along, if you want," she suggested.

"It's okay, Maa, I'm fine now. Moreover, you need her here more. I have the address, it's not too far," I said.

Kanchi closed the main door behind me as I stepped out. I pushed the call button for the elevator. As the elevator door opened, I saw two kids inside; the younger one was crying and the elder one was trying to cheer him up. I smiled at them as I got in. I glowered as soon as I glanced at the operating panel; the kids had pushed the buttons for every floor.

"Why did you do this?" I asked them irately. Neither of them answered and kept looking at me with a puppy face. I smiled and asked them graciously this time.

"*Didi*, he is a guest here and he forgot his flat number and floor, so we are checking every floor to find the house he's visiting," the elder kid replied, looking at me with his eyes wide.

"Oh! Don't worry, I'll also help you look," I said, holding the younger kid's chin.

It reminded me of one of my childhood incidents, when there was an annual function at Paa's college. I was nine then, and playing with the other kids in campus, I forgot the way to Paa's office. I started crying, as I had gone to some other building by mistake, that was entirely secluded. Just then, a boy, who was a little older than I was, came and offered to help me. I felt like God had sent a prince to rescue me. I had an instant crush on him. He placed a chocolate in my hand and consoled me lovingly. We went from one building to another, to locate my father room. I also told him that I would marry him once I grew up, to which he had blushed frantically. It was only later that I understood his intention behind treating me with the chocolate. He just wanted me to keep my mouth shut as I had been screaming my lungs out. Ruminating on that incident, I smiled to myself.

The elevator stopped at every floor and the kids checked every single apartment till we reached the 6th floor, where he found his house.

***

Half an hour later, I found myself in front of the baronial Glory Apartments, which had numerous sky-hugging towers. The guard stopped me and asked me to make an entry in their register. I filled in all the details and inquired him for the way to the community center, where Mitali was supposed to meet me. He pointed towards the lawn, where some girls were sitting on the grass and a lady, who seemed to be in her late thirties, was talking to them, as if delivering a lecture. The lady looked elegant in her off white cotton saree with a pink border.

"Excuse me, Ma'am," I said as I approached her.

"Hey! You are Raahi, aren't you? I was waiting for you," she said cheerfully and extended her hand towards me to shake. I took it shyly. "Call me Mitali," she said. She had a soothing voice. I was flabbergasted by the way she greeted me, as if she had known me for a long time.

"Yeah, Shreya told me to hand this over to you," I took out the cheque from my bag and extended it towards her.

"Ah! Thank you so much. You know, it's people like you who make us believe that humanity still exists," she said as she took the cheque from my hand.

I was perplexed at her remark, as I had no idea what purpose the cheque was for. Before I could ask, she read my expression and answered herself, "Actually, we are planning the admission of these girls to some philanthropic chains of renowned schools here in NCR, and we are collecting funds for the same." She gestured towards the girls sitting in the lawn. They looked like they came from poor families.

"Do you teach these girls?" I asked.

"Yes, some of the girls work as maids and some are the daughters of maids who work here for various families in this society. We are preparing them for an upcoming entrance exam to get admission into various schools. These kids don't know the importance of education, so it's our duty as a responsible citizen to spread awareness among these kids. I strictly instructed the security not to allow them inside the society if they didn't attend my class," she said rather matter-of-factly.

Mitali had an infectious personality. The way she spoke, it felt as if each of her words was travelling through my nerves, reaching my heart and then touching my soul. Listening to her for some time, I actually forgot my own problems; she had such an aura around her.

"You are really doing a great job, Ma'am. Even I would like to contribute," I said and rummaged through my bag to take out the cash that I had carried.

"Do you really want to contribute?" she asked with an interest.

"Yes, of course, there's no question about it," I insisted, counting the cash in my hand.

"Actually, these girls need time, more than money. Would you like to contribute with your time instead?" she asked.

"Umm… I… I…" I stammered.

"No problem, take your time and think about it. Some of these girls are already earning. Moreover, people these days think that they can fulfil their social responsibility just by bestowing money. So money isn't a big deal, but yes, time is. They need someone who can teach them some basic things," she said and turned towards the girls as one of them had called to her.

I turned my gaze to the other side. *Did I have time for all this? No doubt, she was doing a great job, but she was perhaps a housewife, with ample time on her hands, whereas I had to go to office everyday.* I reasoned with myself. Engrossed in my thoughts, I noticed a nest lying scattered on the ground, right at the base of a building. It had a few broken eggs and two sparrows hovering agitatedly over it. Somebody had knocked the nest down, maybe while cleaning the overhang of a window, I speculated looking up the wall, as there were quite a few windows with exhaust fans installed in them. Soon after, the sparrows started picking up the twigs in their tiny beaks and carried them back to the overhang of a window again.

Was my grief more intense than these little creatures'? The thought joggled my senses. They had lost their home as well as their unborn babies; nevertheless, they had started erecting their nest back immediately, instead of mourning over what had happened. '*Isn't that exactly what I needed to do with my life too? Haven't we learned all through our lives that real happiness comes from doing good to others? And life was actually offering me a chance at it,*' I pondered.

I looked back at Mitali and said, "I'll come tomorrow at six, after my office." She smiled and gestured at me to come closer to her.

"Why tomorrow? Let's start from today. Actually, I have to leave early today, as my son isn't well. Can you please take over today's class?" she pleaded.

"Yes, why not?" I said hesitantly.

"Okay then, let me provide you with a quick overview; we conduct a two hour class here. I'll teach in the first hour and you can take the second one. I want you to prepare them for their upcoming entrance exam. I'll give you all the details about that in a bit. They know the alphabets and their formations. They can write almost all three letter words and a few four to five letter words too. In mathematics..." The next few minutes she explained to me everything that the girls had learned till then.

"Come, let me introduce you to them," Mitali said. "Look here girls," she clapped her hands to get their attention, "See, who is here. This is Raahi Didi and from now, she will teach you too." All of them started looking at me. "Don't bother her too much, or she won't come back," she added and laughed.

"Now, I'm leaving and what you all have to do is to write five words in English, describing Raahi Didi. If you don't know the spellings, try to form them yourself by recognizing the sound. Raahi Didi will tell you the correct spellings later," she instructed and bade goodbye, leaving me with the girls.

The girls started scribbling words on their sheets of paper, throwing furtive glances at me in between. I knew that they were observing me to find the appropriate words to describe me, which made me feel very conscious of my looks. I cursed myself for not having worn something nicer that day. They all took a good ten minutes to describe me in five words on their sheets. Then the first girl handed over her sheet to me. The five words that she had written were: beautiful, good, smart, doll, angel. Though, a few of them were spelled wrong, it still brought a wide smile to my face. I found myself genuinely smiling after days. We girls are always desirous of compliments and they can actually brighten us up, no matter what the circumstances.

"Didi, you should smile all the time…you look pretty when smiling," the girl said in Hindi. In the next few minutes, I had all the sixteen sheets in my hand. The girls looked at me expectantly for my remarks. I genuinely felt good after reading all those sixteen sheets. Each and every word written on them brimmed my heart with positive energy. I gathered all those sheets and preserved them carefully in my bag. The girls gaped at me in surprise, as if asking, 'Why are you pilfering those sheets?' but only I knew the value of those eighty words written on them. Those words made me feel truly worthy and exalted. For the next thirty minutes, I taught them the correct spelling of all those words.

***

The dinner was extremely delicious that night. Maa had put her heart and soul into preparing those dishes and the upshot of her effort reflected on our gratified faces. Ebullience was once again in the air; it was after a long time that all of us were having dinner together. Everyone wished for Aadit to be there at that moment. Even I missed him. Aisha dialed his number. He was getting ready for office and was baffled by the odd-timing of the call, while Aisha took full advantage of his edginess by vexing him even further. Before their talk could turn into ugly fight, Maa took the phone from her and pacified him. Having a complete family is truly a blessing; you find happiness even in the petty fights. I had been deprived of this experience all my life and I thanked my stars for having bestowed upon me a chance to get involved in such blissful moments. Suresh uncle then briefed Aadit about his Calcutta visit and hung up after a small talk.

Soon after, all of us went to our respective rooms. I was actually feeling elated after so many days. The ordeal of the last week had drained the life out of me and now it was time to bring my life back on track.

The first thing I did was get rid of all of Abhimanyu's memories. He had already unfriended me and I avenged him by blocking him on Facebook as well as WhatsApp. I also deleted all my WhatsApp chats, as I didn't want to see his mention on any of my chats with close friends. I also made an exit from all our common groups on WhatsApp. I even deleted all the photographs of us that I had saved on my phone, though it wasn't easy because with every picture, all those moments we had shared seemed to come alive and wreck my balance, but I held strong. I took out all his greeting cards and letters that he had filled up with honey coated words, went to my balcony and burnt them. Warm tears rolled down my cheeks as I saw them turn into ashes. "You have done enough damage to me Mr. Abhimanyu Singh, now I won't let you affect me anymore," I murmured.

I stood there for some time, looking at the stars. It was a little cool and windy outside. The swaying of trees and the rustling sound of leaves was very noticeable. A wave of pleasure ran through my body as a gust of cool wind blew through my hair. I turned the other way to let my hair blow away from my face and my eyes suddenly fell on the door of Aadit's room. I had spent so many memorable moments with Aadit in this very balcony. However, at dinner before, while talking to everyone else, he hadn't even bothered to ask about me. And he claimed to love me. 'All these boys are the same: heartless and insidious. They only know how to damage relations and injure hearts...or perhaps, I am no longer worthy of anyone's love,' I thought.

I looked up at the sky again. It was clear and I could see the shining diamonds sprinkled over the dark and endless sky of twilight. Suddenly, my mind started playing with a string of words. I ran inside the room, took out my diary and furiously jotted down a few lines on it.

When life seems like a strife
And the unravels are like walking on a knife
When despair starts brimming over eyes
What to do when all hope dies...?
Look at the stars shining in the night
Despite knowing that they'll die in the light
They hold on to the hope of the next twilight
And inculcate endurance, shining bright.
Look at the birds that have lost their nests
Engulfed in distraught, yet they never rest
They start from scratch and build up the nest again
Isn't it better than dying in the pain?
So the next time when everything seems grey
Reminisce what these things convey
Dusk has never been the end of the day
It heralds the dawn with a promising ray.

A buzz on my phone caught my attention then; I picked it up and checked the notifications bar. There were two messages on my blank WhatsApp page from an unknown number. As I opened the chat, I frowned upon seeing the first message, which was a picture of me, clicked at the time when I was teaching those girls. In the picture, I was holding a sheet in my hand and talking to one of the girls standing beside me. The second message was a text which read: ***The good work you do for others is like an investment, which isn't subject to market risks. You will surely get the return with a huge interest, much more than what you had invested. Thank you for your good work.***

I opened the True Caller App and tried to look for the owner of the number. I couldn't get any information, except that it was a local number. *Who could it be and how did anyone get my number?* I quizzed myself. *Mitali?* I tapped on WhatsApp again to look for Mitali's number that Shreya had shared with me on our chat, but I soon realized that the conversation was lost since I had just deleted all my chats. I called Shreya and she picked up instantly.

"Hello darling, how are you?" she giggled. I could hear some loud music reverberating in the background. It sounded like she was at some gathering.

"Hey...where are you?" I asked.

"It's Kartik's birthday today, so we are getting high at a party," she effused and elongated the word 'party'.

"Aww...you enjoy your party then and don't forget to wish him from my side," I said.

"By the way, why did you call? Is everything alright?" she asked.

"Yeah, all's well here. Listen, can you send me Mitali's number once again?" I asked her.

“Yeah, sure, wait a sec,” she paused for a few seconds and then said, “Done! Check it out.”

“Thank a lot, dear,” I said and disconnected the call. Immediately, I tallied the number that she sent with the one from which I had received the texts, but the digits didn’t match; it wasn’t Mitali’s number. I thought of calling her, but it was too late. I typed a message to that anonymous number: ***Clicking someone’s pictures without their knowledge or permission is an offence. You may end up landing in jail.*** But I deleted it instantly.

‘It’s just a message, Raahi...why are you getting so hyper over a message? Maybe, someone got your number from the entry you made at the security register and messaged you. Perhaps, it is indeed Mitali texting from some other number,’ I thought and tried to relax. We shouldn’t reveal our personal contact details everywhere. I made a mental note of it. I decided to join back at office from the very next day. The more I’d keep myself busy, the less I would think about Abhimanyu.

***

Chapter 13

Two Good Things

After attending office the next day, I came straight to Glory Apartments where I was supposed to teach the girls again. I reached there 10 minutes before the time I had committed to the evening before. Again, the security guard asked me to enter my details in their register and this time, I changed a few digits of my mobile number. As I walked in, I saw Mitali taking the class. She waved at me as soon as she saw me approaching.

"Hey Raahi, how are you?" she asked.

"I'm good. How is your son now?"

"He is better now, thank you," she replied.

"I need to ask you something. Yesterday, I got a message from an unknown number; someone had clicked a picture of me while I was teaching here and WhatsApp'd it to me late last night," I told her and rummaged through my bag to look for my phone.

"With a Thank You note?" she asked casually as if it was a normal occurrence, her attention still occupied in examining the notebook of one of the girls.

"Yeah, how do you know?" I asked, surprised.

"Don't worry, it's completely harmless. Even I used to get such messages when I started teaching. Consider it a compliment from a secret admirer," she said and winked at me.

"What does that mean?"

"Raahi, I'm not the only one who teaches these underprivileged kids; it's a huge group. I'm just a volunteer. Whosoever volunteers for this cause, gets these encouraging messages."

She wound up her class quickly and told me to sit with her for some time. "Girls, it's a ten minute break for you," she said loudly, addressing the girls. Both of us sat there on the bench perched at the side of the park, then Mitali started, "You know Raahi, everyone around us is going through some pain, some struggle, some fight in their lives. Do you know what makes them strong enough to go through all this?" She looked at me expectantly and I shook my head. She continued, "Their will power, their belief that everything will be all right, their trust in God, and above all, the love of the people around them. Sometimes when we are in extreme distress, we start undermining all these things that give us the strength to fight back. It's not our fault, our brain works that way, we tend to notice the negativity around us more, because we take for granted everything that spreads positivity."

I was clueless as to why she had suddenly started this topic with me. It felt like she had read my mind through my eyes. I avoided any further eye contact with her and kept my gaze locked towards the ground.

"Are you surprised, why I'm suddenly telling you all this?" She read my mind again. I nodded. "Yesterday when I saw you, I sensed a kind of affliction in your eyes. I felt like you are going through some kind of depression and are barricading all the positivity around from entering you that can actually give you the strength to combat these bad times," she said and added after a pause, "But I must say, you are truly a fighter. It's not easy to do something for others when you yourself are going through a tough time in your life." I turned my gaze to the other side as my eyes got moistened.

"Do you want to share something with me?" she asked, gently placing her hand on my shoulder.

I shook my head in a vague 'no'. I wanted to open my heart to her, but something stopped me, maybe the fear of being judged. Wasn't it too early to trust someone I had met just a day ago? She didn't prod any further. An awkward silence followed.

"Consider it like a phase is your life Raahi, it will be over soon. Life is like a sinusoidal wave,"— she drew an imaginary sine wave in the air with her index finger—"You can't stay at the crest forever, neither at the trough. Falling from a crest to a trough is always easy, but regaining your position again from the trough to a crest takes a lot of effort, but it's not impossible. Trust me. Just allow the people around you to hold your hand and help you, share your problems with them. You will be surprised to know that everyone around you has gone through a similar phase at some point in their lives. So, stay strong," she said and patted my back. There was a welcoming assurance in her words, which convinced me to trust her.

She then took her leave and I started taking the class. I asked all the girls their names along with what they wanted to become when they grew up. I was surprised to know that most of them had no idea what they wanted to do. According to them, they were already grown up and were satisfied with what they were already doing. So, I asked them about their hobbies and taught them about the different professions that they could pursue according to their hobbies. I noticed a different kind of enthusiasm in them as they started discussing their desired professions and teased each other about their choices. I smiled to myself.

One of the girls came to me and asked, "Didi, can I become a teacher just like you, if I study hard?"

"Of course, why not? Trust me, you are going to be an amazing teacher," I replied and she beamed happily, as if someone had given wings to her desire.

"What's your name?" I asked again, as I couldn't recall.

"Megha," she smiled.

***

"Raahi, thank God you are back. Now go and get changed quickly," Maa said, as soon as I entered the house.

"Why? What happened?" I asked.

"Girish and his family are coming today to discuss and finalize the wedding programs and the venue. Actually Girish's father is going out of the country for some business next week, so we need to finalize everything before that," she said, arranging the flowers in the vase.

The house looked extraordinarily clean that evening, everything was exactly in its place and the aroma was just out of the world. I came to my room and changed into some decent Indian wear. When I stepped out, I saw Aisha dressed in a magenta Punjabi suit. She looked fabulous in that attire. It was the first time that I was seeing her dressed in Indian wear.

Soon, Girish and his family arrived; his father was the exact replica of him, whereas his mother looked like a typical kitty-party kind of a lady, who loved to flaunt her affluence all the time. They started discussing the programs and finalizing the venues for each event. I couldn't be part of their discussion as I had no idea of their customs and Delhi's popular venues for events like these were still alien to me. Girish's mom was more concerned about the venues and the arrangements there for the sake of her reputation in the so-called rich and affluent circles of the Delhi's most elite. They decided on a common and grand reception at a five star hotel in Delhi. Girish's father remained quiet for most of the discussion and agreed to everything that his wife finalized.

The discussion continued even at the dining table. After dinner, I went to the kitchen to help Maa. She handed me a tray with two bowls of ice cream and told me to serve it to Girish and Aisha, who were sitting in Aisha's room. Perhaps she felt a little hesitant to go there herself. So I took the tray from her and ambled towards Aisha's room. I entered after a knock and found them sitting on the bed and watching something on Aisha's laptop, perhaps her pictures. Aisha gestured at me to keep the tray on the side table and to sit beside her. I did as she asked.

I was expecting to see some pictures of her displayed on the screen, but the color of my face immediately drained away when I saw Aadit on video chat. He was dressed in office wear. We had a momentary eye contact, following which, both of us averted our eyes. My own words that I had screamed at him a few days ago ricocheted in my head and his intense expression told me that his mind was replaying the same thing in his head too. Girish sensed the awkwardness that had suddenly formalized since the moment I came to sit next to Aisha.

"Is something wrong between you two? Why are you behaving like strangers?" Girish asked, looking first at Aadit and then at me.

"There is nothing like that. Hi Raahi, how are you?" Aadit said, turning his gaze from Girish to me.

"I'm good," I replied with a dead expression on my face.

"What's wrong with you guys? Such a formal hi-hello. Who could say that you guys performed a rapturous dance together just a few days ago?" chimed in Aisha. We locked our gazes for a few moments again and then Aadit looked down and sniggered.

"Nothing is wrong. Now will you tell me what all happened today? I don't have that much time to stay," said Aadit.

"I really have no idea," said Girish animatedly. "As you can see, women are in majority here, so they decided the programs according to their dresses and jewelry, while us men are left with just one program in our hands, which is the bachelor party."

"For your kind information, it won't be a boys-only event. We girls are going to be a part of it too. So basically, it's a combined bachelor and bachelorette party. And guess what? Papa agreed to this. Can you imagine?" exclaimed Aisha.

"Then give this event some other name, it's neither a bachelor nor a bachelorette party," snapped Aadit.

"Whatever," Aisha replied, chipping at her nail paint.

I felt a little out of place there, so I quietly excused myself. I noticed Aadit looking at me when I got up to leave and it appeared from his expression that he wanted me to stay. Perhaps it was just my assumption because somewhere deep inside, I sought his attention too. He hadn't cared to talk to me even once after that night.

They kept discussing the day's happenings. I came back to my room as everyone else was busy conversing and I couldn't make myself fit anywhere.

I grabbed my phone and found a couple of messages from the same unknown number again. There was a picture of me from that day's class again and a text which read: ***Genuineness of people appears from the sincerity of their work...Thank you for unveiling a new sky of dreams to them.***

My pleasure ☺, I typed back.

***

Two weeks passed by and the Glory Apartments, Mitali, my sixteen students and of course the anonymous messenger quickly became an integral part of my life. The day I had first met Mitali now seemed like God's plan to salvage me from the mess I was in. Those ten minutes of motivational talk with Mitali, helping those girls look for their dreams and most importantly, the two texts from that anonymous messenger really boosted my confidence. I slowly got habitual of their presence in my life. As for that anonymous messenger, I felt like someone was always there around me, watching me and guiding me in whatever I was doing. Gradually and unknowingly, I started to feel drawn towards that anonymous messenger. I tried my best to spy on this secret admirer, but failed miserably each time.

I had also asked Mitali to look for a shared flat for me at the same apartment, as it would save half an hour of my time further. Though living without Maa and Aisha would be a little difficult, I felt that it was the right time to move out. It was their generosity that they let me stay like their own daughter in their house, but at the end of the day, they were a family and I was an outsider.

"Raahi, I'm leaving early today. Will you please handle things if anything comes up?" Ankita asked, hauling me out of my thoughts.

"Yeah, sure. Good bye."

I was sitting in my cubicle, waiting for the clock to hit 5:30. I opened the Facebook app on my phone and started scrolling through the news feed torpidly to while away the time. Just then, one particular post caught my attention. One of my college friends had posted twenty-five new photographs of his recent trip to Goa in an album named 'Gang in Goa'. The cover picture of the album had five boys holding beer glasses in their hands. All of them were from my batch, but the one face which captivated my attention was that of Abhimanyu Singh. I started tapping each picture one by one, holding my sight for a few extra seconds on the ones where Abhimanyu was present. I even zoomed in to his pictures to get the clearest view of his expressions. He looked happy and content. There were girls there too, but all of them were unknown to me.

Then came the most bizarre picture that undid all my efforts of the last two weeks to lift my spirits. The picture had Abhimanyu holding a girl in his arms at a beach in Goa, their clothes all drenched. The caption of the picture read 'love birds'. The picture had received 25 likes, 9 hearts, 6 wows and 12 comments. I quickly tapped on the comments. The one that caught my eye was 'Such a cute picture of *us* Maan...Muaaaah' by Neeti Gupta. I cursed myself for not having given him a love name while we were dating. I used to call him just by his name, like everyone else. I opened her profile and realized that I wasn't blocked there as I could see many pictures of her.

What did she have that I didn't?

It wasn't hard to guess. She was bold, beautiful, confident and so much more. *What was I? Nothing.* I was nothing compared to her. May be the best available option in that small town...and options are meant to be replaced. Perhaps that was the reason why Abhimanyu chose her over me. This is what love does to you...when you have it, you feel like the most deserving person in the world and once it's gone, you doubt your own worth.

Would I ever have gone to Goa with him?

No. Although I had been in a relationship with him, I never crossed my limits. Every girl has an unspoken promise with her family to never cross that moral boundary and I had kept my promise. I had let him touch my soul and heart, but perhaps that hadn't been enough to keep the relationship alive. My phone started ringing as people were waiting for me in the cab. I grabbed my bag and left the office, but before leaving, I deactivated my Facebook account.

I skipped my visit to Glory Apartments that day and informed Mitali of my absence. I came to my room and took out my phone. I had a strong urge to call Abhimanyu and ask him why he had done this to me, but I curbed that urge by shedding some tears. My phone buzzed with a message from the anonymous number again. I wiped my eyes hastily and clapped my eyes on the screen of my phone, hastily blinking the mist of tears away. There was a picture again, but this time, it was of an empty lawn and the text that followed read:

Excuses are the most viperous enemies, Raahi, that not only trouble you but also the people around you. See...one excuse from you has deprived them of a day's education.

I had never replied to these anonymous messages with more than one or two words, but this time, I replied: ***I'm already feeling low, don't make me feel worse. Not everyone is as strong as you.***

I saw the online status turn to '*typing...*' and then popped a reply: ***No matter how strong, how positive, how passionate you are, there always comes a day when you feel like giving up. It happens to test your determination. There is nothing wrong in that. Just don't give up.***

I rolled my eyes and replied: ***That's easier said than done.***

People say this because they know. They just want you to learn from their mistakes. No one is responsible for your happiness, neither for your sorrows, except you yourself, came a quick reply.

Okay then, can you suggest what I should do? I asked with sarcasm.

Do two good things daily; one for others and the second for yourself. You are already doing the first. Now start doing the second one too.

And what's that? I asked.

Anything that makes you happy. ☺

'What does make me happy? Dancing? Painting? Music? Reading? But I like doing these things when I'm already happy. What's that one thing that I love to do even when I'm stressed? Writing? Yes...I like to write poems,' I introspected. I opened my diary where I had scribbled hundreds of poems. Half of them had been written for Abhimanyu. Each one of them was a depiction of my attitude towards some particular happening in my life. Next, I registered myself on Wordpress and started writing a blog. I published my first poem there. I didn't publicize it as I was writing only for myself, not for others. I also decided to start going for a morning walk from the next day. Over the last few days, I had eaten chocolates like a demon and it had started showing its effect around my waist and thighs. This breakup had not only ruined me, but also my metabolism.

After dinner, I checked my page on Wordpress again. A few people had viewed my blog, I could see in the stats. I published another poem immediately and curled-up on my bed to sleep. This new excitement of publishing my work made me forget what had been tormenting me just a few moments ago.

The first thing I did after waking up the next morning was to check my website on Wordpress. A wave of ecstasy rushed through my body when I saw that four bloggers had already started following me. I also saw a comment on my page that read, *Very motivational, keep it up.* I was really amused; my own words that had somehow failed to motivate me, were actually motivating someone else. I opened my WhatsApp and quickly typed a Thank You message along with a link to my blog and sent it to the anonymous number. I didn't get a reply immediately, neither was I expecting one. I got out of bed and changed my clothes for a morning walk.

I was on the way to office when I received a reply from the anonymous number saying, ***Very well composed.***

Thank you! What should I call you? I messaged instantly.

Friend.

But I don't even know your name, I messaged back.

Can't two people just be friends, without knowing the identity of each other? came a quick response.

Who are you, a boy or a girl? I messaged.

Who do you want me to be, a boy or a girl? I got another question for a reply that I couldn't answer. I ended the conversation without a goodbye as I reached my office, because a goodbye would have ruined my chance of messaging him again during the day. *Did I use 'him'?* Why had I even asked that last question, if I had already assumed in my mind that it was a boy.

***

Chapter 14

Finding True Love

People say that all happy love stories end in marriages. However, what if love fades away after marriage? Every time I saw Ankita, I felt the same way. Ankita and her husband Pranav had been college sweethearts and after dating for six years, they finally got married. But the issues they hadn't faced in the six years of their pre-wedding relationship, had suddenly started to sprout within a single year post their wedding. Not a single day passed by when they didn't have a tiff. That day was no different.

I saw Ankita resting her head down on the desk. It wasn't the first time I was seeing her that way, but this time, I decided to approach her and ask why she was so upset. I placed my hand on her shoulder and she looked up at me in response; I noticed that her eyes were moist. When I asked her what was wrong, she replied, "I don't know Raahi, whether this problem is just mine or whether everyone goes through this. Ever since I got married, I have been feeling as if I'm no longer with the person I fell in love with," she paused for a moment to clear her throat and then added, "I had never thought that Pranav would change this much after marriage. There isn't much I want from him; a little bit of attention, a little bit of support, a little bit of his time.

Is that too much to ask for? He used to do so many things to woo me before the wedding, but not anymore. We didn't even go anywhere for our honeymoon. Can you imagine? Just because I'm a part of his life now, doesn't mean that he can take me for granted."

She took out her handkerchief from her bag and continued, "I'm a team leader here and everyone appreciates me for my work. I have an identity here, but what am I at home? Nothing. I'm just a useless lady who doesn't even know how to cook *karela*. Like seriously?"—she threw up her hands in defeat—"You know, I push myself beyond my limits everyday just to make him and his family happy but I fail every time. And I'm not afraid of failure; I'm afraid of the day I decide to give up. No one appreciates the ninety-nine things I do daily, but they don't forget to make me feel guilty for that single thing that I forget," she sobbed.

"It's our wedding anniversary tomorrow. I wanted to go away for a small vacation with him, so that we could spend some alone time away from his family. I even booked the tickets for a three-day trip to Nainital. And now at the end moment, he is backing off because he feels that we are being selfish and should rather celebrate it with everyone."

I had nothing to say as I felt myself too inexperienced to advise her on anything. I couldn't do anything besides lending her my ear and listened to her while she cried her heart out. The way she blurted everything out seemed as if her heart and her mind had been cluttered for days and she finally got a chance that day to hurl everything out of her.

"I don't know why I'm telling all this to you…but trust me, I'm actually feeling a lot better after extricating my mind from all this turmoil. Thanks for listening, Raahi," Ankita said, wiping away her tears with the handkerchief. I responded with a smile.

***

Later that evening, I found myself sitting on the same bench in the lawns of Glory Apartments. Mitali was busy taking her class. As usual, I had reached before time. Though I was physically present there, my mind kept replaying what Ankita had told me earlier that day. *'Is this what happens after marriage? Does every relationship go through the same? What must hurt more; the kind of separation that I had faced, or living with a person you love and feeling no love in his eyes, actions or words in return?'* I questioned myself. Of course, the latter was more dreadful. I came out of my trance when I felt Mitali coming to sit beside me.

"So, what's cooking in your mind today?" she asked mischievously, noticing that I was engrossed in some deep thought. I shook my head and grinned at her.

"Nothing, I was just thinking about a friend from work. She is not happy in her marriage. They loved each other a lot, but after they got married, her husband changed completely. He doesn't care for her anymore," I said, twirling the pen between my fingers. "Does true love really exist at all, or does it only exist in stories? Sometimes I feel as if marriage is the worst thing that can happen to you because no matter what they say or how special they make you feel, in the end, these boys are all the same. You can't trust them. Happily ever after is nothing but a fallacy."

"I would say don't jump to conclusions without listening to both the sides. Marriage is truly a beautiful and sacred relation, Raahi. But it needs patience, that your generation lacks. Your generation seeks instant gratification and is quick of the opinion of 'It's not working' when they face problems. There is a difference between spending a few hours with someone everyday and living with them or seeing them around you all the time. And you know what kills most relationships? Expectations. Expectations are like the shackles around your feet that don't allow a relationship to move efficaciously, eventually causing its death. You have to give everything up to make a relationship flourish, but today's generation just wants to be at the receiving end. Moreover, people need to change their perception of things." She stopped as one of the girls came to her with her notebook.

"See, I'm writing ten words here, tell all the girls to copy them and learn them by tomorrow. There will be a test," she said to the girl and started writing some words in the note book. The spelling of the second word she wrote was wrong, so I tried to interrupt her, but she ignored me and kept on writing the other words. I tried to bring her attention to the word that she had spelled wrong again, but she didn't listen. She handed the copy over to that girl and asked her to go. I called the girl back and corrected the spelling error myself. I looked at Mitali and found her looking at me with her eyebrows raised.

"Do you remember any other words that I wrote in the notebook?" she asked.

I then realized that I hadn't paid attention to any of the other words after my attention was caught by the one spelled wrongly. There were hardly 2-3 words that I could recall from the list of those ten words and one of them was the word that was spelled incorrectly itself. I shook my head.

"This is a human tendency Raahi, I wrote ten words down and you noticed only the one that was incorrectly written. This is the way we look at our lives too, we see only one thing that is going wrong in our life and are so consumed by that one wrong thing, that we effortlessly ignore the other nine things that make our lives blissful. We remember that one curse that made us go through hell and overlook the numerous other blessings that give us the strength to overcome those impediments in life. We remember only that one person in our life who made us feel bad and we lose ourself so much in that soreness that we simply ignore the efforts of the other nine people around us who are fighting for our happiness. We judge a person by their one characteristic that we find annoying, ignoring the other nine qualities that make them loveable. The day we will start appreciating those nine other good things, instead of criticizing the one bad thing in others, life will become beautiful and worth living again," she said, enlightening me.

"You know Raahi, it's not necessary for what is there in your mind, to actually exist. Sometimes the situations that seem utterly unfavourable in your mind, are actually not so in reality. The negative thoughts that we hoard in our minds often prevent us from seeing the positivity around us. That's why I say, you should certainly clear your mind and share your thoughts with someone reliable if something detrimental is going on in your mind, because this is the only way to get rid of your pessimism."

***

Today I have a query for you Raahi and I want you to find the answer yourself. Do you really think that true love exists only in stories? My eyes were clapped on the message that I had just received from the anonymous number. Had he been eavesdropping? This was the exact question that I had asked Mitali. However, it was true that I had started to believe that true love only existed in fictitious or incomplete stories. I hadn't seen a lot of real love stories to make me believe otherwise. Rather, the one I had lived myself was testimony to this opinion of mine. I had seen so many people in my college getting together, breaking up and then getting together with someone else. That's definitely not how true love was supposed to function. I had seen my Paa loving my mother even after her death, but that was an incomplete story. What if she had still been alive; would they really be happy with each other? Would my Paa have loved her the same way he loves her now? I didn't have an answer to that, but I had started to believe that true love was just an illusion.

"Raahi," I heard Maa calling my name.

"Yes, Maa?" I went to her room the very next moment.

"Come here and help me to decide which saree I should wear," she said, gesturing towards her wardrobe which was full of sarees.

"What's the occasion?" I asked.

"It's my friend's 25th wedding anniversary," she said. I carefully examined her wardrobe and picked an off-white saree with a golden embellished border.

"This one," I said, pulling out the saree from the wardrobe.

"Thank you. This is one of Suresh's favorite sarees," she beamed and started getting ready. I came out of the room and watched TV for a bit with Kanchi, who was chopping vegetables in the living room. Aisha was out for her workout session. I was still not sure whether it was best for her to lose or gain some weight. After some time, Maa came out of her room, all dressed up. She was actually looking very beautiful and elegant.

"Maa, can I ask you something?"

"What is it?" she asked, arranging the pleats of her saree.

"Was yours a love marriage or arranged?"

"It was arranged. Why do you ask?"

"Nothing, I was just wondering, Suresh uncle must have lost his heart to you in the very first meeting. You are so beautiful," I giggled.

"And now he doesn't even have the time to take my calls. I've been calling him for the last half an hour," she said, irritated. A few minutes later, Suresh uncle called to inform her that he wouldn't be able to make it to the party as he was caught up with some work at the Hospital. Maa was visibly upset upon hearing this.

"He always does that. I don't know why I married this man. He never keeps his promises," Maa said resentfully. She went back to her room to change. I felt really bad for her; she had been so excited. Aisha came back after some time. We all had dinner together, while uncle was still at the hospital. Then we all went to sleep; I don't know when uncle came back.

***

I woke up to the beeping sound of my alarm. I quickly got dressed into my workout clothes. As I came out of my room, I saw Suresh uncle cooking something in the kitchen. This was the first time I had seen him in the kitchen.

"Good morning Uncle, do you need any help?" I asked.

"No, your Maa is angry with me. She isn't talking to me, so I'm preparing her favorite masala tea for her," he said.

"Oh…o…so you are trying to please her now?" I prodded.

"That's right, this is my tested formula. It always works on her," he smirked.

"All the best." I gave him the thumbs up.

"Raahi, I actually need a bit of your help," he stopped me just as I was about to leave for my walk. "Will you please go and give this to your Maa?" he asked gesturing towards the cup he had just poured the tea into.

"Why me? I think you should do this," I said.

"She won't take it from me, she is fuming right now. Tell her that you made it," he said.

"Okay," I said. I took the tray from him and went to Maa's bedroom. She was reading a book.

"Good morning, Maa. Look what I have brought for you. *Garma garam* chai," I said as I entered her room.

"Ah! Thank you so much," she said, removing her spectacles. "You made this?" she asked as soon as she took the first sip. I nodded.

"Liar! I know this taste very well. It's been thirty years now, but this man still doesn't know how to make tea. Yet, he claims that this is my favorite tea," she said, making a face. I giggled. Just then, uncle came into the room holding his ears.

"Please Suresh, I request you, don't you ever try to make such a pathetic cup of tea for me again," she warned.

"That's why I say, you shouldn't get angry with me. See, both of us are suffering now, you with that tasteless cup of tea and me with no tea at all," Uncle said and she beamed.

"Ah! Now it's really morning for me. I have seen my sun rising," he said, looking at Maa's blooming face. "And Raahi, it's a gentleman's promise, with you as a witness, that next year I'm taking her to Goa for our 31st honeymoon," he added. I sniggered at the way he said it.

"Suresh, stop this drama now, you said that last year too," Maa said and then turned her gaze to me, saying, "Don't trust him, Raahi."

If that wasn't true love, then what was it? Thirty years of togetherness and still love was shining ever so brightly, even in their fights. I smiled looking at them.

"Okay, you guys enjoy your patch-up now and I'll leave for my walk," I said and left.

It was a lovely morning that day. Due to the previous night's light drizzle, the otherwise polluted environment looked fresh and extra clean. I ran two rounds of the park and then sat on the bench to relax and inhale some fresh air. There were many other people around; a few were busy walking, strolling, jogging, while a few were occupied with the *pranayama*, and yet others were sweating it out doing jumping jacks and push-ups. The kids were playing at the swings as I could hear the churning sound of metal rubbing against metal. Just then, I noticed an elderly couple, perhaps in their eighties, enter the park. The lady was unable to walk properly and her husband held onto her hand, encouraging her to take baby steps. The lady held her husband's hand firmly and kept cursing him for pushing her to walk. The wrinkles on their faces were testimony to the kind of emotions they had experienced together in life. I rested my chin over my clasped hands and looked at them attentively. *Wasn't that true love?* They would have seen around fifty years of life together; loving each other, fighting with each other, fighting for each other, cursing each other, understanding each other, taking each other for granted too and caring for each other nonetheless. After going through so much in life, they were still together. I realized then that true love isn't just what we see in stories, because they show only the choicest few moments from the life of those characters that are decidedly good. True love was this, living even the very last moments of life holding onto each other and supporting each other.

I immediately took my phone out of my pocket and clicked the couple's picture. I typed a reply to my anonymous friend and sent it along with the picture: ***True love is everywhere; we just need an eye to assay it.***

A smiley came back as a quick reply. I noticed that my anonymous friend had a display picture now. I tapped on it to reveal an angel emoticon. *The perfect display picture.* I quickly saved his contact with a name most suitable to it.

***

I was sitting in my cubicle later that day, when Ankita came and waved her hand in front of me. She was wearing a new diamond ring.

"My anniversary gift! Pranav got this for me," she gleamed. *Diamonds and women truly have a miraculous connection.*

"Wow, it's lovely," I said, gawking at her ring.

"And you know what"—she paused and smiled to herself—"I'm going to Singapore for a vacation next week. My mother in law sponsored it as our first anniversary gift."

"Awesome! I'm so happy for you, Ankita."

"And I am sorry for yesterday…I don't know what all I blabbered; I was a bit upset. Actually, after marriage, us girls have to go through such a drastic change and I think I wasn't ready for it. I wanted to continue living the way I had lived my life before marriage. But now, I'll definitely work on it. I won't give up that easily. Thanks for listening to me yesterday."

"Anytime Ankita, I'm glad to see you bounce back with such a positive attitude," I said. How true each and every word of Mitali was! We always notice the adversities in our lives and take all the propitious things for granted. Once the clouds of negativity are cleared, we start welcoming the positivity again.

***

Chapter 15

The Guardian Angel

"Happy Birthday!" I heard his words, full of the truest form of love and care. It was the 21st of December, my birthday. A birthday is a special day in anyone's life and it becomes all the more special when the first wish is from the only man in your life, the one who loves you from his soul. It was midnight and Paa had called to wish me.

"Thank you, Paa…I love you and I really miss you a lot," I said, opening my eyes wider in an attempt to subdue my tears. I didn't know why I had started to cry so much those days. My emotions were getting defiant with every passing day. My phone beeped in the middle of our call and I noticed that Shreya was calling me too.

"Paa, I'll talk to you later. It's Shreya's call," I said.

"It's okay, good night and take care."

"You too, Paa. Bye."

I switched the call from Paa to Shreya.

"Hey sweetheart! Wish you a very happy 23rd birthday," she sang.

"Thank you so much," I smiled.

"So, whom were you talking to? I mean, who was the first one to wish you?" she asked mischievously.

"Paa, who else would it be?" I said and took a deep breath before adding, "The one who was the first to wish me last year is no longer in my life and has completely expunged me, not only from his life, but also from his memories. I'm not sure if he even remembers that it's my birthday today."

"Let's not talk about that bastard on your special day. You know, I'm just waiting for a chance to get to him once, I have a perfect plan for him."

"Hmm…to teach him a lesson?"

"No. He is way past that punishment."

"Then?"

"To kill him. And I have even figured out where we are going to hide his body. No one will ever come to know about this," she said in a brutal voice, scaring the hell out of me. I knew how determined she was. And when I say 'determined', I mean it literally. She hadn't even spared Paa, after he refused to permit me to attend her birthday party in Chandigarh during our first year of college. My only mistake was that I ended up crying in front of her. I don't know what she did with Paa's car, but it didn't start when he was leaving for college one morning and he ended up missing his first lecture. And I knew what it meant for Paa to miss his lecture.

"Shreya, stop it. Don't even think about it," I squealed.

"Don't worry. He deserves this. Forget him for now and tell me, what are you going to do on your special day?"

"Nothing, no celebrations this time. No one here even knows that it's my birthday."

"*Arey*, how come? Remember in school, you used to broadcast your birthday by announcing it to everyone daily, starting a week before."

"True…I was damn stupid," I laughed at the memory. "But the times have changed now, Shreya."

"Maybe...but it will always be same for us. So we are going to celebrate your birthday whenever we meet next."

"Sure thing."

"Bye, take care."

"You too...bye."

***

"Aha! What's so special today?" asked Maa, seeing me dressed in an embellished suit salwar.

"It's my birthday today," I replied and bowed to touch her feet.

"Aha! God bless you and wish you a very happy birthday," she said, kissing my forehead.

"Maa, I'm going to the temple," I said and left for the temple in the society. As I reached there, I knelt down and touched my forehead to the first step of the entrance. I prayed for some time and sat there in silence. The pure and divine environment inside the temple had the power to endow one with a clear mind and body, free from all the upheaval in one's life. I felt immensely peaceful. The last time I had visited a temple on my birthday with Paa, Abhimanyu was also there, despite my disapproval of it. I was afraid that Paa would come to know about him, but that didn't happen. Paa considered him no more than a fellow worshiper in the temple. The little moments that he stole with me there, like grabbing a chance to hold my hand when Paa had closed his eyes in prayer, making me touch the offerings before putting them in the donation box, sharing a part of his *prasad* with me, made me feel absolutely blissful. How fortunate I had felt in that moment, when both the men in my life were sitting beside me and praying for me. The good moments spent with a loved one are a treasure as long as you keep receiving the same emotions from them that you formed those memories with, while the same memories come back to haunt you when you realize that all of that was just a pretense; that there wasn't a single element of emotion in them in the first place. All the love that had been mine till a few months ago, was now being showered on someone else.

***

I had just entered my office when all the birthday wishes started flooding my way one after the other. I was wrong that no one knew my birthday here. The internal portal of the company had announced it to everyone first thing in the morning. When I entered my cubicle, I saw a huge bouquet of roses, twenty-three in number, placed neatly on my desk.

"Who has sent these flowers?" I asked Ankita.

"How would I know? Check the tag, there must be a name," she said, pointing towards a card hidden between the flowers. There was a note: *Happy birthday, Raahi. From- A Friend.* Now I knew who it was, my anonymous angel who had asked me to call him 'A Friend'. *Did I use 'him' again?*

I had a cheerful and happening day at office and on my way to Glory Apartments, I bought a bunch of chocolates for my girls. Mitali had gone to her maternal house for a few days, so there was only a one-hour class that day. I distributed the chocolates among the girls and they sang the birthday song for me. Nobody was in the mood to study, so we all started playing dumb charades. We were having massive fun when a delivery boy came to us along with the security guard.

"Ma'am, there is a delivery for you," he said, gesturing towards the boxes that he was holding in his hands. It looked like a cake box with some other eatables.

"But we didn't order anything," I said.

"Ma'am, someone else has ordered it and the payment has already been made," he replied.

"Who has ordered them?" I asked.

"He said he is your friend."

"Are you sure it was a 'he', I mean, was it a boy?" I probed.

"Yes ma'am. It was definitely a male voice. I took this order over the phone myself," he replied.

So my guess was right, it was a 'he'.

"Actually, I can't accept it—" I started, but he cut me off.

"Ma'am, this order is for these girls, not for you," he said, shutting me up. I couldn't protest after that. I didn't know why, but I felt happy knowing that the anonymous messenger was a boy. Had I started falling in love with him? No. It wasn't love; it was just my curiosity to know him because he was still such a mystery to me. The reason behind my happiness was perhaps just his gesture that made me feel desirable and lovable again. Somewhere in my heart, this feeling was healing the wounds that Abhimanyu had given me.

***

Your smile is the only thing that brightens your face and lightens my mood. Wear it everyday, you look beautiful. I smiled as I read that day's text from my anonymous friend, along with a picture of me cutting the cake with a broad smile on my face, with all the girls around me. This was the first time he had complimented me for my looks.

Thank you for making my day extra special with your effort, I replied.

My pleasure.

Why didn't you join the celebration if you were around?

Did you want me to join?

Yes. Do you treat everyone like this?

No.

Then why are you doing all this for me?

I'm doing it for myself, because I find my happiness in your delight.

Do you love me? I typed, but before hitting the send button, I replaced the word 'love' with 'like'.

Of course I like you. Who wouldn't?

He cleverly twisted the answer.

Have you ever fallen in love? I asked indirectly.

No, he replied. I wasn't expecting a 'yes' but such a direct 'no' unsettled me a bit. My phone buzzed with another message after a few seconds.

Because falling in love isn't something I believe in.

So you don't believe in love?

Of course, I do. But I believe in rising in love. Love isn't love if it doesn't make you grow as a person. I smiled at his response.

You know, I read somewhere that we all have Guardian Angels. We can't always see them, but they are always around us, guiding and inspiring us. I don't know why, but I have started to see my Guardian Angel in you. And that's how your name is saved in my phone book. I wrote all that was there in my mind.

Do you know why you see a Guardian Angel in me? Because I'm anonymous to you. If you look around, you will realize there already are so many Guardian Angels around you, but you don't trust them because they are known to you; we take them for granted and fail to appreciate the value of their efforts. Think about today, I wasn't the only one who made your day special.

Yeah...true that, I replied.

I understood what he meant to say; we trust God, who is unseen, more than the human beings whom we can see, touch and feel around us. We tend to trust anonymity more than veracity. Later that evening, I had yet another celebration. Maa prepared special food for my birthday and we all had dinner together. I didn't get any call or message from Abhimanyu, neither from Aadit.

***

"Didi, I won't come from tomorrow," Megha said with a blush on her face as she came to me during my class the next evening.

"Why?" I asked. She didn't say anything. I asked again, "Megha, why did you say that?" She looked down and whispered, "It's my wedding." All the girls started giggling.

"Do you even know what are you saying?" I said, giving a fierce stare to the other girls who had started tittering behind her. "You are too young to get married. Now stop giving these lame excuses and complete your work. Remember what you said that day? That you want to become a teacher. What happened now?"

"Didi, it's not an excuse. She is really getting married," chimed in another girl. I was shocked to hear that. She wasn't even eighteen. *How could they get her married? Isn't it illegal?*

"What's your age?" I asked Megha.

"Fifteen," she replied.

"Look Megha, you are too young to get married. Where are your parents? I'll go talk to them myself," I told her.

"She stays in the slums behind these buildings. Her parents live there only," one of the girls replied.

"Okay, I'll come home with you today," I said.

I called Maa to inform her that I would be late. It was already dark. I thought of calling Mitali to ask her what I should do, but I dropped the idea as I concluded that she would be busy with her family. I went to the slum area nearby. It was very congested and full of small and windowless single room tenements with tin roofs. The sewage water was stagnating in the culvert. I also noticed a few filthy drunk men ogling at us from a distance. Crossing over a broken sidewalk, we reached Megha's house. Her mother was washing some utensils outside the house and her father was busy laying down a cot inside. He was a rickshaw puller. Megha went inside and called her father, while her mother rushed towards me when she saw me standing in front of their house.

"What happened, Madam? Did Megha do something wrong?" she asked me in Hindi, drying her hands with a corner of her saree.

"No, she didn't do anything. I just want to know whether she is really getting married," I asked her. She gaped at her husband, who emerged out of the room just then.

"What happened?" he asked as soon as he came out.

"Do you know that it's illegal to get a girl married before she's eighteen?" I asked ferociously.

"Madam, we are helpless. We would never have done it if our elder daughter were alive. She died a few months ago, leaving her three young kids behind. Her husband is unable to look after them alone, so we decided to get her married to him so that she may look after all of them." I was startled at their justification, as if a woman was only made to serve men.

"She will take care of the kids?" I asked angrily, gesturing towards Megha. "She is a kid herself. How will she look after them? Why don't you get him married to a girl of his age? I'm sure he wouldn't be any less than double her age."

"Madam, you don't understand what we are saying—" Megha's mother started, but I cut her off.

"No. You need to understand what I'm saying. Otherwise, get ready to rot in jail," I threatened. They got a little scared on the mention of jail.

"Okay Madam, we will stall this wedding, please don't call the police," her father pleaded with folded hands. I nodded and after warning them for the last time, I left the place. It had gotten quite dark by then and cold too. I was frightened as hell because that area was completely unknown to me and to add to that, all the hostile and predatory stares I was receiving had started to make me feel twitchy. I had only taken a few steps when I noticed a security guard from Glory Apartments coming towards me. A wave of relief washed through me.

"Madam, we had been looking for you. You shouldn't have come here alone. It's not a safe," he said and started walking with me.

"How come you are here?" I asked, surprised because I hadn't told anyone where I was going.

"Mitali Madam told us to go with you," he said.

I frowned. I hadn't informed anyone of this trip, not even Mitali. Then how could she call and send them to escort me back? "Are you sure Mitali madam called?" I asked.

"No. It was some guy, but he told us that Mitali madam had instructed him to convey the message to us," he said. *Oh, how could I forget my Guardian Angel?* I smiled.

"Thank you, Bhaiya," I said as he hailed an auto for me and instructed the driver to drop me at my place safely.

I received a text: ***Helping others is a good thing, but don't do it at the risk of your own safety.*** So he was around me again, but why could I never find him? I typed a Thank You message back.

The next day, I was delighted to see Megha back in class. She told me that her elder sister had been twenty-two years old when she died delivering her third baby, because she was too weak. Her other kids were aged five and three years. She also told me that her father had cancelled the wedding for good and that she was committed to attending the class daily from then on. I was immensely pleased for her. It was Friday and Maa had asked me to keep my weekend free, as we were going to start the shopping for Aisha's wedding.

***

Shopping is exciting if you are doing it for yourself, but is extremely painful when it is being done for unknown people. We shopped for the close relatives of Aisha's in-laws, and so my weekend went by more frenzied than even the weekdays. After attending office the following Monday, I found myself at Glory Apartments again, where Mitali was already taking her class. She came to me as soon as she finished, and we greeted each other with a warm hug and talked for sometime. Sitting there, I noticed that Megha wasn't present among the girls.

"Did Megha not come today?" I asked Mitali. She placed her hand on my back and said, "I know Raahi, you tried your level best, but sometimes it's just impossible to make these people understand what is wrong and what is right." She paused and let out a huge sigh. "She got married yesterday."

Her words felt like someone had dropped a heavy weight on my chest and my breath got caught in a knot. I couldn't believe what I had just heard.

"Are you sure?" I asked in disbelief. She nodded with a wretched expression. My eyes brimmed with tears of rage. I felt completely helpless in that moment. A girl of merely fifteen years, got married against her will to a man almost double her age and I couldn't do anything. I shouldn't have trusted her parents.

"What happened has happened, Raahi. There is nothing we can do to change it now," Mitali said looking at me.

"Let's go to the police. We need to report this," I said.

"Do you really think that would help? They aren't criminals, Raahi. They are just uneducated and unmindful. Going to the police at this moment will only make Megha's life worse. They did what they felt was right. It's better to leave them to it, maybe with time they will realize their mistake some day," said Mitali. I hadn't expected this kind of a response from her.

"I need to go," I said, getting up from my seat.

"Where?" she asked.

"To Megha's house," I said, looking at her. "They did what they felt was right, now I'll do what I feel is right." I grabbed my bag and was about to leave when Mitali called out to me, "Raahi wait, I'll come with you too."

Soon after, we reached Megha's house. The door was shut, so we knocked. Her mother opened the door and scowled upon seeing us there.

"Where is Megha?' I asked in a stern voice.

"She has gone to the village to visit her grandfather," she mumbled. I stared at her furiously.

"When is she coming back?" I asked.

"She won't come back. She has decided to stay in the village," she replied. My blood boiled with rage inside me.

"Okay, let me call the police. Now they will find out where Megha really is," I said, taking out my phone and feigning to dial. She started crying and knelt down at my feet.

"Please madam, don't do this to us. The marriage was already fixed and calling it off at the end moment would have ruined our honor in the community. We were helpless," she blubbered.

"Is your so-called honor more important than the life of your own daughter?" I asked, fuming.

She kept weeping without a response. "Where is she now?" I asked.

"With her in-laws," she replied, sobbing.

"Take me there right away," I said and she looked at me astonished.

"Madam, she is married now. Please don't ruin her life," she pleaded.

"It's you"—I pointed at her—"who has ruined her life, not me. What kind of a mother are you? You already lost your elder daughter to an early marriage and repeated pregnancies and now you have thrown your younger one into the same sludge. I don't want to hear anything, either take me there or I'm going to call the police," I threatened her.

"What's going on here?" I heard a deep voice and turned to see Megha's father standing behind me.

"Madam, please leave from here. You have no right to interfere in our personal matters. And don't threaten us with the name of police. It won't make a difference now. The wedding has already happened," he retorted, I noticed a remarkable change in his tone from the last time I had met him.

"Yes, I know it's already happened. But for your information, this wedding is illegal and illegitimate. I'm a lawyer and I'll personally look into this case to make sure that you and your son-in-law get at least 5-6 years of imprisonment as punishment. I'll make sure that both of you rot in jail," I threatened. Sudden drops of sweat appeared on his forehead. He was certainly intimidated by my words. I waited for his response and when I didn't get any, I held Mitali's hand and said, "Let's go from here; I think they won't understand anything till they're punished."

"Madam wait," he stopped us as soon as we turned to go. "She is already married. What we can do now?" he asked, pleadingly.

"Call her back. Let her complete her studies. Once she turns eighteen, I'll stop interfering in her life, but until then, she has to stay here," I said firmly.

"Madam, what about my elder daughter's kids then? Their father is absolutely useless. He won't look after them and they will have to live like orphans," her mother appealed.

"Bring them here along with Megha. You all can look after them yourself," I proposed.

"Madam, we are poor people. We don't have the money to feed ourselves properly, how will we nourish them?" her father asked.

"Tell their father to send money for them. If he can't look after them, he should at least take the responsibility of their expenses. From tomorrow, I want to see Megha in our class and this is my last warning. The next time I come, it'll be with the police and an arrest warrant against you," I said and left that place with Mitali.

"Are you really a lawyer? I thought you were a software engineer," said Mitali, surprised.

"No. I don't even know the ABC of law. I lied. I hope it worked out," I said.

"I can see it working already," Mitali said pleased.

I took an auto from there to my place. That whole night, I prayed for Megha to return to class the next day. The thought of Megha and her sister's predicament actually made me feel quite depressed. The presence of a woman is crucial in any family, yet there is no value for her existence; she is easily replaceable.

Megha was back to her parent's house and came to attend my class the very next day. She hugged me tight when she saw me. The bright vermillion in the parting of her hair irked me and made me feel exasperated for a bit, but I didn't let it reflect on my face.

***

Chapter 16

When It Started All Over Again

"Guys! Let's begin the countdown now…ten…nine…eight…seven…" prompted the host on the dance floor where till a few minutes ago people were dancing like crazy, but had now stopped in anticipation of the clock to strike in the New Year.

"Four…three…two…one…Welcome 2017! Wish you all a very happy new year!" cheered the elated host and the crowd responded with loud hooting and applause. It was the New Year's Eve and the celebrations were at their pinnacle. The Oasis Society Club had organized a big event in the prodigious lawns of the apartment complex. Girish was also there to celebrate with the family, as Suresh uncle hadn't allowed Aisha to be out late that night. So she called Girish over. While everyone was busy wishing and hugging each other, I made my way out of the hullabaloo, so I could call Paa and wish him.

"Happy New Year, Paa," I warbled as soon as he picked up the phone.

"Same to you, Gudiya," he said in a rough voice.

"Were you sleeping?" I asked.

"Normal people sleep at this time, don't they?"

"Sure, but on a normal day. Who goes to sleep so early on New Year Eve?"

"It's for young people like you. For us, it's just another year."

"Stop talking like an oldie, now. Did I disturb you?"

"No, when are you coming here?"

"Very soon, maybe next weekend."

"Hmm, we need to discuss something."

"Like what?"

"That I'll tell you later. Good night."

"Good night Paa. Take care," I said and disconnected the line.

I then decided to send greeting messages to the rest of my contacts. I typed a short verse that I had composed that very day specially for the New Year and sent it to all my contacts one by one. Soon however, I found myself in a quandary, stuck at one contact, indecisive of whether to send him the message or not. He hadn't wished me on my birthday, neither at any other occasion. He hadn't even cared to call back and make things clear with me after that night. I am talking about Aadit. I had already gotten rid of Abhimanyu's contact a long time ago.

Should I send him a greeting even after what he did that day? I asked myself. But wasn't that my fault in the first place? He had stood beside me all through my tough times and instead of appreciating his effort, I had impetuously lashed my anger out on him. It wasn't a sin to be infatuated with someone. I was reminded over and over again of Mitali's words that we tend to ruminate more lucidly when our mind is free from all kinds of negativities. I decided to keep my ego aside and sent him the message. The double tick appeared almost as soon as I hit the send button. I immediately deleted the message because I knew I would become too anxious otherwise for the ticks to turn blue, checking it every now and then and would even curse myself for having made the first move if he didn't reply at all.

I kept my phone inside the pocket of my jacket that I had been wearing due to the frigid winter cold and joined Girish and Aisha on the dance floor. I had started liking Girish over time. He was the most caring and understanding person I had ever met, not only towards Aisha but for everyone around him. For Aisha, he was more of a friend than fiancé anyway, always ready to do anything for her. My thoughts about him had completely changed since the first time I had met him. Who says that the first impression is the last impression? Judging someone by his or her appearance is the most imprudent thing one can do; appearance doesn't matter, if you have a heart of gold.

We danced there for some time and after dinner, we came back to our apartment. Once I was on my bed, I grabbed my phone and noticed two messages from Aadit. A smile appeared on my face as soon as I saw his name on the screen.

Aadit: ***Ah! At last you remembered me.***

Thanks a lot for messaging me. Really!! And I wish you the same. It's a lovely poem you sent, where did you copy it from?

Me: ***I wrote it myself. It's not copied. And I'm really sorry for that day.***

Aadit: ***Don't be. Can I call you now? It's been ages since I last heard your voice.***

Me: Yeah...sure.

Within a flash, my phone started ringing and I felt the familiar harmonious ardor again as I heard him say, "Hello Miss Raahi Sharma, how are you?"

"I'm good. How are you?" I giggled.

"Why are you laughing, Miss Raahi Sharma?"

"Stop calling me that way. You can call me just Raahi."

"Okay, so just Raahi, why were you laughing?"

"You are incorrigible, Aadit," I said and added after a pause, "I'm really sorry for being so rude to you that day. I didn't even give you a chance to explain."

"It's okay, I have been habitual of your rude behavior ever since the day we first met. You hadn't given me a chance to explain that day either."

"Oh God! That was epically disastrous," I snickered.

"After that long and tiring journey, you made me sit outside the building in sweltering heat. You have always been harsh on me," he carped. I winced at the memory.

"There is nothing like that, I was just being cautious. That's what everyone had crammed into my mind, to always stay alert as it was not a safe place."

"Hmm, I am just kidding."

"Why did you never try to talk to me after that night?"

"You told me not to."

"What if I hadn't messaged you today? Would you not have called me ever?"

"Perhaps."

"I'm really sorry, Aadit."

"It's okay, Raahi. Don't repeat it over and over again. So tell me now, shall I take this moment as your 'yes' to my proposal?" he asked jocularly.

I had always felt like running away from questions that were difficult to answer, but this time, I decided to keep the conversation light.

"Not yet, but keep trying. You never know when I might change my mind."

He laughed and I joined him.

***

"Paa, I really can't come home this weekend. I know I told you, but that time I wasn't aware of this one-day training program scheduled for Saturday. I'll definitely be there next weekend," I told Paa apologetically. Those days, Paa was getting more and more insistent on my visit to Solan, either he was missing me a lot or something vicious was cooking up in his mind.

At my evening classes at Glory Apartments, Megha had started to come regularly again. My warning had started to show its impact and I was extremely glad because this was the first time I had done something that courageous, and without Shreya too. As I reached home after the class, I noticed that the whole living room was full of shopping bags.

"Maa, did you purchase a whole shop?" I asked astonished. The previous weekend we had searched the market all day and came back with just two-three shopping bags, but that afternoon she went along with her friend and brought back the whole market into the living room.

"This is the drawback of going shopping with you youngsters. You browse the whole market and choose nothing," she replied, proud of her day's shopping as if she had just won a battle. I came to my room and checked my phone for new messages. A smile crept onto my face as I read the sweet words of my Guardian Angel.

Will I ever get to see you? I typed back.

Certainly. But at the right time, he replied.

Another message was from Mitali that said: ***There is a 3BHK flat available on my floor. Two girls are already sharing it. They need a third companion. Are you interested?***

I quickly went to Maa, who was still busy with the shopping bags.

"Maa, there is a vacant room in a shared 3BHK flat in Glory apartments, where I go to teach the kids. I was thinking about shifting there," I said.

"Why? Do you have any problem living here?" she said, carefully placing the folded sarees in envelopes.

"No, absolutely not. But Aisha's wedding is coming up and soon the guests will start arriving too. I was thinking perhaps it would be better for me to shift out before that," I suggested.

"You don't need to worry about the arrangements at all. Moreover, I need you here all the time. We have already planned everything. All the guests will be staying at the hotel. Only Suresh's aunt will stay with us at home for a few days as she is the eldest in the family and is aware of all our customs and traditions. For that, Aisha and you can share one room and she will be accommodated in the other."

"Umm, but still I think…"

"You aren't going anywhere, Raahi. We will talk about it after Aisha's wedding," she said.

***

A Week Later

The best thing about being at home is that no matter how old you get, a parent will still treat you like a kid.

"Paa, can I sleep in your room today?" I asked as I entered his room. He smiled looking over his spectacles and I cozied myself up in his quilt and rested my head on his lap. He removed his spectacles and placed them on the side table, along with the book that he had been reading.

"Raahi," he said, making circles with his fingers in my hair.

"Hmm?" I replied sluggishly with my eyes closed, relishing the head massage.

"I want you to meet someone tomorrow."

"Meet who?" I asked.

"One of my colleagues has invited us for lunch. I want you to meet his family," he replied. This was the first time ever that he was asking me to meet a colleague's family, and that too in such a skeptical way. He had been an introvert all his life.

"But why? I mean, we have never done that before, so why now?" I asked, lifting my head to look at him.

"Umm, actually I want you to meet his son. He is also a software engineer and is well placed at a governmental organization," he replied persuasively.

"I don't want to meet anyone." I said in an apathetic tone and rested my head on his lap again.

"Why?"

"Because I know why you want me to meet him. I don't want to get married so early," I protested.

"Okay, then don't get married, but at least meet him once. They can wait. Besides, he is planning on his own startup, so even he isn't in a hurry to get married," he replied calmly.

"Paa, I can't get married to some random unknown guy," I stressed, lifting my head from his lap again.

"He isn't a random unknown guy. I have known him since the day he was born. And trust me, you will like him." His voice was still relaxed.

"Whatever, no means no," I said, irately.

"Raahi." He gave me a fierce stare.

"Why are you doing this, Paa? Why do you always foist all your decisions on me? You can't force me to do anything, I'm not a kid anymore," I said, pointing my finger at him. The moment those words escaped my mouth, I realized the harshness loaded in them.

"Raahi, what kind of language is this?" he said, his voice almost intimidating now.

"I'm sorry," I said, looking down. I had never talked to Paa in this manner. "I know I have became a burden on you now that you just want to get rid of as soon as possible," I mumbled, but he heard me and gave a ferocious look in response.

"We are meeting them tomorrow and that's final. End of story. I don't want to discuss it any further," he asserted.

"Okay then," I said and clambered off the bed in anger.

"Where are you going?" he asked, looking up at me.

"I'm going to sleep in my room," I said and scampered out of his room.

The next morning, I was sitting on the porch. The rose plant that I had planted had withered already, so I took it out and planted a marigold in its place. I didn't feel any revolting emotions while doing that. Time is the best remedy for any emotional injury; it cures you and makes you strong enough to deal with all kinds of agonizing situations in future.

"Raahi…" Paa called out from inside the house. I ignored him and continued working on my new plant. He called again; I got up reluctantly and went inside.

"Yes?" I asked.

"I want you to wear this today." He handed over a new silk saree to me. I was furious, but didn't say anything. '*Why does he always try to control my life? Don't I have a right to take my own decisions?*' I argued in my head. I took that saree from him, went to my room, slumped on my bed with a thud and tossed the saree to the other side of the bed.

"Raahi, I know you are offended right now. But remember one thing, whatever I do, it is always keeping your best interests in mind," he said, entering my room. I walked towards him and with eyes full of tears, I started, "I just want to—" but a sudden vertigo made me feel so dizzy that my knees wobbled under my weight and I collapsed onto the ground.

When I opened my eyes a few moments later, I found Paa caressing my forehead. I was lying on my bed and a doctor was scribbling something on a notepad beside me.

"It's just weakness. I have prescribed some multivitamins for her. Take them daily. Girls nowadays are so obsessed with dieting that they end up deteriorating their own health. Eat properly, *beta*," the Doctor suggested. I nodded meekly in response.

"Paa, what about our meeting today?" I asked as soon as the doctor left.

"I have cancelled that. You can't meet them in this condition," he responded. I smiled and pursed my lips instantly to stifle it.

"You take rest," he said and left my room.

***

That evening, I was still lying in bed as Paa hadn't allowed me to move all day. I was reading a random WhatsApp post when my phone buzzed with a new message. It was a good morning message from Aadit, sent according to his time.

Me: *Not well* ☹

Aadit: *What happened?*

Me: *Collapsed. Dizziness.*

Aadit: *Really?*

I was typing a reply when my phone started ringing. It was Aadit.

"Hey, what happened to you? Are you okay?" he asked, a little worried.

"I'm fine now," I replied.

"Aren't you taking a proper diet?" he asked.

"There's nothing like that, I'm absolutely fine."

"Vertigo doesn't just happen to absolutely fine people."

"Actually, nothing really happened to me," I sniggered.

"What does that mean?"

"Umm, shall I tell you the truth or a lie?" I teased.

"The truth."

"Can't tell you now. Paa is around," I whispered, holding the phone's speaker close to my mouth, as I saw Paa entering my room.

"Okay then, tell me a lie, I'll surmise the truth."

"Hmm, actually what happened this morning was that I suddenly felt like my head was spinning and then I collapsed."

"Okay, does that mean you faked it?" he laughed.

"Yeah…absolutely."

"Why did you do that?"

"We were supposed to meet the family of Paa's friend today and I was so excited to meet them. But you know, we couldn't because of my health." Paa glared at me with suspicion, as I used the word 'excited'. '*Raahi, don't overact,*' I scolded myself.

"So you faked it because you didn't want to meet them?" he speculated.

"Correct."

"Was it a marriage proposal?" he asked.

"Hmm..." I nodded.

"Going good girl, keep it up. Now trying your hand at acting too?" he said playfully.

"Ok, bye. I need to rest, I'm still feeling very weak," I said and cut the line.

Paa gave me a glass of milk and sat beside me, gazing at me suspiciously or maybe my guilty conscience needed no accuser. I sipped my milk quietly, not meeting his eyes.

"I have cancelled your ticket to Delhi tomorrow," he said.

"Why?" I asked, surprised.

"Because you need to rest, you are still feeling very weak. Isn't it?" He used the same words I had just used with Aadit.

"Hmm, but I'll be fine by tomorrow. Moreover, I have office to attend on Monday," I said, still sipping my milk.

"Health is more important than work. You aren't going anywhere till you are perfectly fine," he said, taking the empty glass from my hand and left the room. *At least I got rid of that unsolicited suitor; not a bad deal overall,* I thought.

***

"Raahi, get up and take a shower," Paa commanded. I was lying on the sofa, lazily flipping through the channels on TV. "And wear a nice dress," he added. The last bit of his sentence irked me.

"Why? Are we going somewhere?" I inquired.

"No. We aren't going anywhere, but someone is coming here," he said.

"Who?" I asked, pulling myself up from the couch.

"The same family which you were so excited to meet yesterday," he taunted, elongating the 'so excited' a bit.

"Paa, I'm still not well," I stressed.

"I can see that," he said, assessing me from top to toe. "Anyway, they are coming here, so it won't be too much work for you. Now go and change your clothes. They will be here in half an hour."

"Don't try that illness drama again. It won't work this time," he added. He knew everything and I patted my back for being over-smart. Now I understood why *chacha* had been so busy in the kitchen since morning.

I called Shreya as soon as I entered my room; only she could tell me how to get out of such a situation.

"Shreya, I'm in a mess. I need your help," I said as soon as she picked up my phone.

"Raahi, wait a minute. I'll call you back," she whispered.

I paced around my room apprehensively before she called me eleven minutes later.

"Hey, what happened? I was in class, so couldn't take your call at that time," she said.

I explained the whole situation to her.

"Look Raahi, they are about to reach your house, so we can't do much now. But you can make sure that the guy rejects you."

"How?" I asked.

"Okay, so here is a five step formula for that. Don't worry, it's tested and tried. It will definitely work."

"What is it?" I asked and picked up a paper and pen to note it down.

"Okay, so here you go…

Step 1: When they leave you alone with him, make sure that you are the one to start the conversation. These arranged marriage seeking people generally look for a cow-like girl; they can't take it when a girl takes initiative.

Step 2: Tell him that you will neither change your surname nor your address after marriage and it is he, who will have to change his surname as well as his address. No men will stand by this demand because of their ginormous yet delicate egos. But in case he agrees, we have a step 3.

Step 3: Tell him that you are addicted to all kinds of bad habits and have no intention of leaving them even after marriage. He will definitely be out after this. But if somehow he agrees to this too, there is a step 4.

Step 4: Tell him that your current boyfriend is far hotter and sexier than him. After this, I don't think you will need to do anything. Yet, if he still doesn't react badly to this, step 5 is your last hope.

Step 5: Tell him that you are pregnant and want him to accept you with your baby…

And it's done," she explained.

"What if he agrees to that too?" I asked.

"Then marry him, darling. You won't ever find a guy better than him," she said.

"What if he reveals all these things to Paa," I asked.

"Tell him you were testing him. Marriage isn't something you can undo later. It's your right to test him before saying 'yes,'" she said.

"Okay, thanks. Let's see how it goes," I said and disconnected the line.

***

He soon arrived at my home with his parents. Paa made me do everything needed to evince myself the best available option for their son. No, I didn't wear saree, but a decent salwar suit instead. The family was quite cultured and conducted themselves well. The guy had on a beige jacket, with a black tee and denims underneath. The light stubble on his face complimented his personality. Overall, he was good-looking. I caught him looking furtively at me. I could tell from the expressions on our parents' faces that they had already fixed this alliance in their heads. Then came the moment I had been waiting for. His mother said, “Raahi *beta*, why don’t you show him the small garden that you have build up outside? He is very fond of gardening.” She looked at Paa for his approval and he nodded in response. I looked at Paa, grinding my teeth slightly, and he smiled. In all of my life, I had planted just one little rose sapling, that too for my own selfish reasons, and he had exaggerated that tiny activity into ‘gardening’. I smiled at his mother and stood up to go out. He stood up too and followed me outside. I reminded myself of the first step. I had to start the conversation, but somehow I found myself hog-tied. I took a deep breath and gestured towards the marigold plant that I had planted just the day before.

“This is the only plant I have ever planted. Rest is all maintained by Devrath *chacha*. I’m not all that fond of gardening,” I said and he smiled in response, admiring my honesty perhaps. *Bad start.*

“What’s your name?” I tried to be a bit rude.

“I’m Harsh,” he said looking into my eyes, which made me nervous. I instantly averted my gaze.

“I’m Raahi,” I said.

“I know that,” he said and came to stand in front of me. I took a step back.

“See, before we proceed, I need to make a few things very clear,” I said in a stern voice. He cocked his head to one side and crossed his arms over his chest. The mild frown on his face gave me the much-needed confidence to go ahead with Shreya’s plan.

“Umm, okay?”

“I won’t change my surname—”

“No issues-” he started, but I cut him off.

"Let me complete first, please. It is you, who will have to change his surname to mine. Do you agree to it?" I asked, searching his eyes for a response. He sniggered.

"What's so funny?" I asked, snubbed.

"Nothing. I agree."

"You have no problem with changing your surname to mine?" I asked him, surprised.

"Why would I have a problem? Replacing my 'Sharma' with your 'Sharma' won't make much difference, would it?" he said, frivolously. *Oh! I had made a fool of myself.*

"Do you drink?" I asked then.

"Yes, I occasionally do. Is that a problem?" he asked, sliding a hand into his jacket's pocket.

"No. I don't have any problem, but you might just do. I drink daily, you see." I looked at him for a reaction. He looked away for a brief moment with his tongue in cheek and then asked me, "Which brand?"

My eyes grew wide as I was caught unawares. This question was out of syllabus.

"Let's not discuss the brands. Tell me if you are okay with that," I insisted.

He shook his head slightly, giving me a slight hope before stubbing it by saying, "Yeah…I'm fine with that. I'll also get company for my occasional drinks. Won't I?" He winked, tilting his body slightly towards me.

"What about smoking?" I asked, immediately taking a step back.

"I don't," he responded.

"Oh! Well I do it occasionally. I hope you are okay with that too." I knew of a cigarette brand that my *mamu* smoked. I was ready for that question, but he never asked.

"Yes, I'm fine with that too," he replied, "So now you—"

"I have a boyfriend too, and he is way better looking than you!" I exclaimed, cutting him off.

"Great! I would like to meet him," he said calmly. I was only left with step 5 now.

"I want to tell you one more thing—" I was about to say when he broke in.

"I think you have asked me enough questions. It's my turn now."

"Okay," I acknowledged in a low voice.

"Are you still bad at remembering your ways?" he asked with a soothing smile on his face.

"Huh?" I didn't understand what he was referring to. I gave him a confused shrug.

"Do you still scream the same way you used to, fourteen years ago? If yes, then it might be a serious problem." He smiled slyly. I shook my head, trying to connect the dots in my head with the incident that happened fourteen years ago.

"Will you agree to marry me if I offer you some chocolates again, the way you proposed fourteen years back?" he asked, holding my gaze with his for a response.

"Don't tell me, you are…" I started. He nodded in affirmation with a broad smile on his face, revealing his dimples. So this was the same guy who had helped me find Paa's office when I got lost in campus fourteen years before. I couldn't stop smiling, recollecting the memories of that day. The same emotions were glistening on his face.

"Small world. Eh?"

"How did you recognize me?" I asked astounded.

"I inferred from your father's name. However, I became absolutely certain when I saw a childhood picture of you in your living room. Solan isn't a big city anyway," he said.

"Yeah, true," I said and suddenly felt embarrassed about everything that I had told him about myself.

"Actually, whatever I told you, all of it was a lie. I'm not that kind of a girl. I just wanted you to reject me," I confessed.

"Well, I know that. You are quite bad at lying. But you don't need to do all this. You have an equal right to reject me too," he said.

"But I don't have a single reason to justify my rejection," I said looking at him.

"I'm flattered to hear that, but may I know why you want me to do all this?" he asked.

"I'm not ready for marriage yet."

"I can wait," he responded immediately.

"I don't think I'll ever be ready for it. I hope you understand. Please tell everyone that you don't like me," I requested him.

"Let's take time for a day or two and then we can announce it to everyone."

"I don't think that will make a difference. I have decided."

"Is it your final decision?"

I nodded.

"Okay, then let's go," he said and turned towards the entrance.

We walked inside where Paa and his parents had already started discussing the feasible dates for an engagement. All of them looked at us expectantly and I turned to look at harsh.

"Umm, I don't think that we are all that compatible. We need some time to reach a decision," he said assertively.

"How can you decide this in just one meeting? Don't take any decisions in haste. See, both of you make such a good pair," his mother wheedled.

"Mummy, that's why I asked for some time, because we don't want to take any decisions in haste," he elucidated. His mother threw her hands up in disappointment.

"It's okay, I think we shouldn't force them for anything. After all, it's their life," his father reasoned. My Paa was tongue-tied; I could see the lines of discontent emerging on his forehead. Soon, they all left. I went to my room and started packing my bag.

"Why did you do that, Raahi?" I heard my Paa's voice behind me.

"What did I do?" I turned to face him and tried to look innocent.

"Whatever harsh said, those were your words," he accused.

"Paa… I… I just…" I trailed off.

"Do you think I'm a fool? You have become so mature, so independent now that you don't even trust your father's decisions?" he said sarcastically.

"No Paa, I trust you. But right now, I'm not in a state to trust anyone else." My voice cracked at the last word.

"Raahi, this is just an initial hesitation. You aren't the only one to be facing it. Just give it some time. I promise, you won't regret this decision," he said persuasively.

"I can't Paa, I can't do it. I have decided," I said.

"Raahi, look here." He placed his hands on my shoulders and continued, "If your mother had thought the same way, would I ever have gotten the happiness of holding you in my arms for the first time?"

"That's because you never broke her trust. Would she have been able to trust someone else ever again, had you broken her trust first?" I asked as my lip quivered and my eyes twinkled with fresh tears. He understood that I was no longer talking about my mother, but myself.

“Is something wrong? Are you hiding something from me, Raahi?” he asked with concern.

I hugged him tight and sobbed on his shoulder. He caressed my back and asked again.

“Don’t ask me anything, Paa. I won’t be able to tell you.” My voice broke.

“Okay, don’t cry. I won’t ask anything.” He cupped my face and said, “Do you want me to come there and live with you? I can do that *beta*. I’ll take voluntary retirement.”

I shook my head. “I’ll be fine, Paa. You don’t worry.”

“Listen Gudiya, no matter what happens, I’ll always trust you and I’m always with you. You aren’t alone,” he said. His eyes were full of concern and discomfort.

“I know that, you don’t worry, please. I’m fine.” I tried to calm him down.

We always presume that our parents won’t understand us, but the reality is that no one can understand us better than them, despite the generation gap. They are our roots and they don’t need words to know what’s going on within us.

***

Chapter 17

The Day Of Love

Mother's day, Father's day, Friendship day, Women's day and many more; aren't they worth celebrating every day? Why have we dedicated just one out of the 365 days in a year for each of them? And so ridiculous is the way we celebrate these days, by just posting some nice lines on social networking sites and relieving ourselves of all responsibility. Is that worth it? Another such day has arrived in my life, the day of love: Valentine's Day. Do we really need a day to celebrate love? I mean, if there is love between two people, isn't every day a celebration of love itself, and if there is no love, what's the use of wasting one precious day of your life to it? My thoughts were rambling in my head and I couldn't decide whether I really meant it or if it was just my frustration, as I had no one to share it with and make myself feel special. I was sitting in the office canteen, where all the office romances were at their zenith. Ankita and I were having lunch and she was telling me all about her special Valentine's Day plans. Her relationship with her in-laws had drastically improved and by extension, with Pranav too, especially after their Singapore trip. Some petty issues were still there, but she had learned to ignore them. On that day, she was planning a surprise for Pranav that included some nasty stuff I was least interested in listening to. After lunch, we walked back to our respective cubicles, where I noticed a big bouquet of red roses on my table.

"Ahem, ahem...so our Raahi madam has started dating someone," teased Ankita.

"There is nothing like that. I don't even know who these are from," I clarified. I carefully examined the bouquet and found a tag with just two sentences written on it: ***What could be a better day than this to meet you. See you today at Cafe On The Rocks at 5 P.M.***

Is this from my Guardian Angel? He had told me that he would meet me at the right time. *Then why did he choose Valentine's Day for it?* I wondered and my heart started to race fast.

"Is everything alright, Raahi?" asked Ankita, tapping on my shoulder.

"Yeah," I smiled.

The café was at a walking distance from my office. *Should I even go there? I don't even know him. What if he turns out to be a psycho? Who sends messages like this anyway? First, he did this with Mitali and now me. God knows how many other women he might have stranded in his ruse.* My overly cautious mind went into an overdrive and suddenly, the image of the Guardian Angel turned into a Devil in my thoughts. However, I decided to go anyway, because I didn't want to miss the opportunity of meeting him. *Moreover, he wouldn't be able to do anything tricky amidst so many people*, I thought. I called Mitali to inform her.

"Hello Mitali, I called to inform you that I won't be coming for the class today," I said.

"It's okay dear, enjoy your date," she replied. Did she say *date? How did she know?*

"Why did you say 'date'?" I asked.

"It's obvious, it is Valentine's Day today, isn't it?" she replied.

"Oh! Yes…but this isn't a date. I'm going to meet a friend," I clarified.

"Okay, then enjoy your meeting," she said, after which I hung up. My phone's screen displayed a message from some unknown number that said: *Happy Valentine's Day*. I did a background check on that number and came to know that it was registered to Hyderabad. *Hyderabad…could this be Abhimanyu?* The thought made me shudder. I had deleted his contact and didn't remember his Hyderabad mobile number either. I checked the tag on the bouquet again. The last time I had received a bouquet, he had mentioned 'A friend' as the signature, but this time it was a simple message without any name underneath. I took out the previous card from the drawer and matched the handwriting. It didn't match. *Could it be Abhimanyu?* But I knew Abhimanyu's handwriting and this wasn't it. *Maybe he sent it through someone else*. I read the message again, 'W*hat could be a better day than this to meet you*.' A sudden chill ran down my spine. *What if it is Abhimanyu? Why now, when I finally have started to get used to his non-existence in my life?* I sighed. *But didn't I always know that he would come back?* The little excitement I had of meeting my Guardian Angel, now turned to anxiety. I wasn't ready for Abhimanyu.

I left office a little early, so that I might reach the café on time. I managed to reach exactly five minutes before five. It wasn't all that crowded. I looked around impatiently for a familiar face when a waiter approached me and asked, "Are you Ms. Raahi Sharma?"

"Yes," I replied.

"Come this way, ma'am. There is a table booked for you," he said. He took me to a table at one extreme corner of the café. "Can you please tell me whose name this table is booked under?" I asked him curiously. His expression told me that this was the first time he was dealing with someone on a blind date. "Certainly Ma'am," he replied and went to check the details.

I took a seat and was fidgeting with a spoon and a knife when I heard a familiar voice, "Hello, Miss Raahi Sharma."

"Aadit?" I frowned. This wasn't something I had expected in the least. "What are you doing here?"

"We are on a date, aren't we?" he said, narrowing his eyes playfully.

"Very funny! So those flowers were from you?" I asked.

"Yes madam, were you expecting them to be from someone else?" he asked.

"Yeah. Actually, I thought they were from some other friend."

"Have you started dating someone?" he asked warily.

"No. Just a friend. How come you are here? Weren't you supposed to arrive on the seventeenth?" I gawked at him in disbelief.

"Yeah, then I thought of surprising everyone, so I changed my plan," he said wittily.

"Typical you," I shook my head. Once the initial sense of shock passed, I realised that I was actually quite happy to see him again and the dazzling smile on his impeccable face told me that he felt the same. We ordered pizza and cold coffee, as the café was popular for its Italian menu.

"Ah! I forgot. I have something for you," he said and took a gift pack out of a large envelope.

"It's your Valentine's Day gift and I want you to wear it this evening. It's a dress that I have meticulously chosen for you," he said with a sanguine glint in his eyes.

"Okay, I'll accept it as a friend," I stressed on the word 'friend' to make it clear that there still wasn't any possibility of us being together. He looked at me with a disheartened expression and then averted his gaze. We sipped our coffee in silence for a few minutes.

"Raahi," he said.

"Hmm," I looked at him.

"I want you to seriously consider the prospect of us. I still feel for you," he said with an intense look, which was hard to ignore.

"That's not possible, Aadit." I closed my eyes for a moment and then added, "We share a beautiful bond Aadit, please don't ruin it with such expectations," I pleaded.

"I'm not ruining it, Raahi. I'm just asking you to take it a step ahead," he said persuasively. I shook my head in exasperation. *Why was he so bent on complicating things between us?*

"This is where the end is. Why don't you understand a simple thing?" I yelled at him. I took a deep breath to calm myself down and slid the gift back towards him, "I'm sorry, but I can't accept it. Neither this, nor the one you left in my drawer," I said and got up to leave.

"Raahi," he stood up, blocking my way. He forced the gift pack back into my hands and said, "I brought it for you, please keep it." He paused for a moment to study my expression and then added, "Wear it the day you feel that you are ready to take the next step with me." I could see in his eyes that I had crushed his heart, but I couldn't let him dwell on empty promises.

"I don't think that day will ever come," I said, swallowing the entangled emotions that had started to grow as a lump in my throat.

"Then gift it to someone else. I can't take it back," he said.

The pain was visibly evident on his face, but I couldn't help it. What he wanted from me, had already been crumbled by another a long time ago: my heart, my soul and my trust. I had taken a step ahead with Abhimanyu, which not only ruined my friendship with him, but my trust too. I didn't want to take a chance with Aadit because people who don't learn from their mistakes are fools. I took the package and made my way to the exit. He followed me.

Once we were out, I waved my hand to hail an auto.

"Don't do that. I have a car," he said.

"I'm not coming with you, Aadit. I don't want to give any false hopes to Maa," I said without looking at him and slid inside an auto. He stood there, his gaze fixed at the back of my auto. He rested his hands on his hips and clenched his jaw in annoyance, I noticed from the rear view mirror.

***

Back home, I was surprised to see him back to being his old self again, laughing and jesting with everyone. *How on earth could someone be so composed in life!* He was exactly such a person from whom you could snatch away his most precious thing and he'd be sad for a moment, but the very next second you'd see him celebrating, having found something positive in that too. From his actions, it seemed like nothing had affected him at all. Was it because he never let himself get emotionally attached to another person? But if he had nothing emotional towards me, what could explain the pain I had seen in his eyes a few hours before. Was that just pretence to make me fall for him, just as Abhimanyu had? Or was this a facade that he wore for the world, while staying broken inside, just like me?

Somewhere in my heart however, I was sure that he was the only person in the world, after Paa, who would never hurt me. Did that mean he was hiding the plight of his heart behind a mask of an I-Don't-Care attitude? I stood in my doorway, glancing at him from a distance, while he was busy pestering Aisha about how-fat-her-groom-was? We were going out for dinner that night. Girish was supposed to join us at the restaurant. I was feeling a little hesitant in facing Aadit after what happened back at the café. I would have declined the offer to join them for dinner too, but I didn't want to ruin the evening for Aisha, so I said yes for her sake. I decided to act the same way as Aadit, like nothing had happened. I smiled at Aisha and him as I entered the living room. He carefully gazed at me from top to bottom, making me feel weak in my knees. No, I wasn't wearing the dress he had gifted. I hadn't even opened the gift pack. I wore white denims with an orange top, with my hair tied up in a ponytail.

"Ask Raahi," Aisha pointed towards me and said, "Raahi, tell him how much weight Girish has lost."

I was caught off guard and fell short of words to answer her question immediately. The one thing she was expecting from me in that moment was to support her. So I replied with a nod, "Yes, he has lost around 3-4 kgs." Aisha wiggled her brows at him with an I-told-you-so smile. Aadit started laughing at our response.

'What's so funny?' I asked.

"Losing 3-4 kgs for him is like removing a drop from a bucket-full," he chuckled.

"At least he is trying for me. Don't ridicule if you can't appreciate his effort," Aisha yelled, smacking his shoulder.

"Okay, let's go now. Otherwise, he will lose a few grams further, simply waiting for you there," he teased. I tried to keep my laugh in check, but couldn't resist a grin at his jibe. Aisha glared at me in exasperation.

On our way to the restaurant, Aisha took the front seat with Aadit and I settled in the back seat. The brother-sister fight was on the whole way. Aadit didn't leave a single chance to inflame her and she kept retorting in defense. *Do all siblings fight the same way?* I wondered. I thanked my stars for being a single child.

We soon reached DLF Mall of India, where Girish was supposed to meet us. Aisha stepped out of the car as soon as she spotted Girish. Aadit and I climbed down too. After exchanging some casual pleasantries, Aadit plopped down on the driving seat again. Maybe to park the car, I thought. But I was wrong. I had been kept in the dark again about the hidden agenda behind this group dinner. The Valentine's Day date was only meant for Aisha and Girish. Aadit and I were just a medium to buy them some extra time together. Aadit blew the horn and signaled me to sit back in the car.

"So? What should we do now?" asked Aadit, as I plopped back into the car. I thought for a while and then suggested, "Let's go for a movie." It was the only place where we would have been able to spend time together without talking much. I didn't want to have the same discussion with him over and over again. He agreed to my suggestion, so we headed over to Wave Cinemas and bought two tickets for a recent Bollywood movie. We grabbed our seats. I noticed that most people in the hall were couples.

"Whoa! She is hot," exclaimed Aadit. I followed his gaze and found that he was looking at a girl who was wearing hot pants with a spaghetti top. I shook my head in disbelief. *Who could wear such clothes in the month of February?* I was shocked at Aadit's remarks too. I turned to look at him, his eyes were still glued to that girl. *Was I feeling jealous?* Perhaps a little.

"Damn hot!!" I said, matching his tone. He looked back at me instantly.

"She is just perfect, isn't she?"

"She?" I frowned, "I was talking about him." I gestured with my eyebrows towards the guy just behind that girl and looked at him the same way that Aadit had been staring at the girl. Aadit looked at me, tongue-tied.

"Bad luck for both of us!" I said and crinkled my nose, turning to him. "They are together," I added. He didn't turn his head to look back at them this time and a slow smile crept on to his face.

"Why are you smiling?" I asked.

"I see, the small town girl has started exploring the big city boys," he said with a hint of sarcasm in his voice. I giggled facetiously in response.

I hated to admit this, but the level of comfort I felt with Aadit, I had never felt with anyone before him, not even Abhimanyu. I could be myself with him without any pretense.

We quieted down and turned our heads towards the screen as the movie started. With each passing moment, the environment inside the movie hall grew more and more amorous, which was a bit hard for me to take. The couple sitting diagonally down the next row started making out.

Sometimes I feel that my mind is the most rebellious part of my body. Whenever I instruct my body to refrain from certain impulses, my mind commands the exact opposite and the body blindly follows. I controlled myself hard not to look at them, but I couldn't peel my eyes away and yet, the thing that was bothering me most was that I didn't want Aadit to notice me noticing them. I blocked my view by shielding my eyes with a hand in such a way that I could only see the screen, but this activity was equally embarrassing. When I couldn't take it anymore, I thought of excusing myself to visit the washroom. I turned my head to look at Aadit and saw him watching that kissing couple shamelessly, without even realising that I was staring at him.

"What are you doing Aadit?" I asked sternly.

"Huh?" he turned his gaze to me, clueless.

"What are you doing?" I asked again, adding a little pause after every word.

"Watching the movie," he shrugged.

"Which movie?" I asked again, raising my eyebrows.

He shook his head and then sniggered. I wasn't expecting him to answer, but he answered blatantly with tongue in cheek, "The more interesting one."

I glared at him in disbelief and said, "Let's go."

"Huh? Where?" he asked, dumbfounded.

"I don't want to watch the film anymore. I don't understand why these people have to do everything in the open, can't they get a room?" I said, more to myself than him, and got up grabbing my bag. He remained sitting there. I gave him a fierce stare, crossing my arms and that was it. He stood up instantly and followed me out like a kid follows his mother after having received a good scolding. He looked so cute that I wanted to just...*leave it.*

We came out of the theater. None of us spoke for a while. As we came down to the first floor, a bright hoarding of an eating joint caught my attention. The tempting pictures of *chat, Panipuri* and *Rajkachauri* were enough to induce a loud growl in my stomach. I grabbed his hand and pulled him to its entrance. He looked utterly dazed by my sudden gesture. I felt comfortable holding his hand as it perfectly fit around my own.

The very next instant, we found ourselves standing near the billing counter. I dug my face into the menu and ordered almost everything that tempted me. Soon, all the food was on our table and I started gobbling it up right away. Paa never allowed me to eat this kind of food outside; nonetheless, I used to have it secretly with Shreya and Abhimanyu. It had been months however, since I last had that kind of spicy stuff. I relished every bite with my eyes literally shut, till each and every taste receptor cell on my tongue felt completely satiated. Aadit was a little startled to see me like that, but I didn't care. I just enjoyed the meal.

***

It was already past midnight and we waited for Aisha to call. Almost all the shops and stores had closed by then. We were sitting outside the mall on a marbled platform and waiting for Aisha as she was supposed to meet us there. It was getting colder with each passing second. Though I was wearing a full sleeved top, it wasn't sufficient to keep me warm against the dropping temperature. I started rubbing my hands up and down my arms in an attempt to keep myself warm, but it didn't make a lot of difference. I suddenly felt relief as someone placed a jacket around my shoulders from behind. I looked over my shoulder to find Aadit standing behind me.

"Don't worry, I'm wearing sufficient layers," he said, pointing to his sweatshirt.

"Thanks," I whispered with a smile. I could feel the warmth of his body in the jacket that had now enveloped me whole and drove all my chill away. He walked over to the front to face me. He held my gaze and I couldn't avert my eyes away from his, as there was a certain assurance in his eyes that he wouldn't let anything bad ever happen to me as long as he was around. He parted his lips in an attempt to say something, but didn't. I knew what was coming next, so before he could say anything, I started, "You know Aadit, this is so beautiful what we have between us right now. It's just perfect, like the Panipuri we just had." He laughed at my weird analogy. "Adding anything to it will ruin the taste and I don't want that to happen. The relation I share with you now is special and very close to my heart. I feel very comfortable with you. Please don't turn it the other way," I said, shaking my head slowly. He nodded with a fake smile on his face and a twinge in his eyes. He didn't say anything in response.

Soon, Aisha and Girish joined us. Aisha was draped in Girish's jacket herself, but was still shivering as she was in a knee length dress. We quickly moved into out respective cars and reached home at around 2 A.M. Maa was still awake, waiting for us. She scolded us for being reckless, but a scolding doesn't hurt as much when you're not the only one at the receiving end.

***

Chapter 18

A Closed Chapter

Why didn't you message me yesterday? I checked the status of the message that I had sent him a day ago. It was still unchecked. The first thing I did after reaching office that day was to make a futile effort to call the Guardian Angel, because I hadn't received a message from him in the last two days. It was unusual. I had grown so habituated of his messages that his sudden absence had started bothering me. I kept my phone aside and resumed my work. After lunch, my phone buzzed with Aadit's call.

"Hey, come down. I'm waiting here in front of your office," he said.

"Why? I mean…what are you doing here?"

"Oh God! You ask too many questions. Come fast or you'll miss something incredible."

"Okay, wait a minute."

"Bring all your belongings too. We are going somewhere," he added.

"Where? My office time isn't over yet," I said, twisting my wrist to check my watch, it was half past three in the afternoon.

"Come-on, Raahi! They won't expel you if you leave a bit early one day."

"Okay. I'm coming," I said and started collecting my things.

As I exited out the front gate, I saw him wearing shades and reclining against a lavish bike. I was astounded by the sight and my jaw dropped down in incredulity.

"Oh. My. God! Is that a Hayabusa? Whose bike is that?" I asked him, still slack-jawed.

"Yeah, it's Girish's. Wanna go for a ride, baby?" he asked in a funky tone. I chuckled.

"Hmm, but on one condition," I said, tugging my shirt's sleeves up to my elbows.

"What's that?" he pursed his lips.

"I'll ride, you sit pillion," I said with a sly smile and tied my hair up in a tight ponytail.

"Are you mad? It's not a toy," he raised his voice a bit and knitted his brows together.

"I know how to ride. Now you either let me do it or I'm going back to my office. Your call. Decide quickly," I countered. He shook his head.

"Raahi *beta*, this isn't the time to throw tantrums. Now please sit?" he said, patting the back seat.

I shook my head in a clear refusal, crossing my arms over my chest. He let out a huge sigh.

"Are you sure, you can drive?"

"Hundred and one percent, now may I please?" I said, literally jumping with excitement.

He quickly explained the controls, as this bike was new to me. I adjusted the helmet on my head, turned the key in the ignition and then carefully pushed the start button. I grinned as I heard him chant the *Hanuman Chalisa*, sitting behind me. I slowly shifted down to the first gear and let go of the clutch. The bike started to roll forward. Aadit was amazed to see that I could actually drive. He guided me the way and I followed his directions. Soon, we found ourselves on the Yamuna Expressway.

"Whoa! You can actually drive, eh? You are so full of surprises," he shouted over the wind. I giggled. I drove down a few kilometers and we stopped near a toll plaza for some tea and snacks.

"Where did you learn to ride a bike?" he asked, stirring sugar in his tea.

"Abhimanyu taught me. He used to have a bike back in college," I said smiling.

His eyes bored into mine, making me a bit uncomfortable.

"What?" I asked.

"You know, this is a sign of maturity. When you talk about your ex and smile, instead of getting emotional or upset," he said. I shrugged in response.

"Yeah, I have learned to keep myself happy," I said and it reminded me of my Guardian Angel's words that no one was responsible for my happiness, except for me. He had no idea what each and every word of his meant to me. Just thinking about him warmed my heart. I quickly took out my phone from my handbag and checked for any new messages. There was a single reply from him that said: ***Because you don't need me anymore.***

Now what did that mean? Was he being sarcastic or genuine? I wanted to text him, but avoided it in front of Aadit, because telling him about my anonymous friend would have meant listening to another lecture on safety rules. It was hard to explain my relationship with this unseen messenger to anyone.

On our way back home, Aadit rode the bike. I told him to drop me at Glory apartment. He was surprised to find out that I had started teaching kids. I narrated the whole story to him, right from how I met Mitali, but skipped everything about my Guardian Angel. Reminiscing about that day, it dawned on me that Shreya had unknowingly done me a favor by having forced me to meet Mitali.

"How will you come back?" Aadit asked, as I alighted from the bike.

"By auto," I replied.

"Umm, don't come by auto. I'll come to pick you up at seven," he said.

"Okay," I smiled and waved him goodbye.

Mitali was busy teaching when I reached. I quietly took a seat and opened WhatsApp to reply to my Guardian Angel.

Why did you say that? He didn't reply. I turned the screen of my phone down as I saw Mitali approaching me. We smiled at each other.

"Hey, remember you told me that you got some messages from an anonymous number when you started teaching here?" I asked as she took a seat next to me.

"Yeah. What happened?" she asked.

"When did he stop texting you?"

She looked at me as if reading my face and then smiled. I felt nervous for an instant.

"Are you still getting those texts?" she asked. I shook my head slightly.

"No. He stopped texting a day before yesterday."

"He stopped because you don't need them anymore," she replied and my face went blank. This was exactly what the Guardian Angel had told me too. Did that mean the chapter of my Guardian Angel was about to be over in my life? My heart sank.

***

I was lost deep in my own thoughts when Aadit's voice jolted me out of them. "Raahi, we have reached."

I noticed we were in the parking of Oasis Apartments. I hadn't realized when we reached there. "What happened?" Aadit snapped his fingers at me. I simply shook my head and smiled.

"Let's go. You are going to meet another member of our family today," he said as we entered the elevator.

"Who?" I asked.

"My Dadi. She is Papa's aunt, actually."

"Oh yes! Maa told me about her," I gave a half smile.

As we entered the house, we saw everyone sitting on the sofa in complete silence. I quickly noticed the new addition to the family, an elderly lady with henna colored hair, a fair complexion and a dead serious look on her face. She appeared to be a strict one. I folded my hands in salutation and greeted her with a smile, but in return, I was greeted with a furrowed brow and an annoyed expression. Aadit was standing right next to me.

"Is she the girl you were talking about?" she asked in an intimidating voice, turning her eyes to Maa. I noticed that Maa had covered her head.

"Yes, *Chachi Ji*," Maa replied. The look on Dadi's face told me that she wasn't too pleased about me staying here.

"What was she doing with Aadit?" she questioned again.

"Aadit went to pick her up. She teaches kids in a society nearby," Maa replied and sensed from my expression that I wasn't feeling comfortable under Dadi's constant stare.

"Raahi *beta*, you go and get changed. I'll send in some tea for you in your room," she said. I nodded. I didn't like the way Dadi looked at me.

Later that evening, Maa called me out for dinner. She also told me not to mind whatever Dadi said. We all took our places at the dining table and I noticed Dadi glaring at me occasionally.

"Oh! I forgot the salad in the kitchen," Maa said and was about to get up, when Dadi stopped her and turned to look at me "*Aye ladki*, go and bring the salad from the kitchen," she commanded.

The way she addressed me, drained all the color off my face. I looked down and was about to get up, when Aadit said, "You sit, Raahi, I'll bring it." Dadi's eyes followed Aadit closely, as he got up and went to the kitchen.

"Her name is Raahi, Dadi," Aadit said, placing the salad plate on the table.

"Why are you looking at me like this? She stays here, eats here, sleeps here, when she isn't even paying for anything. Doing a little work at home won't hurt her," Dadi said heatedly. My throat tightened up, but I kept a check on my tears.

"*Chachi Ji*, she is just like my daughter," Maa said.

"So? Don't you ask your daughter for help?" Dadi said and a muscle in her jaw twitched.

"*Chachi Ji*, calm down, you already have a high blood pressure," said Suresh uncle and everyone fell quiet. Suddenly I lost all my appetite, the food placed in front of me made me nauseous, but getting up at that point would have called for another argument. At that moment, I had a huge urge to pack my bags and leave their house immediately, but somehow I managed to keep my composure.

I cried after coming back to my room and messaged the Guardian Angel again.

Please reply, I need you.

I quickly wiped my tears off as I heard a sharp knock on my door. It was Aisha with her pillow.

"I'm supposed to sleep here with you. Dadi wants my room," she said, making a face. "And Raahi, please don't mind whatever she said at the dining table. She is a bit tenacious, so just ignore her," she added.

***

I started spending extra time out of the house and at my walk, or office or Glory Apartments since the dinner table incident, just to avoid bumping into Dadi again. Maa understood why I had suddenly started working overtime, but didn't say anything. Rather, she started caring a bit more for me so that I didn't feel too bad about Dadi's continuous taunts, but she couldn't say anything to Dadi. All she wanted was peace at home. I didn't like the sarcastic tone that Dadi always used when I was around. I was also aware that she talked ill of me behind my back, but no one paid attention to what she said. Their behavior with me was the same as before. Surprisingly, every time she said something harsh to me, Aadit was the only one to take a stand for me and that made the situation even worst, as she started thinking that I had done some black magic on him. I even heard her say once that 'Small town girls are experts in these kind of tactics, especially the one who come from hills'. I knew she was referring to me, but I chose to ignore it. I also came to know that day that Raj *mamu* wasn't coming to the wedding due to heavy snowfall in Shimla, and Paa had already declined the invitation as he was taking extra classes to prepare his students for exams.

'It's just a matter of a few days, Raahi,' I said to myself. I was literally marking the days on a calendar for Dadi's departure. I was so entrapped in this Dadi episode that I didn't even get time to think about my Guardian Angel, who had completely stopped messaging me.

All this was running in my head, while I lay on a comfy chair in a saloon and got my facial done. The beautician applied a third cream on my face meant to make my skin glow. According to her, my skin was dull and tanned. This was the first time in my life that I was getting such a treatment done. Aisha was there in the next room, getting her skin waxed. It was the nineteenth of that month and the wedding programs were going to start from the next day.

The first was the Shagun ceremony that was to take place at Girish's house, followed by the combined bachelor and bachelorette party arranged at some hotel. The second day was some other ceremony, where the groom's family was supposed to bring the *Mehndi* and the wedding dress for the bride, and on the twenty-second, *Haldi* and a grand reception were arranged.

"Ma'am, please keep your eyes closed," said the lady, placing cucumber slices on my eyes. In a short while however, I had to remove those cucumber slices, as my phone started buzzing in my hand. I opened one eye just enough to have a peek at my phone and immediately felt a burning sensation, perhaps due to the chemicals in the face pack that she had applied on my face. I narrowed my eyes in an attempt to reduce the burning sensation and checked the message. As soon as I saw the sender's name, I quickly got up and washed my face clean. It was from Guardian Angel. I read the message which read: ***How about meeting tomorrow at the Shagun Ceremony?***

Frowning, I quickly typed a reply: ***That's a private function. It would be difficult for you to come there.***

The next instant, he replied: ***Who said I'm not invited?***

***

Chapter 19
An Accident

"Aisha, please help me," I called out, struggling to attach the hooks of my *choli* on the backside. I was getting ready for Shagun ceremony.

"This is really, really bad. It's my wedding and everyone is getting ready except for me," fumed Aisha, attaching the hooks of my choli in place. According to tradition, the bride wasn't allowed in the groom's house before the wedding, 'it's ominous' in Dadi's words. Ever since Dadi had arrived, she had put so many restrictions, especially on Aisha. Fortunately, she wasn't aware of our bachelorette party plans for the night, or God knows how would she have reacted.

"Raahi, come fast," Maa rapped at our door.

"Just a minute, Maa," I said, looking at my reflection in the mirror and arranging the pleats of my *duppatta*. I quickly put on my danglers and lightly brushed my freshly curled hair again with my fingers.

"Bye bye, Aisha, I'm leaving now," I sang, elongating every word to tease her.

She latched the door shut as soon as I came out. "Get lost," I heard her say and I giggled in response. Maa was waiting for me in the living room. She looked beautiful in an orange saree. "Come fast, everyone else has already left," she said with a worried expression plastered on the face.

I trotted past her towards the main door, spreading the pleats of my *duppatta*, in order to cover the exposed part of my waist between the *choli* and the *lehenga*. Suddenly, the hem of my *lehenga* got stuck in my heel and I stumbled. "Careful, Raahi!" Maa said as she rushed towards me to lift me back up. "Are you okay?" she asked, helping me stand up. I realised that the hook of my lehenga that had been holding it in place was broken. "Shit! Maa, I'll have to change my dress," I said, holding the lehenga up with my left hand. Maa looked at the broken hook and quickly hunted through her handbag for safety pins. "This will do. Now go and secure it with pins, quickly."

I turned to go to my room, but Aisha had latched the door. I knocked it once, but she didn't open. "Raahi, go to Aadit's room. We don't have time," Maa said, looking at her watch. His room's door was a little ajar, so I ambled towards it. As I was about to enter, Dadi's voice interrupted me.

,"Why are you going to Aadit's room?"

I turned to face her. She was staying at home with Aisha that day.

"Aisha has latched the door from the inside. I need to fix my dress. That's why," I said timorously.

"Aadit isn't there in his room, Chachi Ji," Maa clarified and then turning her eyes to me, she said, "Raahi, please go fast, *beta*, Suresh and Aadit are waiting downstairs." I nodded and latched the door upon entering his room. I quickly removed my duppatta, tossed it over the bed and started to fix my lehenga with safety pins. Just then, I heard the washroom door click open. As I turned my head, I saw Aadit coming out of the washroom. I quickly grabbed my duppatta and wore it around my chest with my right hand, while holding the lehenga in place with my left.

"What are you doing here?" I whispered, so that my voice didn't go out.

"Excuse me! If I'm not wrong, it's my room." He snapped back in a slightly louder voice.

"Can't you speak a bit low?" I hushed him. He looked at me dumbfounded.

"Go out, I need to fix my dress," I said, resuming my attention to the broken hook of my lehenga.

He walked towards the door, shaking his head and was about to unlatch the door when I grabbed his arm and pulled him back. "Dadi is standing outside, stay here," I whispered, clutching the front of his shirt. I didn't want to create another scene. She had indicated enough times in her taunts that I had my eyes laid on her handsome and eligible grandson. As I looked up at him, I realized that I was standing so close to him that I could feel his breath against my face. His hooded eyes were glancing at me with flared pupils. I loosened my grip on his shirt and took a step back hesitantly. My heart started racing as he moved forward towards me. He held my forearm and pulled me into his chest, wrapping his other arm firmly around my waist. I fidgeted to get out of his grip, but all effort was futile under his strong hold. He released my forearm, still keeping his other arm wrapped around me, and tucked a tendril of my hair behind my ear with his fingers. Then he slowly brushed the back of his fingers over my cheek. I wanted to stop him, but my defiant mind suddenly stopped listening to me and I couldn't do anything. My heart started pounding so fast that anyone standing near me at that moment would probably have been able to hear my heartbeat. He moved his fingers down to my neck slowly and traced them over my collarbone, proceeding to my shoulder and then my arm, feeling my skin against his touch. His eyes followed the movement of his hand. As his hand travelled down my hand, he entwined his little finger around mine and clenched it. The burning look of desire on his face made my stomach flutter and turn. I noticed his eyes drifting from my hand to my bare waist. When he released my finger, I intuitively guessed where his hand was going to land next, but before he could reach there, my mind came back into its senses and I yelled, "Aadit, don't."

He stopped and hastily released me as if suddenly drawn out of a trance. "I…I'm sorry," he whispered, turning his back to me. I could imagine the expression on his face. I quickly picked up my duppatta that had dropped down to the floor and marched towards the washroom.

After I shut the washroom door behind me, I looked at myself in the mirror and brushed the tips my fingers gently across the same path where his fingers had been grazing a minute ago.

'*Why did I let him touch me?*' I asked myself. '*Do I love him?*' another question immediately followed. I had no answer to them. I had no strong or valid reason for pushing him away. Perhaps, I was too scared to take a chance again. I couldn't trust myself, as I had failed to recognize Abhimanyu before. I closed my eyes and calmed myself down, inhaling and exhaling deep breaths. I quickly fixed my dress and came out. I couldn't meet his eyes after that moment, so I looked everywhere but at him.

"You go first and signal me if Dadi isn't around," he said. I nodded and opened the door carefully so as not to make any noise. Dadi and Maa were both sitting on the sofa in the living room; Maa was sitting facing my direction, whereas Dadi sat with her back towards me. I gesticulated at Maa to keep quite by touching a finger to my lips and signaled Aadit to go out. He walked out and quickly disappeared behind the door of Maa's room. I banged the door of Aadit's room purposely, for Dadi to see me coming out alone.

"Maa let's go. I'm ready," I said.

"See, they have all gotten late just because of you," Dadi continued with her taunts.

As we were leaving, Aadit stepped out of Maa's room. Dadi glanced at him with suspicion. "Papa forgot his phone up here, so I came to fetch it," he clarified before Dadi could ask anything. She nodded. We heaved a sigh of relief and walked out.

"What were you both doing inside?" Maa asked, raising an eyebrow as we entered the elevator.

"I didn't know that he was there in the washroom," I said.

"And I didn't know she was going to put in my room." Aadit said, looking at me. This was the first time since that moment that we shared an eye-contact.

***

As we reached Girish's place, we received a warm welcome from his family. Arrangements for the *Shagun* ceremony had been made in the main hall. His house was luxurious and the hall was quite spacious and tastefully designed. It looked like a typical bungalow straight from the sets of Rajshree Productions, where the protagonist is linked to some royal family. The ceremony started with the priest chanting some holy *mantras*. Then he called forth Aadit and handed him a silver tray that contained vermillion, some rice gains, dry fruits and a coconut wrapped in a golden foil. Aadit applied the *tilak* on Girish's forehead and handed over to him some gifts that we had brought with us.

The photo session started soon after the Shagun ceremony. I clicked a few pictures of everyone at the event and sent them to Aisha. I was also making a video for Aisha to see, when it got interrupted by a message. It was from the Guardian Angel,

So, it's time for me to meet you, Miss Raahi Sharma. Meet me outside, near the swimming pool.

The way he addressed me reminded me of Aadit. I turned to look at him across the hall and found him busy with Utkarsh and his friends. *Well, that's my name and anyone can call me by it,* I thought.

I got up and walked out of the house. There was a lavish arrangement for lunch in the lawn outside. Many people had already started having their meal there. I stopped one of the waiters and asked him the way to the swimming pool. He pointed towards a small passage at one corner of the lawn that opened to the backside, where the swimming pool was. I ambled towards the small passage, carefully holding up my lehenga. When I reached there, I couldn't see anyone around. I knew there was nothing to get nervous about, but I was frazzled nonetheless. I took out my phone to text him, but before I could start typing, his message popped in. I frowned upon reading the first few lines of the message; it was the same poem that I had sent to Abhimanyu right after he broke up with me.

"With a broken heart................

...................*I'm falling apart*"

I typed a quick message: ***Who are you? Where did you get this?***

But before I could tap on send, I received another message from him:

The only creation of yours that I hate the most, because this isn't you. If you really want to deem your worth, look into my eyes: the twinkle, the hope, the bliss you see there, is all because of you. You are the sunshine that kindles hope. You are that missing piece of me that makes me complete. Words would never be enough to express how much I love you, because I believe that if you can define love in words, you are yet to really experience it.

This was the first time that he was confessing his love for me. I swallowed and shut my eyes.

"Raahi..." I heard his deep voice coming from behind me.

Hearing my name from his lips after all this time was enough to make me feel wistful. How could I ever have forgotten that voice? He had met me when I was yet to experience the word called 'love'. He had been the one who induced the first sensation of love in me. I couldn't turn my head to face him. I squeezed my eyes shut as I heard his footsteps approaching.

"How are you, Raahi?" I heard him say again.

'How should I be after what you did with me? I'm still alive, but something has died inside me...forever. I'm unable to fall in love again, because I'm too scared of the pain that love causes. You made me feel like trash: worthless and unwanted, something that you use and throw after having found something better.' I wanted to scream my lungs out, but I was too traumatized to say anything.

I opened my eyes and found him standing in front of me, with the same smile on his face, the same twinkling eyes and that same charming face that I had fallen for once. Looking into his eyes, I felt like his name was still etched on my heart. All my effort towards expunging that one name and the memories allied to it became futile and fell apart in a flash. The endless tears I had shed for this man were testimony to my true love for him. However, what he did with me wasn't something I was ready to forget so easily. I still remembered his words that had ripped me apart. I had gone to meet him that evening with such hopes, but he didn't think twice before shattering all my expectations and feelings. And now when he had come to stand in front of me, I had nothing to give him.

I knew that my eyes were moist, but I didn't let any tears fall because I didn't want to show him how badly he had affected me. He took a step ahead and grabbed my hand. I yanked it away instantly. "It's too late, Abhimanyu," I said. I turned around right away and started walking away from him. I heard him call my name twice, but I didn't turn to look back at him. I thanked God that he didn't come running after me, because I didn't want to create a scene at the ceremony. There was no way I could discuss anything with him without falling apart at that point. I had an overwhelming urge to cry. As I took a turn around the corner towards that small passage, I bumped into Aadit and without a second thought, I hugged him tight. I needed a shoulder to cry my heart out and who could have been a better support than Aadit at that moment. I couldn't hold myself anymore and a surge of tears broke forth and started streaming down my face. He didn't ask me why I was crying, neither did I tell him anything. He just held me, placing one hand at the small of my back and the other at the back of my head, gently caressing it.

***

I had been pacing around my room since Aadit dropped me back home. On our way, he did ask me once if I was okay and I had replied with a nod. Except for that, we didn't share a single word. He then left for the hotel to make sure that all the arrangements for the night's party were in place. I was still unable to digest the fact that my Guardian Angel had been Abhimanyu all along. After having broken me into pieces, what the hell was he trying to prove? How could I not have figured it out? I then remembered that back in college, we once had a week's vacation and I had gone to Shimla to spend some time with Raj mamu. Abhimanyu had done the same thing then too. He had all my information, where I went, what I had, and even what clothes I wore. He sent me photographs of me too. And when I had asked him how? He had replied, "I have my own ways". Later, I came to know that he had a friend over there, who lived in the same area as my Mamu. Maybe this time too there was someone here who had been helping him all along, I thought. But who could it be? *Mitali?* She had told me that she got the same kind of messages when she started teaching. Was that a lie, constructed to prevent me from doubting her? She had clearly told me that it was harmless. That was the reason I never tried to dig too deep into this matter. How did I not get it earlier? Did that mean he acted as a support system for me when I was on the verge of breaking? But why did he do it if I didn't matter to him anymore? All these questions were bugging me and only Abhimanyu could answer them. I was sure that he would definitely try to contact me again.

My phone buzzed just then, flashing an unknown number. As I had anticipated, it was him on the other side.

"Raahi, I need to talk to you, not over phone, but face to face," he said.

"Why? And what on earth you are doing here?" I asked.

"Utkarsh is my friend from Hyderabad and he insisted that I come to this wedding. But I came here for you, Raahi, because I wanted to talk to you. Please meet me once," he pleaded.

"There is nothing to talk about anymore. Remember what you said? 'Loving me was a mistake', then why are you here making that same mistake all over again?" I snapped back.

"That wasn't a mistake, Raahi, that was the most beautiful phase of my life. Leaving you was a mistake," he said. His guilt laced words fell like raindrops over my parched heart.

"You can't imagine what I have gone through over the past month," he said miserably, yammering about his distress, wholly unaware of what I had gone through over the past four months.

"There is nothing I can do about that, Abhimanyu. Goodbye and all the best," I said and cut the line. He called again, but I didn't pick up. It was hard to understand why my life was playing such a game with me. I had never wronged anyone, then why was I being punished so? Aisha entered the room just them and I quickly blinked away my tears.

"Have you decided what you are going to wear tonight?" she asked. I shook my head.

"Oh God! Raahi, you've got to be kidding me. What are you doing? We have to leave for the parlor soon."

"I have no idea, what should I wear? Why don't you pick a dress for me?" I requested, because I was neither in the state nor the mood to think about clothes.

"Okay, wait," she said and rummaged through my wardrobe to find an appropriate dress for me. I shifted my gaze from her to my phone, when a message popped in: ***Please don't avoid me. I just need a few minutes with you. See you tonight at the party, Abhimanyu.***

***

Chapter 20
A Night Of Delusion

Aisha laid down three dresses at the edge of my bed for me to pick from and wear at the Bachelorette party. There was a *Ladies' Sangeet* function organised back at the hotel, where all the guests had been staying. Suresh Uncle, Maa and Dadi had already left to go there. Only Aisha and I were there at home. Aadit was busy with the arrangement of the night's event. Our plan was to go to the beauty parlor first, from where, Aisha's cousins were supposed to pick us up. Suresh Uncle had instructed us to come back home before their arrival so as not to let Dadi get suspicious about the party. According to her, for the groom to meet the bride before the wedding was terribly inauspicious.

"I think you should go for this one." Aisha pointed at the red dress out of three lying on my bed.

"Is it yours?" I asked, because I had never seen it before.

"No. It's yours. I picked it from your wardrobe."

"But I never bought this one," I shrugged, holding the dress in my hand, examining it carefully. It was brand-new, even the tag hadn't been removed yet.

"I think it was a gift, because it was wrapped in a gift pack," she said and then it dawned on me that it must be the same dress that Aadit had gifted me.

"No. I can't wear this. I'll wear this one," I said instantly, picking up a black dress next to it.

"The red one is way prettier than this one. Why don't you try it once?" she said, taking out her purple gown from the closet that she was supposed to wear that evening. The red dress was indeed the most appealing among the others and I would have worn it without a second thought had Aadit not gifted it to me.

"Don't think too much, Raahi. Trust me, you are going to grab all the limelight at today's party in this dress," Aisha said. I was still confused. So I tried on all the three dresses, but the way the red one complimented my body-line, hugging perfectly at all the right places and ending just an inch above my knees, none of the others could match it, and all I wanted in that moment was to look the best. I wanted to make Abhimanyu realize what he had lost. Somewhere in my head, I had started to get competitive towards his new girlfriend, Neeti. *But what if Aadit takes it in the wrong way?* I didn't want to take a chance.

But I can explain this to him. I'm sure he will understand my perspective, once he comes to know why I did this. The other voice in my head reasoned.

***

Aisha was getting continuous calls from Girish, as we were late to the party. We were struck in a terrible traffic jam along with the Aisha's cousins. The party had already started and everyone was waiting for the would-be-bride. I, too, was getting calls from the same unknown number, but I didn't pick any. I knew he was waiting for me and I was ready to face him, unlike the last time when he had caught me off guard. I couldn't overlook the fact that he had been concerned about me even after the breakup and that was the reason why he ensured that I didn't end up getting myself in trouble. But I also couldn't ignore that he was the one who put me in that situation in the first place. I could never forgive him for cheating on me. The one who could cheat once, could cheat again. I had lost my trust in him.

"Why are you shaking your leg?" Aisha hauled me out of my thoughts, placing her hand on my knee. I realized suddenly that I had actually been shaking my legs. I had a habit of doing that whenever I had an urgent requirement to use the loo. My mind had been so entangled with these thoughts that I didn't realize what was going on inside my bladder. But now that my mind was back to its senses, it started to get all the more difficult to control.

"How much longer?" I impatiently asked one of Aisha's cousins who was driving the car.

"We are almost here," he replied.

As we entered the hotel with Aisha's other cousins who had been waiting for us, everyone from the groom's side started hooting cheering, seeing the bride. She was looking perfect in her purple off shoulder gown with her hair tied into a chignon, topped with a diamond tiara. The first thing I did upon entering was to look for a washroom. After relieving myself, I came out of the washroom and found Abhimanyu right outside, wearing blue denims and a grey blazer, leaning against the wall with one foot resting against it. He was completely engrossed in his mobile phone, tapping furiously on it. I ignored him completely and walked past him with shaky legs. Despite my prolonged preparation, I was still not ready to face him.

It took him a while to realize that I was out of the washroom.

"Raahi, wait," he called out and rushed after me.

"I need to talk to you," he said, catching up to me and blocking my way.

"There is nothing left to talk now, Abhi. Get out of my way," I said, irately.

"Please Raahi, I need you," he begged.

"You need me? ME?" I said, pointing my index finger at my chest. "What happened to Neeti?" I asked and saw the color of his face draining away.

"You know about her?" he asked. I crossed my arms over my chest and quirked a brow at him. He stared blankly at the wall for a moment before looking back at me.

"That was my mistake, Raahi. You have no idea what I have gone through."

"That's none of my business, but I'm really pleased that you realized in just six months that she was a mistake. In my case, it took you two years to realize the same. Now get the fuck out of my way," I retorted and pushed him aside before making my way back inside the hall without looking back at him.

Upon entering the main hall, I urgently looked around for a familiar face to go to, in order to avoid Abhimanyu from trying to approach me again. Aisha was busy meeting Girish's friends and I was still not that well acquainted with her cousins. As I walked a little ahead, I saw Aadit talking to someone I didn't know. I waved my hand to catch his attention and he responded to it immediately. He looked at me with such intense fervor as if I was the 8th wonder of the world. It took me a while to realize that beckoning him was a mistake. It wasn't I who had caught his attention, but the dress I was wearing, the same dress that he had gifted me on Valentine's Day. With every step he took towards me, I felt like someone was pulling away the ground from beneath my feet. I decided to tell him everything the instant he would reach my side.

"You look beautiful," he whispered in my ear, leaning in, as if to kiss my cheek. My heart started racing like a bullet train. I knew he had started to misunderstand the whole situation and I needed to make everything clear as soon as possible.

"Umm Aadit, I need to tell you something—" I was about to say, when the host made a loud announcement for the couple's dance and interrupted my words.

"Dance with me," he said with his eyes gleaming, ignoring completely what I was about to tell him.

"Wait, Aadit, listen, I want to tell you something very important. Actually, I—" I was interrupted again as he placed his finger on my lips.

"Hush! Even I'm dying to hear it, but this isn't the right moment," he whispered, rubbing the back of his index finger across my jawline. I shook my head. "You don't understand..." I trailed off, when I noticed Abhimanyu right behind Aadit. I could tell what was going on in his mind from his resentful expression. A seed of doubt had already been planted in his mind the day he saw my profile picture with Aadit and this was the time for me to water the weed. I wanted Abhimanyu to feel the same pain that I had gone through, seeing him with someone else. It was the time to give him a taste of his own medicine.

"Let's burn the dance floor again," Aadit broke my trance, raising his hand in invitation for mine. I smiled and placed my hand in his. He pulled me to the dance floor and as soon as we stepped on it, we recreated the same magic as before, only with more passion and coziness this time. I noticed Abhimanyu watching us from a distance, which made me draw even closer to Aadit while dancing. I wrapped my arms around his neck, while he held me close by wrapping his arms around my waist. I could feel the heat of Abhimanyu's burning heart, even from a distance of a hundred meters. *Love is a cruel thing and revenge in love is even more ruinous; it awakens that devilish side of you, that you were unaware of till then.* ***It forces you to do such a thing, after which you have no choice but to repent."***

. I knew what I was doing was certainly going to affect my relationship with Aadit, but I did it nevertheless because in that moment, I had lost my sense of judgement. The only thing I could see then was the despair and jealousy in Abhimanyu's eyes, but the thing I overlooked was the love and trust in Aadit's eyes.

After the dance, Aadit grabbed my arm guided me out of the crammed hall. We stepped out into the hotel lobby that connected the main hall to the front lawns. Once we were out, he pulled me into an enveloping embrace and held me tight in his arms.

"Aadit, leave me, please," I tried to wriggle out. He loosened his grip, but kept holding on to me. He brought his face close to my ear and I felt a tingling sensation as his breath tickled my earlobe.

"Even though I can see it in your eyes, your gestures, and your moves, I still want to hear it from your lips," he whispered.

"What?" I yelled, pushing him away from me. He released me and took a step back in utter shock and confusion. The exhilaration that had been there in his eyes a moment ago went away instantly. I looked away, fidgeting with my fingers.

"Why did you wear this dress, Raahi?" he asked in a skeptical way.

"I ...actually...umm..." I stammered. I knew that next few minutes were going to be the toughest for me and that there was no way to get out of it without falling apart. I had to tell him everything honestly. I was sure until a few minutes ago that he would understand, but the way he was looking at me at that moment evaporated all my confidence away. I took a deep breath, squeezed my eyes shut and blurted everything out in one breath, "I didn't wear it for you, Aadit. I wore it for someone else." I opened my eyes and added, "Abhimanyu is here and I just wanted to make him feel jealous. And that's why I—"

"That's why you played with my feeling, huh?" Aadit cut me off. The way he was looking at me with a sense of incredulity, was hard for me to bear.

"I wanted to tell you this right at the beginning, but you didn't let me. I know I'm hurting you, but please try to understand—"

"Understand what, Raahi?" he yelled, "That you used me, so that your ex could come back to you?" The tortured expression on his face was enough to tear me apart. And the worst part was, I was the reason behind his pain.

"No. I didn't mean that…" I shook my head vigorously.

"Then what did you mean?" his anger and hurt filled eyes bored into mine.

"Listen Aadit, I can explain everything," I looked down, unable to meet his eyes.

"What will you explain, *haan?*" He stared at me in disbelief. "Don't you dare treat me like just another option in your life, MISS RAAHI SHARMA," he gritted his teeth in an attempt to control his anger. I had never seen him like this before and it scared me out of my wits.

"Thank you, thank you very much, Miss Raahi Sharma, for showing me the real you. Otherwise, I would have lived in the delusion that you are different from other girls. But you know what? You are no different. You are just like any other girl—selfish and mean." For a brief moment he averted his eyes and then looked back at me, saying, "Well, it's over now, whatever little there was between us. I know it was just my unrequited feelings for you. But after knowing THE REAL YOU, I can safely say that I don't love you anymore." A humorless laugh escaped his lips. "I don't even like you," he raked his hands through his hair and took a step back. Each and every word of his pierced through my heart. I stood there, completely numb, still trying to grasp whether it was real life or a nightmare. It wasn't something I had anticipated. I opened my mouth, trying to push out the words I wanted to say, but failed. Somewhere deep down I had come to realize that it was too late now to unring the bell. Teardrops started trickling down my cheeks, but they couldn't melt him this time.

"You are mistaken, Aadit. It's not like that..." I sobbed.

"No. I'm not mistaken. I'm a fool. I was living a myth. You played with my feelings. You used me to get back your love. Gosh! This thought is making me sick," he said, running his fingers through his hair again in exasperation. What I saw next broke me completely from inside; his eyes welled up with tears too. As he turned to leave, I gathered some courage and blocked his way, "Don't blame me Aadit, I was only doing what you taught me, making him jealous to make him realize my worth. Remember? Didn't you say it yourself that day?"

"I never taught you to play with the feelings of others," he said.

He took a step towards me and placed his hands on my shoulders. "And for whom are you doing all this? The one who didn't think twice before leaving you for someone else."

I was stunned to hear his words as I had never told him about Abhimanyu's other relationship or anyone for that matter. Then how did he know that Abhimanyu had left me for someone else?

"But he still loves me…he never left me. He was always around to support me like a Guardian Angel," I said.

There was an instant change in his expression that I couldn't read or understand. He looked at me with disgust and released my shoulders with a jerk.

"You have made your bed with delusions, Raahi. Now go lie in it. I'm so done with you," he said and left me stranded there.

***

Sometimes, it's not fate that shapes your destiny, but your own deeds. To what extent your gestures could break someone's trust, I had witnessed for myself that day. The indifference I saw in Aadit's eyes towards me on our way back from the party was enough to shatter my heart into pieces. I knew it was entirely my fault and that I had to make everything right as soon as possible. It was very hard for me to see him like that. I couldn't afford to lose him at that moment. I couldn't let him give up on the relationship we shared. I pulled my phone out of my purse and messaged him: ***I'm waiting for you in the balcony. Please come. I need to talk to you.***

It was quarter to two at night and I was lying on my bed awake. Aisha had long since gone to bed, not wanting to compromise on her beauty sleep before her big day. For me however, sleep was the last thing I wanted at that moment. I figured I wouldn't be able to sleep till I cleared everything with Aadit. As I saw the ticks turn blue on my WhatsApp message to him, I quickly grabbed my shawl and unlatched the door as quietly as possible so as not to wake Aisha up from her sleep. I stepped on to the balcony and the cool February breeze made me wrap the shawl tighter around my shoulders. I made myself comfortable on a chair that was already there in the balcony. I waited for him for some time, but when he didn't turn up, I messaged him again: ***Aadit, please come out. I'm waiting here and I won't go back until I've had a talk with you.*** I raised my feet and placed them on the chair. I wrapped my arms around my knees in an attempt to chase the chill out. I was so tired from the day's events that I didn't realize when I collapsed into slumber.

I opened my eyes as I heard the sound of a door clicking open and realized that it was morning already. My body ached and my head was throbbing. With eyes still shut, I unfurled my arms and legs to stretch them after an uncomfortable sleep on the chair, but quickly withdrew them in a knee jerk reaction, as I realized that my hand had knocked at his groin. He was standing in front of me holding a damp towel in his hand, small droplets of water dripping from his hair. He looked at me with an expression that was hard to read. He looked concerned, surprised, exasperated and angry, all at the same time. I couldn't tell whether he was annoyed or stupefied. He broke the eye contact and set his towel to dry on the clothesline. I had so much to say in my mind, but at that moment, I felt as if someone had zipped my lips up. He quickly turned to go back to his room. When I called after him, "Aadit, I…" he snubbed me and slammed his door shut.

***

Chapter 21

Unraveling The Secret

"Aisha, please call Girish and ask them when they are arriving with the *Mehndi*. It has already gotten very late," Maa said to Aisha, as she was busy attending to the guests. All of us were at the hotel and were supposed to stay there until the wedding. Most of the guests had already arrived and a few were supposed to arrive the next day. The Mehndi ceremony was scheduled for this day, which was to be followed by the Sangeet ceremony. According to tradition, the Mehndi for the bride's ceremony had to be sent by the groom's side, along with some dry fruits and sweets. We were all still waiting for somebody from Girish's side to arrive with the Mehendi, so that we could start with the ceremony. We hadn't decided on a dress code, but somehow most of us were wearing green, including Aisha and me. The professional Mehndi artist had arrived already and grew visibly restless with time as he was booked for some other bride too. The elderly ladies started singing the traditional songs associated with this occasion to the earthy beat of a *Dholak*.

I had desperately been looking for Aadit since morning, but couldn't find him anywhere. Maa told me that he had gone to see the arrangements for the next day's reception. I needed to talk to him, but he had been acting so aloof and detached as if I was a stranger to him. Nevertheless, my instincts were telling me that everything would be all right.

A big smile crept on my face as I saw my girl students at the entrance of the hotel. I quickly marched towards them to welcome them in. As they saw me, they all scurried towards me and hugged me one by one. I was so enthralled to see them and so were they. In only a few months, we had become such an integral part of each other's lives.

"Didi, you are looking very beautiful in this dress," said Megha, appreciating my embellished green Punjabi suit.

"But not more than you," I replied, pulling her cheeks. Everything had been going smoothly on Megha's part. I had kept a close eye on her parents by secretly visiting her place occasionally.

"How is your preparation for exams going on?" I asked, looking at all of them. Some of them were soon going to appear for the entrance exam to get admission into schools.

"Didi, we have so many doubts. I don't think we'll be able to pass."

"Why so? Work hard and I'm damn sure you all will get through. Next week onwards, we will start studying on weekends too." They all smiled. "Now let's go, yummy food is waiting for all of you," I said and guided them towards the lawn, where the lunch was arranged.

While I was heading towards the function hall, I saw Mitali entering the premises. I had invited her, but she had politely declined saying that there was some other wedding in her family that she had to attend the same day. I was truly delighted to see her. I hugged her as she approached me. She looked dazzling in her green and blue saree...*another green!* The first thing I wanted to ask her was about Abhimanyu, but I bridled the urge. No matter how she was connected to

Abhimanyu, it could never alter the special place she held in my heart because she was the one to provide me with emotional succour in times of my misery.

"I'm so happy to see you here. Come, I'll introduce you to Maa," I said, breaking the hug and pulling her towards the hall where the Mehndi ceremony was about to start, as the Mehndi had finally arrived.

"Hello Dr. Shrivastva, what a pleasant surprise!" exclaimed Suresh uncle as he saw Mitali and me entering the room. I was surprised that Suresh uncle knew Mitali already, but why did he address her as Doctor?

"Reena, look who's here!" Suresh uncle turned to Maa. Maa looked visibly ecstatic as she saw Mitali.

"Welcome, Dr. Shrivastva. I'm so happy to see you here. Thanks a lot for joining us."

"Ah! Mrs. Kashyap. I had to come. You invited me so cordially. Many, many congratulations," said Mitali, hugging Maa.

I was unable to understand what was going on around me. They were meeting as if they had known each other for ages and here I thought that she had come on my invitation. I was still standing dumbfounded beside her when Maa and uncle took their leave to attend to the other guests.

"What happened to you now?" asked Mitali, looking at my astounded expression.

"Nothing, I was just wondering why they called you Dr. Shrivastva? I mean, are you a Doctor?" I asked hesitantly.

"Yes, I'm a doctor and Shrivastva is my surname," she said, confident and clear.

"But you never told me that—"

"Because you never asked me that," she cut me off.

I had presumed her to be a housewife and never felt the need to dig any further. I smiled at her.

"Can I ask you something?"

"Yeah sure, but let's get seated first" she said, gesturing towards the chairs.

"Oh! I'm so sorry. I didn't offer you," I apologized.

"It's okay," she said. Once we were settled comfortably on the seats, she asked me, "Now tell me, what's bothering you?"

"Umm, how do you know Abhimanyu?" I asked, looking straight into her eyes.

"Who is Abhimanyu?"

"Look, I know everything now. There is no need to hide it from me anymore," I said as a matter of fact.

"I genuinely don't know who Abhimanyu is," she said and there was a gist of honesty in her tone. *If not her, then who else?*

"The one who used to send me messages after every class. You said that you got the same kind of messages too," I rambled.

She didn't say anything for a moment and then smiled. "Raahi, do you trust me?"

"Of course, more than myself," I replied immediately.

"Then mark my words; it's very difficult to find someone who loves you truly. Don't take those people for granted who love you unconditionally and selflessly, because they are the ones who will stand by you in all kinds of circumstances," she said and then placed her hand over mine. "Don't let him go."

"What's this all about? Just now you said that you don't know Abhimanyu."

"It's about Aadit, not Abhimanyu. He loves you Raahi. Don't push him away," she said, looking deep into my eyes.

"But how do you know Aadit?" I asked, stunned. She smiled and averted her gaze from mine.

"I know Aadit better than anyone else in this room, Raahi. I treated him four years ago. I'm a psychiatrist," she said. The instant she said this, my mind started connecting the dots.

"Did he tell you something?" I tried to probe if he had shared something with her about the previous night.

"No, he didn't. But the way he is always concerned about you, I don't need a verbal clue," she shrugged.

"I…I can't…" Words refused to escape my mouth and I shook my head.

"Why? Because you love someone else? Abhimanyu, right? Just answer this Raahi, does he love you the same way you love him? Do you trust him enough to take him back in your life? Once a cheat is always a cheat," she said. So she knew everything about me. Now I understood why I felt like she could read my mind every time that she looked at me, because she knew everything already. But how did she know this much? She knew Aadit, but even Aadit wasn't aware of the fact that Abhimanyu had cheated on me. A gentle nudge on my shoulder jolted me out of my thoughts.

"No. It's not about him. But—" before I could complete, she cut me off again.

"Then who else, your Guardian Angel?" she raised her eyebrows.

I scowled, how did she know I called him Guardian Angel?

"Do you know who he is? It is none other than Aadit," she said. I looked at her with my eyes wide open, and on the verge of tears. "Remember the day you met me for the first time? It wasn't a coincidence. That was a well-planned encounter. He had called me that morning and requested me to see you. He just wanted to ensure that you were okay, but he didn't want you to meet me as a patient, so he arranged our meeting. He had been so worried when he told me everything about you and calmed down only when I ensured him after meeting you that you were strong enough to deal with it, unlike him."

"But it was Shreya, who told me to meet you."

"I don't know how he arranged for our meeting, but the one thing I can bet on is that he loves you," she said and added after a long pause, "And I am sorry, it was I who clicked your pictures and when I wasn't around, it was the security guard, as I instructed him to do it for attendance purposes."

I was so injudicious to think that it had been Abhimanyu. I was too thunderstruck to respond, but deep inside, my heart ached to run to Aadit and hug him tight. He cared so much for me and in return, I had made his heart crumble. I felt like an insensitive bitch.

"Are you okay?" asked Mitali.

"Yeah," I smiled.

"Let's go, I think the ceremony has started," said Mitali.

***

"Hello, Shreya?"

"Yes darling, how are you?"

"I need to ask you something and I want an honest and forthright answer."

"Hmm, go on."

"Do you know Aadit?"

"Umm, what happened?"

"Answer in a yes or no."

"Umm yes, actually a few months ago, when you came to know about Abhimanyu's relationship, I think you had some issues going on with Aadit at the same time and you both weren't on talking terms. A day before I talked to you,

I got his message on Facebook. We had a chat and I came to know that you weren't okay. He blamed himself for your condition. So he told me to ask you what was bothering you, as you wouldn't have shared it with anyone else. I called you so many times, but you didn't pick up your phone. Then it was Aadit who arranged a call on his mother's number and then we had a conversation—" she paused for a moment and then said, "I'm sorry, Raahi, he was also on the line that day when you told me everything, I couldn't deny him, he was so concerned about you. Then, a few minutes after talking to you, he called me again and told me to coax you into meeting Mitali and that's why I made the excuse and asked you to deliver her a cheque, so that you could meet her."

"You could have told me this later."

"Yeah, but I thought you would get angry with me and Aadit wasn't doing anything wrong anyway. So I didn't tell you."

I had nothing to say. I had made a complete fool of myself. I now understood the expressions he had made when I called Abhimanyu my Guardian Angel.

"Are you okay, Raahi?"

"I'm in a mess, Shreya."

"Oh! What happened?"

"Abhimanyu is here."

"What? What's he doing there?"

"He regrets breaking up with me."

"Don't you fall into his trap again, Raahi. He will do anything to get you back. Just don't listen to him."

"Hmm, and Aadit isn't talking to me."

"Why? Is it because of that douche? I know how he must be feeling, he loves you a lot, Raahi."

"Did he tell you this?"

"No, but the way he cares for you, anyone can guess. Moreover—"

"Hey, I'll call you later," I cut her off as soon as I caught a glimpse of Aadit. I rushed towards him, but was too late. A gaggle of people had come to surround him. I messaged him immediately: ***Please talk to me***. He pulled out his phone from his pocket, checked the message and kept it back, without a single twitch of the eye. I felt a lump rising in my throat. Why do we always realize the worth of people when they start to drift away? I messaged him again: ***Please, Aadit. Don't behave as if you don't care for me.*** This time he didn't even care to check.

He sauntered towards the elevator after Maa instructed him to fetch something from the room. I too made my way towards him. As he unlocked the room's door and entered, I followed in behind him, closed the door from inside and leaned against it so as to block his way out.

He turned to look over his shoulder as he heard the the door clicking shut. His brows pinched upon seeing me.

"What are you doing here?" he asked, picking up a few gift boxes from the table.

"I want to talk to you."

"Listen Raahi, I'm neither in the mood, nor do I have the time for this bullshit. So get out of my way and let me go."

I shook my head. "You can't go unless you talk to me."

He gave me a fierce stare and then pulled me away from the door, grabbing my forearm. He jerked the door open and went out. I tailed him.

"Aadit please listen to me, at least once," I called after him from behind and followed him into the elevator.

"Aadit, this is my last attempt to talk to you. After this, I'll give up and will never show you my face again. Please listen to me," I said and my eyes brimmed with tears. He didn't give me a second look. A meek voice in my head told me that I had lost him, but I decided not to give up. The elevator door opened and he got out. I held on to his forearm to stop him.

"Aadit please..."

"Raahi, what part of it is so difficult for you to understand? Dammit, it's my sister's wedding and I'm busy. For God's sake, STAY AWAY FROM ME!" he yelled. The pitch of his voice made me shudder and I released his hand instantaneously.

"What's going on here?" My heart stopped throbbing the moment I heard Dadi's voice. I wasn't in the state to handle anything from her at that moment. I looked at Aadit whose gaze moved from me to Dadi and then back to me. There was the gist of concern in his eyes, or so I felt.

"See, this is the reason why I told you to stay away from her. From day one I knew what was going on in her filthy mind," said Dadi looking at Aadit and pointing her finger towards me.

"Dadi, I need to go..." he said and left me there with her. This was a big change in his behavior; he had been the only one to always take a stand against Dadi for me, but this time he didn't say anything, almost as if he was approving of her quip. All my senses went numb the moment I saw him turn his back on me. Dadi continued to say something, but none of her words fell on my ears, as there was already too much noise in my head.

***

I came to my room in the hotel and cried my heart out. I felt lonely and empty. Till that moment, I had never felt that Aadit mattered to me so much. The hurt and rage in his eyes was something beyond my power of tolerance. He had never spoken in that tone to me, or anyone else for that matter. I spent the next two hours lying in bed and staring at the ceiling. I could hear the stifled sound of traditional songs that wafted into my room from the ceremony hall. But I didn't go there. Suddenly, I felt like I didn't belong to this place, I didn't belong to these people, I felt like an outsider. A buzz on my phone caught my attention and relief washed through my body as I saw Aadit's name flash on the screen. I picked up the call in the blink of an eye.

"Hello, Raahi?" His voice was calm, but I felt my throat too choked to spurt a word out of it.

"Hmm," I replied, the back of my throat aching with emotion.

"Where are you?"

"Why?" I asked, trying to hold back my tears.

"Can we talk?"

"Hmm." I squeezed my eyes shut as tears escaped the brim of my eye.

"Where are you?"

"My room."

"Will be there in two minutes."

The pit of anxiety sitting deep in my gut roiled as I heard a knock at my door. However, it all vanished with one look in his eyes when I opened the door.

"Thank God…I…I…" I choked on my tears and stammered. He looked back and forth into my eyes as if trying to find an answer to the turmoil that was going on in his mind. I wanted him to say something, I wanted to hear from him so badly, but he chose to be quiet. His nostrils flared and he pursed his lips, as if fighting something within. I wanted his heart to win this fight, because I knew his heart would always be on my side. I looked at him expectantly, but he was still quiet. When he called me, I thought he had forgiven me, but the way he was looking at me standing there in the doorway, I was no surer.

"Aadit, I wasn't thinking that day. I swear, I never intended to hurt you, but the fact is, I already have…I'm really sorry, I'm so sorry," I started and a fresh tear made its way down my cheek. He swallowed and looked away as if my tears didn't affect him anymore. I wished I could read his mind, but his expressions were too enigmatic. His silence was killing me.

"Please say something, Aadit." I tried to read his eyes. I didn't know what was there in his mind, but I waited for his response patiently, not that I had a choice besides that.

"I'm sorry…please say something…" A surge of tears started to blur my vision, so I wiped them with the back of my hand. I heard a deep sigh and then felt his hands cupping my face. He gently wiped my tear stained cheeks with his thumbs.

"It's okay," he broke his icy silence and those two words felt like petrichor that follows the rains after a dry and sweltering day. I smiled, my eyes still swimming with tears, but what he said next drowned me further into misery and took my soul away.

***

Chapter 22
Letting Go

AADIT

"Thank God...I...I..." she tried to say something, but choked on the tears that she was trying to hold as she opened the door. *Letting go* is the easiest thing to say and the most difficult to do. Every time I looked at her I failed to understand why I loved this girl so much. It isn't like she was the most beautiful girl I had ever seen or someone just out of the world, but she owned my heart and despite my endless endeavors, I couldn't get her out of my mind. My God knew how hard I had tried to tear my heart away from her, but failed miserably every time and now it felt like she was running in my blood.

"Aadit, I wasn't thinking that day. I swear, I never intended to hurt you, but the fact is, I already have...I'm really sorry, I'm so sorry," she said. I wanted to kiss her tear away, the instant it started rolling down her cheek. I swallowed the urge and turned my gaze away from her. She continued to stare at me with her big child-like eyes, attempting to read my mind, but I knew she could never do that because she could not think beyond the one person she loved. I looked back into her eyes when I heard a sob escape her lips. Every time

I looked into those sparkling eyes, I felt as if I was connected to her soul, but it had all been my misconception. She never belonged to me. She had been certain from day one that she didn't want me in her life, but I had still hoped that one day she would see my love for her. The previous day, when I had called her by the swimming pool and she hugged me tight, I thought she finally accepted my love for her. I didn't ask her anything because I wanted to hear it from her without any pressure from my side. Later that night, I found myself on cloud nine when I saw her wearing the dress that I had asked her to wear the day she felt ready to take a step ahead with me. But again, all of that proved to be my misconception. She never loved me. *Never.*

"Please say something, Aadit," she pleaded again, nibbling on her lower lip and fidgeting with her fingers. She did that every time she was anxious. This look on her face reminded me of the day I met her for the first time. After having made me wait for hours outside my house and splashing water on me, she had stood in my doorway exactly the same way as she was standing now.

So much had changed since then. Love is the most unpredictable thing in life; it doesn't knock before entering your life and you break all the barricades that you yourself had created around you. You welcome love, despite knowing how much pain it causes. After Ruhani, I had shut all the doors to my heart, but she managed to enter anyway. I loved her and I had tried everything to make her see the love that I carried for her. Yet, she had been so in love with someone else that she could never see the effort that I had made for her out of my love.

That evening, it had almost killed me to turn my back on her and leave her alone with Dadi. She hated Raahi because somewhere she knew that I loved her. I left her there because

I wanted her to fight her own battles.

Those eyes still looked at me expectantly, demanding my words, but I didn't have anything to say, not now at least, when I knew that I had to let her go for the sake of her happiness.

"I'm sorry…please say something," she said again, wiping her tears with the back of her hands, smudging her kajal in the processs. The color from her face drained with every passing second as the silence between us stretched out.

"It's okay," I said, taking her face in the palm of my hands. Those two words did the magic, as the corner of her lips turned up immediately. Her eyes regained their glimmer and they too smiled with her lips. Her enchanted smile told me how badly she wanted me in her life, the only difference was…she didn't want me the way I wanted her in my life.

"Keep smiling this way and don't ever forget that your happiness is my delight, even though I'm not a part of it." I said. She looked at me surprised.

"Go now, Abhimanyu is waiting for you downstairs. Talk to him and sort things out," I said with a heavy heart.

"No," she sobbed, shaking her head.

"Raahi, remember what you said? If your love is true and you are meant to be together, love will lead you back to each other. And look, he is back in your life now."

"Do you really want me to go?" she asked.

No…

"Yes. Life doesn't give second chances to everyone. Go before it's too late," I said, releasing her face from my palms.

"Okay, I'll go then…I'll go if you want me to go," she said, gritting her teeth and turning around to pick her duppatta from the bed. This girl was beyond my understanding, she behaved so silly sometimes. All this time she kept crying over that boy and now she behaved as if I was forcing her to go to him.

"Are you going like this?" I asked.

"Hmm, is there a problem?" she said, her eyes still moist.

"Fix your makeup first, otherwise you will scare him," I laughed and she cried. I wanted to hug her, but didn't. She wasn't mine. *She was never mine.*

"Okay, I'm leaving. I need to make an urgent call," I made an excuse and turned around.

"Aadit, can I please hug you once?" she said, twiddling the corner of her duppatta. "Please..." she added, when I didn't respond. She drew closer to me and hugged me without waiting for my reply.

"Thank you for everything you did for me...and I'm so bad, I made you cry. I'm so sorry," she mumbled, resting her face on my chest. My hands remained fisted at my sides. No, I didn't hug her back. *I just couldn't.*

***

Chapter 23
I'm Pregnant!

So he wanted me to go to Abhimanyu and added insult to injury further by telling me to fix my makeup. Did that mean he didn't love me anymore? He hadn't even hugged me back. Did that mean that he really meant whatever he had told me at the bachelorette night? And why was it bothering me at all? All I wanted was for Abhimanyu to come back in my life, I should have been happy that the person I loved was back in my life. Why was I getting agitated? Life seemed completely chaotic in that moment, I knew where to go and what to do, but it felt like I had kept myself tied in manacles. Reluctantly, I got up and looked at myself in the mirror and then I realised why he had asked me to fix my makeup. I would definitely have scared Abhimanyu. I looked horrible because of all that ugly crying.

After fixing my face, I hustled to the main hall where the Mehndi function was going on. The mehndi on Aisha's hands and feet was done already and the other guests were getting their hands done.

"Raahi, where have you been? I was looking for you," Maa chided.

"I wasn't feeling well, so I slept for some time," I lied.

"Why haven't you applied mehndi yet? Go and get it done quickly," she ordered.

I ambled towards the artist who was applying mehndi. I needed something to occupy me anyway, to stall the meeting with Abhimanyu. I wanted some time to chew the cud.

A sudden buzz on my phone split through my thoughts. It was Abhimanyu's call. Till then I had rejected all his calls, but this time I answered it.

"Thank God, Raahi, you took my call. Where I can meet you?" he asked.

"First floor lobby in ten minutes," I replied in short and hung up.

***

As I padded towards the lobby on the first floor, I saw him. He was sitting on the sofa perched in the corner, flipping through the pages of a magazine. He stood upright when he saw me approaching. I couldn't quell the sting of exasperation that pierced through my chest. I had trusted this man more than myself, while it had taken him just a few days to hop from one relationship to another.

"Hey Raahi…" he stretched his arm out to hug me, but I stopped him by holding my hand up.

"What do you want to talk about? I'm in a hurry."

"I want to talk about us."

"Ahhh! Us," I laughed, "This 'us' was the most beautiful thing that had happened to me till a few months back, but now it's nothing more than a sting in the tail, so let's better not talk about it." My eyes welled up.

"I'm really sorry, Raahi. I know, I fucked up and it's not easy to forget. But for the sake of the time we spent together, please just give it another thought," he said. I shook my head. I didn't want to cry in front of him, but my emotions were beyond my control.

"It's been four months, Raahi, since we ended, but I still remember each and every blissful moment that I've spent with you. I strayed in the glimmer of the new city and new people, but I realized my mistake when the same thing happened to me, that I had done to you"—I noticed moisture in his eyes—"I miss you, Raahi. I miss you every time I breathe. I miss that twinkle in your eyes that used to wash away all my perturbations. I miss your voice that was the most melodious music to my ears. I miss the touch of your hand that used to give me the feeling of home and contentment. You know, words aren't enough to define how much I miss you," he said.

"Give me a single reason, Abhi, why I should trust you again. You have always been good in playing with words, what if it all comes out to be a lie this time too?" I said gazing into his eyes, but a part of me was still desperate to believe him. The quiver in his voice and the tears in his eyes were incessantly coercing me to rely on his words… *once again*. Despite my endless attempts against it, my heart started to melt. I looked down so that he wouldn't take my emotions as my weakness.

"I know, I have messed it up. But trust me, it won't happen again. I was an idiot not to realize that it's only you that I need in my life. Please forgive me." He took a step forward and placed his hand on my shoulder. I shrugged it off instantaneously. Tears started rolling down my eyes, I was about to wipe them, when it occurred to me that there was mehndi on my hands now. He drew near me and wiped my tears with his thumbs and cupped my face in his palms, his hands still trembling. His touch sent a chill down my spine.

"I promise, Raahi, I'll never make you cry. Just give me one chance," he implored.

It was getting hard for me to ignore him. He still had that power to control my heart. It had to be, for the way I was attached to him, it wasn't easy to brush it off in the blink of an eye.

"I need some time to think," I replied.

"Of course, you take your time. I have made a blunder and I don't expect you to forget everything instantly. But trust me, Raahi, I will do anything to get you back in my life."

"I think I should go now," I said.

"Yeah," he nodded.

"By the way, you look gorgeous, just as you always do," he said with a smile plastered on his face. I didn't respond.

***

I spent the whole night tossing and turning in bed. At half past five in the morning, I found myself sitting near the window of my hotel room that I was sharing with Aisha. Sometimes, life seems too complicated for no reason, but the fact is, it's not life that is complicated, but our own ways of dealing with problems that make it so.

Nothing is more beautiful than witnessing the divine moment when the light of dawn devours the endless darkness of the night. It inculcates hope and fortitude, because in life too, it's just a moment, a choice and a state of mind that changes the whole course of life. Gosh! I too had started thinking like Mitali and Aadit: i*ntellectual.* Despite that, I had created such a mess in my own life.

The *Haldi* ceremony was scheduled for that day, and the main event, the wedding, was later the same evening. My head felt heavy due to sleep deprivation. I made myself a cup of tea to get some respite from the headache. I hadn't had any conversation with Aadit after he had asked me to go to Abhimanyu. After that incident, he had gone back to the same aloof and detached mode.

"Hey, why are you up so early?" Aisha asked, lifting her face from the pillow.

"Because I'm so excited for your wedding," I mocked.

"Ha! It's my wedding. Why are you so excited? You aren't going to get anything out of it," she winked.

"You never know, what do they say, '*Saali, aadhi Garhwali'*?" I leaned back in my chair and looked upwards, as if deep in thought. "Moreover, I think I'm in love with him"—I paused for a moment before adding— "and his Hayabusa." I giggled.

"Don't you dare even think about it," she said, throwing a pillow at me and headed towards the washroom. I laughed.

Soon we all assembled at the function hall for the Haldi. Aisha wore a yellow saree, while I had on a long yellow skirt with an off-white cold shoulder crop-top. Aadit was out of sight again. Everyone started applying the haldi paste onto Aisha. They said that it was to make the bride's skin extra glow-y.

"Raahi, please call Aadit. He hasn't applied haldi to Aisha yet," said Maa, as the photographer had been insisting on calling the bride's brother to capture some emotional brother-sister moments. I called him and he picked up the phone instantly.

"I'm driving right now. I'll be there in ten minutes," he said without giving me a chance to speak, and cut the line. However, the one thing that didn't go unnoticed in this conversation was the saccharine voice of a girl in the background, as if she was also there with him in the car. I told Maa that he would be there in ten minutes. Aisha was covered in turmeric paste from top to toe and the remaining paste was applied to all the other eligible girls, because it's said that doing this would bring them a good-looking partner. *Silly.* I too got my cheeks smeared with some turmeric paste. Just then, I saw Aadit entering the function hall with a tremendously gorgeous girl. The way they were talking to each other showed that they were quite close. I felt my heart burning instantaneously. I leaned towards Aisha and asked, "Who is that girl?" gesturing towards the person next to Aadit.

"Oh my God! It's Sakshi. Aadit's childhood friend, they studied together almost all of their school life," she replied with excitement.

The girl approached Aisha and hugged her. Aadit didn't throw a second glance at me, I noticed. Everyone seemed happy meeting Sakshi. Even Dadi had a satisfied expression on her face, seeing her with Aadit and this nearly killed me from inside. After that, Aadit was either busy with the arrangements or with Sakshi and a few other of his friends. I didn't get even a penny-worth of his time throughout the day.

***

"Aisha, you are the prettiest bride I have ever seen in my life," I told Aisha the umpteenth time, as she wasn't satisfied with the way she looked. She had on a deep orange and green coloured wedding lehenga. We were at the grand room of an aristocratic hotel in Delhi and were about to go for the *Jaimala.*

"Are you sure, Raahi? I think this jewelry looks too gaudy with this lehenga," she said, skeptical despite all my praise.

"I'm damn sure. Now smile. It's the only thing missing from your face," I said.

"Aisha, let's go. Everyone is waiting for you," Sakshi said, entering the room. She was looking absolutely gorgeous again in an aqua blue saree, with her perfectly styled pin straight hair swept to the side, flaunting her backless blouse. She was the kind of girl who could make any other girl jealous just with her looks. She was that perfect, which had to be, considering that she was a model.

As we came down, we found Aadit and his cousins there already. He was wearing a tailored fit charcoal grey suit with a deep maroon cravat underneath a white shirt. He looked damn handsome. His eyes glimmered as he saw Aisha in her wedding dress. He gave her a quick side hug and planted a kiss on her head, "I don't think anyone can ever look as beautiful as you are looking right now," he whispered in Aisha's ear.

"Wow, and you look ravishing in blue," he said, quickly glancing at….well, Sakshi. She turned pink in response. I felt like someone had shot me right in my chest. He didn't even care to notice what I was wearing.

Aisha made her entrance at the wedding hall just like a princess. Aadit and her other male cousins escorted her into the hall and towards the stage. They held a sheet of white and red roses above her head.

Once Aisha settled on stage with Girish, the rest of us stepped down. I purposely walked beside Aadit so that we could have a conversation, but he didn't take the initiative.

"Aadit, you look very good today," I said, breaking the ice.

"Thanks, you too," he replied, without looking at me. Now that was quite a hackneyed response. I had expected a little more than just that.

"Umm, so how are you doing?" I winced at my own words, realising what a silly question that was, clearly sounding made-up just for the sake of making conversation.

"Huh?" He looked at me quizzically, narrowing his eyes.

"I mean, what are you going to do now?" I blurted out another stupid question, just to extend our conversation. He looked at me as if asking me to come to the point.

"Actually…I was—"

"Hey Raahi, I have been searching for you," Abhimanyu's voice cut me off.

And I was avoiding bumping into you, I thought.

"Whoa! You look stunning. Didn't I always say, pink is your colour!" Abhimanyu said, appreciating me at an arm's length. I was wearing a baby pink saree embellished with silver stones.

"Excuse me. You guys carry on," said Aadit and left me there with Abhimanyu.

Throughout the evening, Abhimanyu did not leave my side, while Sakshi was always around Aadit. I made many futile attempts to talk to Aadit, but he didn't even look at me. My patience crossed the line when I saw Aadit and Sakshi dancing on the dance floor. He whispered something in her ear and she giggled, throwing her head back in response. I hated that girl, I felt like she had snatched away something that was mine. Tears started pooling in the corner of my eyes. It was hard to understand why I was getting so jealous of that girl, when I knew that it was I who had pushed Aadit away. He had chosen me over her. Why was I even competing with her? Why had it gotten so difficult for me to see Aadit with someone else?

Do I love him?

No. I'm just concerned about his nonchalant behavior towards me…

Really?

Okay…maybe it's just infatuation, but it's definitely not love.

*Oh God! Who am I kidding? Yes, I love him. I love him without a shadow of doubt, I love him more than anyone else and I need to confess it before it's too late, m*y heart screamed at my defiant brain and won the battle.

Bereft of my senses, I padded towards the dance floor. I grabbed his hand and pulled him towards myself. I didn't care what the people around me thought of it.

"What happened?" he shouted over the loud music.

"Can we talk?" I shouted back.

"Now?"

I nodded. He turned to Sakshi and said something in her ear. She giggled again in response. Gosh! This girl had seriously started getting on my nerves.

"Why are you avoiding me?" I asked, once we were away from the boisterous music.

"I'm not," he said, without making eye contact.

"Look at me, Aadit, and spit it out straight on my face. You are lying. You aren't talking to me the way you used to talk before," I said in a shaky voice laced with anger.

"I'm a bit occupied, that's why," he said, looking at me.

"Yeah, I can see that. You are only occupied with regard to me, you have all the time in the world for others," I felt choked with the bulge of emotions in my throat.

"Others?" he asked, puzzled.

"Hmm, your friends," I replied with sarcasm in my tone.

"You mean Sakshi?" he said, resting his hands on his hips.

I averted my eyes in response.

"Are you jealous of her?" he asked, knitting his brows together. It felt like a tight slap on my face.

"No, not at all. Why would I be jealous of her?" I spurted out instantly, to hide what was clearly written all over my face. He looked at me with his brows pinched and crossed his arms over his chest.

"Okay, a little," I confessed, closing my eyes.

"You know better than that, because the look on your face says that you have even planned her murder in your head," he said. I shook my head to regain my composure.

"Are you doing all this on purpose?" I asked.

"Is that all you wanted to talk about?"

"No. Aadit, I only want you to know that I… I… I—" I sighed. Why was it so difficult to confess love, while lashing out anger only took seconds? "I …that I…" I couldn't go on.

"Raahi, is there something you really have to say?" he asked.

"Nothing. You can go," I said with a heavy heart.

"Are you sure? Because I don't want you to behave again the way you behaved on the dance floor just now," he said.

I shook my head. *Please, say it Raahi, before it's too late.* I squeezed my eyes and took a deep breath before starting, "Actually, I want to tell you…"

"Raahi, what are you doing here?" Abhimanyu cut me off again and I felt like smashing his face. "Anything serious?" he asked, looking at the heated expressions on our faces.

"Nothing. I've got to go now," Aadit said, patting Abhimanyu's back.

Once Aadit was gone, Abhimanyu turned to me, "Is there something I need to know, Raahi?" '*Yeah! That you are a jerk, I was going to propose to the guy I actually love and you ruined it,*' my head screamed.

"There is nothing like that…can you please leave me alone for some time? I think you have friends here, don't you?" I said, gesturing towards Utkarsh, who was standing with his friends.

"Is there a problem?"

"I'm not feeling well, actually," I fibbed.

"Can I do something to help?"

"No. I just need some time."

He nodded and took his leave.

***

Aisha clenched my fist anxiously, as the time of her *Vidaai approached*, the most emotional moment of a wedding. The last few rituals of the wedding were being performed, where the friends and cousins of the bride asked the groom for money in return of his shoes that they had stolen before.

"It's okay, Aisha, don't worry, you aren't going to some unknown place and Girish is such a nice boy. I'm sure he will take good care of you," I whispered in her ear, trying to pacify her.

"No, that's not the thing I'm worried about. It's something else that is eating me up," she whispered back.

"What's that?" I asked.

"Do you think these people will judge me if I don't cry during Vidaai. Because I'm literally not feeling like crying at all," she said and I tried to stifle my laughter.

"Should I use something like glycerin for tears?" she asked and I hushed her.

Girish got his shoes back after paying the demanded money and it was soon time to bid the couple adieu. As we all proceeded towards Girish's beautifully decorated car, Aisha threw five handfuls of rice back over her head and it fell over the people standing behind her. This was the last ritual that signified the bride leaving behind prosperity to flourish in the house that she is leaving. Before sitting in the car she hugged her father, and in that moment she actually cried and made everyone else cry a tear or two too. It was an emotional moment, as she crossed over from one family to the other. She then hugged Maa and Aadit.

"This house will always belong to you and you don't need anyone's permission to come here anytime. Nothing will change," Aadit said to Aisha, caressing the back of her head.

She slid gracefully into the car and it soon drove out of sight.

As we came back to the hotel to say good-bye to the guests who were leaving, Abhimanyu came to talk to me.

"Raahi, I'm leaving for Hyderabad and I need to know your decision before leaving," he said, taking my hand in his. I was listening to him, but my eyes were glued to Aadit who was standing at the other end of the lobby, busy on a call. There was no one else around. A peculiar kind of noise in my head wasn't letting Abhimanyu's words register in my mind. I held my head, as I began to feel faint and at the drop of a hat, I was on the floor... *unconscious.*

"Raahi..." shrieked Abhimanyu as he held me in his arms and the next instant, I heard another set of footsteps coming towards me. It was Aadit. He picked me up in his arms and carried me over to a room nearby. He placed me on the bed, patted my cheeks lightly and then asked Abhimanyu to fetch some water.

"Aadit, I think you should go, I can take care of her," Abhimanyu said rudely. I didn't like the tone he used with Aadit. How did I know all these details if I was unconscious? Actually, I wasn't. I just needed some time to formulate a strategy to kick Abhimanyu out of my life and I couldn't think of any other way. He sprinkled some water on my face and I acted as if I was coming back to my senses by opening my eyes slowly. Aadit wasn't around.

"Are you okay?" Abhimanyu asked, as he held my hand and kissed it. I pulled it back immediately.

"I haven't said 'Yes', Abhimanyu," I reminded.

"Hmm, I know you will now say that I'll have to earn your 'Yes'. I remember how you made me go through your weird tests the last time," he chuckled.

Test...should I try Shreya's five-step formula on him? A thought crossed my mind. Would it work on him? He already knew so much about me and I was sure that in that moment he would agree to anything I asked for...*except one*—

"Abhi, the fact is, we are no longer the same people we used to be a few months ago. So much has changed."

"Yeah, I know."

"I'm aware of your relationship with Neeti and you should know that I also started seeing someone after our breakup."

He averted his eyes for a moment and then looked back at me. "Aadit, right?" he said.

I didn't respond, I swallowed audibly and then added, "And I'm—"

"You don't need to say anything, Raahi. It's okay. At least, we are in the same boat now," he said with a smirk on his face.

"No. Abhimanyu, we aren't. You started dating Neeti before our breakup and that is called cheating," I said.

I wasn't in the same boat with Abhimanyu, but with Aadit, yes I was. We had both loved, with all our heart and soul, a person who didn't value our love and trust. We both had warped fates. But there was something good in that too. This twist of fate was to bring us closer, because Aadit and I were destined to be together.

I looked back at Abhimanyu. He was staring blankly at the floor, a wave of embarrassment gushing all over his face. He didn't respond.

"It's okay. I'm ready to accept you despite all this. But before that, I want to tell you something," I said.

"What's that?" he looked back into my eyes.

"I'm pregnant," I spurted and my face turned red with embarrassment.

"That's a lie," he laughed.

"I wish it was…I haven't been feeling well for quite some time and yesterday when I tested, the result was positive," I squeezed my eyes shut. He didn't say anything.

"I don't know how Paa will react to this, I'm so scared, Abhi"—I clenched his hand—"Please tell me Abhi, that you will accept me with this baby," I pleaded, wrapping my other arm around my belly. He pulled his hand out of my grip.

Bingo! It was working.

"I can't believe it. This is exactly why I told you"—he pointed a finger at me—"to stay away from Delhi boys. But you—" he yelled and anxiously ran his fingers through his hair. "Now I understand why you had been running behind Aadit all the time yesterday, while he was avoiding you," he gritted his teeth.

"Please forgive me, Abhi, and let's start afresh," I begged.

"Why don't you go to Aadit and beg him to accept his sin?" he said, scowling.

"I think you are right, I'm just wasting my time on you. Thanks for your suggestion and you may leave now please," I changed my tone. He quietly stood up and left the room. They say that if you love someone, set them free. If they come back to you, they're yours and if they don't, they never were. But, what if they come back and you don't want them in your life anymore? No one has said anything about that, so I did what I felt was right. I quickly grabbed my phone and typed a message to Shreya.

Me: *I kicked him out of my life.*

She replied almost immediately.

Shreya: ***Who? Abhimanyu? Aadit?***

Me: ***Abhimanyu, of course. Dumbo.***

Shreya: ***I'm proud of you. Love you.***

I heard a knock at the door just then and saw Aadit standing there. I smiled at him, but he didn't reciprocate.

"What did you tell Abhimanyu?" he asked, furrowed.

"God! Don't tell me, he told you everything," I said, placing my hand over my mouth. *Shit! Did he tell Aadit that I'm pregnant with his baby?*

He shook his head, "Disgusting! And you faked this illness too, didn't you?"

I nibbled at my lower lip and looked down at my fidgeting fingers. The way he was glaring at me, I wanted earth to open up and swallow me whole.

"Do you know what he said? That a girl would never lie about the father of her child," he snorted.

I felt like laughing the moment it came out of his mouth, but pursed my lips to stifle it instantly.

"And you find it amusing?" he asked, pinching his brows. "Every time I start thinking that you are a nice girl, you do something to make me feel otherwise," he said and stormed out of the room, without listening to my side of the story. All I wanted to say was, 'I did it for you, Aadit.'

***

Chapter 24

A Date With Destiny

It had been thirty-three hours since Abhimanyu left and I was still waiting for Aadit to talk to me. I couldn't entirely blame him, for he truly had been too busy to even breathe. The back-to-back trips to the airport and railway station to drop off the guests, settlement of bills with the hotel, the caterer, the decorators etc. and the post-wedding rituals had all kept him on his toes. That day, everyone had planned to go the Akshardham temple along with Aisha and her new family. It would have been the last chance for me to grab some time with Aadit, but my hard luck, I was at that time of the month when I wasn't supposed to go to a temple, so I was staying at home. My heart was drowning with the every passing second, because it was Aadit's last day here. He had a return flight early the next morning.

"Raahi, why are you not coming with us?" Suresh uncle asked, to which Dadi stared at him as if she would eat him alive.

"Because she isn't feeling too well," Maa answered on my behalf. She knew why I wasn't going.

"What happened to you now?" Aadit whispered from behind me and I turned on my foot in reflex. His tone was skeptical of whether I was faking the illness again or not.

"Actually, I…I…"

"Whatever," he cut me off and went straight to grab his car keys.

"Maa, I'm waiting downstairs. Please come fast," he said, rolling up the sleeves of his shirt. Soon after Aadit left, Maa, uncle and Dadi exited the house too, leaving me alone. Sometimes we take so much time to take a decision, that things start to slip out of our hands. That is exactly what I was feeling at that moment, as if everything was slithering out of the gaps in my fist, like sand in an hourglass. With every passing second, I felt like I was losing something. I ambled towards my room, but turned to Aadit's room instead. His gigantic bag was perched at one corner, along with some other luggage…*all packed.* His passport lying on the top of his bag teased me. The clothes that he had just changed out of were lying on one edge of his bed. Tears started streaming down my eyes as I held his T-shirt in my hands and hugged it. I sat there on his bed and inhaled his fragrance in an attempt to imbue myself with his hue. I didn't want him to go. Not without letting him know how I really felt for him, at least. I wished I could stop time. I wished I could go back in time and set everything right. I wished I could tell him at least once, what he meant to me. I wished, I wished and I wished, but some wishes never come true.

It was quarter to eight, when I heard a ring on the landline phone. I sauntered to the living room to answer the call, not letting go of his T-shirt still. My heart started pumping again when I heard the voice at the other end of the line.

"Why are you not answering your phone?" he asked.

"I didn't hear it ringing."

"Did you have dinner?"

"No. Not yet."

"Then get ready. We are going out for dinner. I'll be there in thirty minutes max."

"Didn't you go to the temple?"

"No. I made up an excuse and came back. I'm driving, can't talk now. You get ready."

"Sure," I said and hung up the phone. I clasped my hands in excitement and swirled on my heels. I felt like dancing and I literally twirled a little, still holding his T-shirt in my hands. I quickly took a shower again and wore the same dress that he had gifted me on Valentine's Day. This time however, I wore it for him...*only for him*. I kept my hair untied as I remembered him saying that he liked me better with my hair untied. I did a quick and light makeup. I also put on the diamond earrings that he had gifted me on Diwali. I did everything I could to make him realize that I belonged to him. It hardly took me twenty minutes to get ready. Waiting for him, I paced around the room impatiently. My heart was beating so fast that I felt like it would explode out of my chest. It was exactly eight-ten when the doorbell rang. I took a deep breath to calm my nerves and heart down, counted till ten and then pulled open the door.

I felt the heebie-jeebies deep down my gut, seeing him standing in front of me. I didn't know whether it was my dress or me that caught his attention which I had been yearning for. Suddenly, I felt weak in my knees as I saw his gaze slowly travel down my body.

"You ready?" he asked, looking back into my eyes.

"Yeah," I smiled.

Soon we were at a restaurant, looking at the menu. Well, it was only he who's eyes bored into the menu as if he was cramming for an exam. I still waited for him to start a conversation. He was sitting across the table from me. The whole way he hadn't uttered a single word. I didn't know what was going on in his mind.

"So what will you have?" he finally spoke.

"Anything," I gave a typical response, still not interested in the menu at all.

"Umm, I don't think they serve 'anything' here," I got the typical reply in return.

I took the menu from him. 'Took' would be an understatement, I actually snatched it from his hands. There was a picture of a delicious looking pizza on the very first page.

"Do you have this?" I asked the waiter, pointing at the picture.

"Certainly, ma'am."

"Okay then, we would like to order this," I said. I didn't want to waste anymore of the time that was already pacing at the speed of light, on discussing the stupid menu. I looked at him, while he scanned the wall behind me. I shook my head in disappointment.

"Aadit, why have we come here?" I asked exasperated, and he finally turned his gaze towards me.

"For dinner," he said.

"Seriously?" I couldn't hide the sarcasm in my tone.

"Okay, you said you want to talk about something."

"And you don't want to talk about anything?" I snorted. I couldn't believe I was sitting with the same guy who had proposed to me a few days ago, but was so indifferent and nonchalant now.

"Can I come and sit there?" he asked, pointing at the seat beside me. I nodded and breathed a sigh of relief, as my man was finally taking the lead. He sat beside me and a shiver ran through my body as his muscular shoulder brushed against mine.

"It's good here," he said, looking straight at the other tables in front of us. "At least I have a view now. Otherwise, it was just the wall to look at and"—he turned to me—"you." The sunniness that had brightened my face just a moment ago, evaporated like a bat out of hell. What did he mean by that? Wasn't I worth glancing at? He started tapping his fingers to the song that was being played at the restaurant. With every passing moment, my heartache was slowly transforming into anger. I felt like shaking him out of his complacence to make him realize our purpose of being there.

My heart picked up its pace as he scooted his face close to mine and whispered in my ear, "I'm so in love with you." Each word from his lips aroused butterflies in my stomach. I looked at him with my heart in my eyes.

"Lovely lyrics, aren't they?"

"Huh?" I asked, heartbroken.

"The lyrics of this song," he said, twirling his finger in the air.

He had just been humming the lyrics of the song that was being played at the restaurant, Let's Stay Together by Al Green.

Was this the same Aadit who used to grab every opportunity to flirt with me and was now behaving completely oblivious to all my hints. I realised that if I continued to sit next to him even for a minute longer, I would start crying. So I excused myself to go to the washroom. As soon as I turned my back on him, the first tear rolled down my cheek. Once I was in the washroom, I locked it behind me and cried. I actually wanted to shed the stock of my tears right there so I wouldn't end up crying in front of him. When I felt a bit lighter, I washed my hands and looked at myself in the mirror. Damn! I looked terrible with those smudged eyes, puffy nose and lips and messed up hair. To top that, I didn't even have my handbag with me. With no other option left, I washed my face, detangled my hair by combing through it with my fingers and returned to my seat. I noticed that our food had arrived on the table. As I took my seat beside Aadit, he looked at me strangely.

"Look here," he said. Somewhere in my heart, I wanted him to know that I had been crying. I looked at him.

"What happened to your face?" he asked. I looked into his eyes and hoped for him to read my mind, but he was far away from understanding me.

"Aha! You removed your makeup, didn't you?" he concluded. "Even your hair is a complete mess."

I angrily rummaged through my handbag for hair ties and tied my hair up in a ponytail. I felt him staring at me and when I turned my gaze towards him, I saw him looking pensively at my ears. So he finally noticed that I was wearing the same earrings that he had gifted me. I felt this to be the right moment to tell him everything.

"Aadit, I want you to know that—"

"Shall we eat first?" he said, gesturing towards the food and then proceeded to place a pizza slice on my plate, followed by another one on his own.

"Let's start. I have to go back and pick everyone up from the temple too," he said, devouring the first slice of pizza.

"I don't feel like eating," I said, sliding my plate away.

"Why?"

"Because I don't like it."

"But you only ordered it. What happened now?"

"Yes, I ordered it, but suddenly I feel like I have no appetite for it. Is there a problem?" I asked angrily, narrowing my eyes at him. He placed his hand on mine and an instant shiver ran down my spine.

"Do you like me?" he asked, holding my hand in his.

I nodded. There was so much I wanted to say, but felt too choked.

"Fine then," he released my hand and resumed eating, "Imagine this isn't a pizza, but me. Eat it now, I'm sure you will like it too," he said with a deadpan expression.

My patience wore thin with every passing moment. I picked up a fork and knife and started slicing through the pizza. '*I don't love this guy. I hate him. I hate you, Aadit Kashyap. I hate you from the core of my heart. You are testing my patience. I know you are playing with me, if you dare speak one more word, I'll kill you with this same fork and knife in the deadliest way you can think of.*'

"Action speaks louder than words, Miss Raahi Sharma." His voice pulled me out of my wicked thoughts. I looked up at him.

"I can see how much you like me," he gestured towards my plate. I followed his gaze and was shocked to see what I had done. The pizza slice was lying dead on my plate. I had chopped it up outrageously. I didn't realize that I had been chopping it to bits until Aadit pointed it out. Soon after, we were out of the restaurant and walked towards the parking lot where he had parked his car. He stopped to answer a phone call, while I kept on walking without giving any attention to what or to whom he was speaking to.

"Raahi...where are you going?" he yelled after me from behind. I then realized that his car was parked where he had stopped. I turned back and found him looking at me with his hands on his hips and a sly smile on his face.

"Wait a sec," he said, as I reached out to open the car door.

He opened the back door and took out a rose bud. He stood straight in front of me, holding it in his hand. '*Don't have any hopes now Raahi, this is just another prank,'* I warned myself. As he extended the bud towards me, I snatched it from his hand and crushed it furiously, before throwing the dead blossom on the road. I turned on my heels and started walking away from him. I knew that I was on the verge of an emotional breakdown. He followed me and grabbed my hand, pulling me into him. I made a futile attempt to wriggle out of his grip. He looked back and forth into my eyes, holding me tight in his arms.

"Leave me, Aadit. I don't love you anymore," I said, still trying to wriggle out of his hold.

"What did you say? You don't love me anymore. ANYMORE?" he raised a questioning eyebrow. "When did you ever say you loved me?" he asked sarcastically and I stopped struggling immediately. I looked up into his eyes and said, "I was about to say it, I tried so many times, but you didn't let me complete," and tears started rolling down my face again. He placed his index finger under my chin and lifted my face up to meet his eyes.

"I know, what you were about to say, and I was just giving you time to think about your decision, because there is no going back once you say 'yes' to me," he said.

"Neither do I intend to go back on my word. I love you, Aadit," I confessed, *finally.*

He locked his eyes with mine and mouthed, "I love you more."

The way he looked at me, I knew what was coming next, but before I could think, blink, act or react, I felt his lips on mine. The touch was so gentle, tender and warm, I savored every moment of it. In that instant, I knew that it was *my forever...my happily-ever-after...*

***

EPILOGUE

A Year Later (New York)

AADIT

It was a beautiful morning. I opened the window blinds and turned to glance over the bed where she lay. She squeezed her eyes shut as the bright rays of the sun filtered into my room. I quickly lowered the blinds and she fell into deep slumber again. Wrapped in a white comforter, she looked like an angel, *my angel,* her long dark brown hair spread over the pillow, her lips a little parted and her breathing, deep and relaxed. I loved watching the baby-like innocence on her face while she slept and I felt lucky to witness it every morning. It was our anniversary today; exactly a year ago she had said 'Yes' to me and changed my life forever.

We got married seven months after Aisha's wedding. Yeah, I told you that I wouldn't get married before twenty-eight, but it just felt like the right thing to do. Besides, there was no point in waiting when both of us knew that we were the ones for each other. The best part was that there was no hindrance or objection from our families. Maa was on cloud nine when we broke the news to her and wanted us to get married immediately. Dadi wasn't exactly pleased with the alliance and took her time to accept this relationship.

One day, she dragged Raahi into the kitchen and told her to prepare *halva*. Oh God! How could I ever forget the day. The look on Raahi's face then was incredible: stunned, confused and unhinged. It was that very day that I came to know that she had no idea how to cook. She then had to go through some torturous cooking classes with Dadi. She told me later that when she was very young, she had burnt her hand trying to cook and after that, her father never allowed her in the kitchen anymore.

After going through my morning routine, I sauntered towards the kitchen. It was a special day for both of us and I didn't want to miss the chance to make it extra special for her. I took out some cheese, butter and veggies for her favorite grilled sandwiches and some strawberries for a smoothie.

I can never forget the day she cooked for me for the first time. She had looked anxiously at me, biting her lower lip, when I took the first morsel of food into my mouth. The taste was disastrous, but I still praised her for her effort, because I didn't want to discourage her. But my face gave me away and I failed the test. Yes, it had been a test.

Ever since we got married, everyday has felt like a made-up test. Shreya crammed her ears daily to keep testing me. According to her theory, it was to keep our relationship fresh and spicy. And my wife was a blind follower of her words. Despite all my efforts, I failed all of her stupid tests, but I enjoyed all her games nevertheless, and I loved her even more. She was everything I could ever have wished for. *My love. My life. My forever.*

Yesterday, she had been a bit agitated as her father's birthday was coming up and she desperately wanted to see him. I knew how close her father was to her, so I told her that she must go to India to see him and immediately booked her tickets to Delhi. It would kill me to not see her around for a few days, but I had vowed to fulfil all her wishes and I meant to keep it till my last breath.

"Raahi, get up, baby. Breakfast is ready." I arranged the breakfast on the table and called her. She didn't respond. It was already ten in the morning and Raahi never slept in till that late. Something was wrong.

I walked back to our room. She was still in bed, her face buried under the comforter. A little movement inside the comforter told me that she was awake. I pulled the comforter down to uncover her face and there she was— *crying.*

CRYING!!!

Why?

What had I done now?

She covered her face with her palms and sobbed. My heart stopped for a moment, seeing her like that.

"What happened, baby?" I asked and slid inside the comforter next to her to hold her in my arms.

"Go away, Aadit. Don't talk to me," she sniveled, pushing me away and turning her back to me. I grabbed her waist instantly and pulled her into me.

"Tell me, what happened?" I asked, spooning her body.

"You don't love me anymore," she carped.

"What makes you think so?" I asked, kissing the crook of her neck.

A test again...

"Yesterday, when I told you that I wanted to see Paa, you immediately booked the tickets for me. You didn't once try to stop me, almost as if you want to get rid of me. All I want is for you to come with me," she seethed, but I just tightened my grip around her.

I had failed a test again...

"I can't come with you, Raahi. You know how my job is," I soothed her.

"Then I'll wait, but I won't go anywhere without you," she purred after a brief hiatus and I nuzzled her hair in response.

No matter how many tests I failed, I knew that our love was all-conquering.

END

Acknowledgement

My heartfelt thanks to my father-in-law, my parents and my nani ji for their endless love and blessings, Anita Vatsal, for always encouraging and guiding me, Ritu Malik and Richa Sharma, for being my support system when I was writing the story. Rajasree Menon, Neetu Bindra and Gagandeep Assal for reading the first draft of the story and giving their valuable suggestions.

Natasha Sehgal, I'm indebted to you for helping me through the editing and working hard on this book with me.

My sincere thanks to team Invincible for making this happen, especially Mr. Ajay Setia, my editor Aditi Saxena and Ruchika Khanna.

My deepest gratitude to all my relatives and friends for teaching me the invaluable lessons of life that helped me in portraying the characters. I am also indebted to all my brothers, sisters and friends for helping me with the book's promotion.

A big thanks to all my Facebook, Instagram and Twitter followers for encouraging me with their likes, comments and messages.

My love and a big thanks to my kids Agastya and Advitya, for putting up with my schedule when I was all engrossed in writing.

And lastly, the love of my life, Amol Malik, I really can't thank you enough for letting me spread my wings and follow my dreams. I couldn't have done this without your love and support.

Author's note

Life is like a play. People will come as per their roles, and once their role is over, they will leave. If you keep mourning their departure, how will the story of your life progress any further? So move on...and cherish the new entries, because you never know when your role itself comes to end.

A special thanks to you for reading this story. I will wait for your reviews, short or long doesn't matter, but do post them. You may connect with me:

Facebook: www.facebook.com/anjum.a.malik

Instagram: @anjumawasthi

Twitter: @anjum_awasthi

Email: anjumawasthi@gmail.com